The Aiken and Burnettown Murders

D. R. BEAVERS

iUniverse®

THE AIKEN AND BURNETTOWN MURDERS

iUniverse books may be ordered through booksellers or by contacting:

iUniverse
1663 Liberty Drive
Bloomington, IN 47403
www.iuniverse.com
1-800-Authors (1-800-288-4677)

ISBN: 978-1-4917-3286-1 (sc)
ISBN: 978-1-4834-0917-7 (e)

Printed in the United States of America.

iUniverse rev. date: 7/14/2014

Dedication

This book is dedicated to my mother, Maxine. She inspired me to attempt many things in my life and this is my attempt at writing a novel. Thanks, Mom.

Chapter 1

Monday Night—William

The police and emergency vehicles were parked in front of the home of Carol and Tom Lowe, a middle-aged couple that had lived in the house next to mine for about three years. Our neighborhood consisted of four- to five-acre lots with large homes. The Lowes' house was situated about two hundred yards from the street, ensconced by a wooded lot. I had a couple of business ventures with Tom in the past and played golf with him fairly often. They often invited me over for dinners, cookouts, neighborhood gatherings, and sometimes just drinks. They apparently felt sympathy for me, a single male.

It was midnight on a Monday in the otherwise sleepy town of Aiken, South Carolina. The moon was full and glowing, competing with the sparkling stars—though the glowing and sparkling were likely due to my Lasik surgery. My future children, if I ever have any, will probably wonder why they're blind as a bat when their old man has twenty-twenty vision. I'll blame it on their mother, if I ever find someone who fits the job description.

I've always been a curious sort, so I threw on jeans, a T-shirt, and my running shoes and headed outside. I saw Ralph and Mary coming across the street. Both were wearing bathrobes. I caught up to them as they started up the neighbor's driveway. Behind us were other neighbors in varied attire.

Ralph said, "Hey, William. Do you know what's going on?"

"I don't have a clue," I responded.

The cops hadn't cordoned off the area yet, so the neighbors and I wandered up the driveway and as close to the Lowes' front door as we dared. A young officer came up to us and said, "Please go back to the street. This is a crime scene."

"What crime?" I asked.

"I can't tell you any details. Please go back to the street."

"Are Carol and Tom okay?"

"As I said, I can't tell you anything. Please move to the street." The polite officer began ushering us down the driveway as more neighbors joined.

Ralph said, "What do you think happened?"

"I don't have a clue. I was at their house last night, and everything was fine."

Crime tape was being put up, and we were about halfway down the long driveway when a black Impala came up and stopped beside our officer. I thought it might be a detective, but it was an attractive woman.

Her voice wasn't as attractive as she said through her open window, "Why aren't these rubbernecking yokels in the street? A good officer would already have these civilians away from the crime scene."

The officer tried to answer, "I'm taking them ..."

The woman didn't give him a chance to finish. "Get them in the street," she said before she continued up the driveway.

I asked the officer, "Who was that?"

"She's a detective from Chicago, helping us out while we're shorthanded."

"What's her name?"

"Jessie. I don't recall her last name."

I turned and walked backward so I could see the Chicago detective get out of her car. She was wearing black jeans, a black shirt, and black boots. Her black hair flowed over her shoulders. Her attitude and demeanor certainly matched her attire. She strode with purpose up to the house.

I asked the officer, "How long has she been in Aiken?"

"She just started a few days ago. She seemed much nicer when I met her at the station."

We all, not to be confused with y'all, waited in the street. More neighbors joined the hoard. The curved driveway to the house was lined with trees, so it was hard to see the front of the house. Thunder and lightning had started in the west, so the gawkers and I would be forced to seek shelter soon.

I saw the Chicago detective marching down the driveway the same time the polite officer saw her. He tensed up as she came close.

I heard a slight Chicago accent as she said to the officer, "Get everyone's name, address, and phone numbers and ask everyone whether they saw any vehicles or persons near the house this evening."

The officer had already been gathering the information and answered, "Yes, ma'am."

I took the opportunity to ask the Chicago detective, "What happened to the Lowes? Are they okay?"

She turned her glare from the officer to me and said, "There's nothing I can tell *you*." She then turned around and headed back up the driveway. She was a lean woman, about five feet seven or eight, and her gait was athletic with long strides.

The polite officer rolled his eyes as she walked away. He turned to the swarm of yokels and continued to gather personal information and ask if anyone had seen or heard anything during the night. No one had. The neighbors talked about the rain getting closer, so I went for my golf umbrella in my car.

Some of us were still in the street an hour later. That's when we saw the ambulance backing up to the house. The EMTs went inside and brought out a gurney with what looked like a body. Quick as could be, they drove down the driveway past the polite officer and us and headed out of the neighborhood toward town. A second ambulance repeated the process, so there were probably two bodies. The polite officer still didn't give us any explanation of what happened in the house, but by then I figured it was because he didn't know any more than we did. I could only assume that the victims must be Carol and Tom, but it wasn't confirmed yet.

By two o'clock, most of the neighbors had gone home, and the storm had moved in. I was the last to leave.

I'm William Bradford of the Appalachian Bradfords. You can be thankful to us for the lights in your home and the juice for your electronic toys. We Bradfords aren't the ones who own the utility company—probably aren't even shareholders—but are the ones who get the coal out of the ground for the power plants. We've been coal miners for generations.

I spent my share of time in the coal mines while I was in college getting my engineering degree. Each summer starting after high school and one Christmas holiday break, I labored in the mines. Using a sledge hammer. Busting rock. Working on the ventilation crews. Operating a belt head. Drilling for methane gas. Cleaning belt sections. It was an experience that all teenagers and students needed to have, if anything so they could feel what it's like to hear the rats scurrying in pitch darkness. Actually, I've seen pitch, and the mines were darker than pitch.

Our part of the Bradford clan was led by a hardworking father, George William Bradford—hence the William for me—and a mother, Maxine, who demanded all of us kids work hard. Children were the source of free labor on farms and businesses in that bygone America, and my family consisted of four sons and one daughter. I'm the youngest.

My childhood and teenage years in the heart of Appalachia involved building houses, remodeling houses, building barns, building outhouses including outdoor toilets, sharecropping, farming, and taking care of the livestock. The garden was massive, with enough vegetables for a whole year. Canning the crops happened all summer long. Mother did let us sleep and go to school. It was very gracious of her. Mother and Dad were religious, so Sundays involved only minimal chores. Sundays were also for pickup football or basketball games or swimming in the river. A favorite was riding in the river in a rooftop cut off a junk car.

Thanks to our mother, all the Bradford children are hardworking and successful adults. I'm thirty-two now, haven't found the perfect mate, and have acquired a sustainable amount of wealth despite my rather frugal upbringing.

Chapter 2

Monday Night—Jessie

I wanted to turn on my sirens and lights to make the locals get off the road, but there wasn't enough traffic in Aiken, South Carolina, to warrant it. It would have been my first opportunity, and it was thwarted by the lack of cars. I was already annoyed by the woman on the GPS giving me directions in a southern drawl and saying please all the time. I had to slow down at the intersections so the woman had time to tell me to turn. "Please take the next right turn on Whiskey Road" took her about twenty seconds to say. The GPS had to be a special order. And Whiskey Road should be a Chicago street and not the main street through Aiken, South Carolina.

The dispatcher called me at 11:50 p.m. and said I should report immediately to 225 Mulberry Drive. I got dressed and programmed my GPS. The county had provided me with a black Impala, and I was wearing all black. In Chicago, everyone dressed in dark clothes. A lime-green shirt stood out like a sore thumb in Chicago unless you were a hooker or a pimp.

I arrived at the house at 12:10 a.m. A young officer was trying unsuccessfully to move the neighborhood locals off the property. I gave him a piece of my mind. The houses on Mulberry Drive were on large lots, unlike Chicago. The house was huge, like those in the elite Chicago suburbs. It was brick and stone, three stories high, with an impressive entrance. The foyer had a marble floor and a wide staircase going to the second floor. An officer directed me to a master bedroom off the foyer. The master bedroom was a large room with tall ceilings, a large poster bed, and a sitting area. The one room was bigger than my apartment in Chicago.

I looked through the doorway, and the officer pointed out the two bodies on the bed. I didn't go in since the forensic techs hadn't shown up yet. I asked the officer for an update.

The officer said, "A 911 call came at 11:30 p.m. stating that there were two people dead at 225 Mulberry Drive. The caller didn't stay on the line and didn't identify himself. Police officers came to the house and found the front door wide open. They went inside and found the bodies in the bedroom. The officers called the dispatcher, who called the EMTs, the coroner, other officers, the shift lieutenant, investigator Bill Hankinson, the captain, and you. The coroner pronounced the couple dead shortly after arriving and said the time of death was about ten thirty. We're now waiting on the forensic techs to arrive to work the scene."

I usually took charge in Chicago. Actually, I always took charge in Chicago. Since I was being mentored by another investigator in Aiken so that I could learn the southern methods for investigating, I didn't take charge.

While waiting for the shift lieutenant, the captain showed up and said "How are you doing, Jessie?"

I had told the captain that I went by Jessie rather than Jessica. The captain was John Thomas, a local who had come up through the ranks in the local police departments. John was in his late fifties, had brown hair with lots of gray, and was about my height at five feet eight inches. John reported to the sheriff, Fred Franklin, another local who was elected sheriff. I had to get used to being asked how I was doing before getting down to business. In Chicago, if there's any small talk, it's usually an insult.

I said, "Fine, Captain."

The captain asked, "Did you find the house okay?"

"As long as my GPS works, I can find my way around. Otherwise, I'd be lost. The streets aren't numbered like Chicago streets."

"Have you been told what happened?"

"Yes, from the officer over there. I'm now waiting on the shift lieutenant."

The shift lieutenant showed up, saw the captain, and came over and said, "Hey, Captain. Hey, Jessie."

I had made a point of meeting the shift officers and crew during the past week. The shift lieutenant was Tom Brown, another local who had come up through the ranks of local police departments. Many of the local officers moved from local town, city, and county police departments during their career. Tom had been with the City of Aiken and County of Aiken Police Departments.

The captain asked, "What's the latest status?"

The shift lieutenant repeated the same information I had heard from the officer.

"Did the neighbors see or hear anything?"

"If they did, they're not telling us."

I continued to test my patience since I usually opened my loud mouth to ask questions. It was probably in my best interest to be less outspoken than I was in Chicago. The pace of living was slower here, and I was trying to adapt. It could cause me to explode, but I was really trying. I kept reminding myself that it was the South. I was on loan from the Chicago Police Department, and I needed to be patient. As an example of my typical lack of patience, I had driven off from a Burger King when my whopper took too long.

The captain asked, "Is the house alarmed and is there video? I saw a camera at the entrance."

The lieutenant answered, "The alarm system was off, and the video system was shut down. It's a digital system, so we may be able to retrieve some information."

I couldn't stand it any longer and asked, "Why isn't the whole house and lot a crime scene?" There were police officers all over the yard.

The lieutenant responded, "Since the yard and house entrance are already contaminated, we excluded them from the crime scene. We'll still look for evidence on the lot."

"Is this a normal practice?"

"It depends on the situation. Each scene is different."

"Have the forensic techs provided any information yet?"

"I haven't gotten anything yet but expect something soon."

As he finished his response, an Aiken County investigator, Bill Hankinson, showed up.

As he walked up, Bill said, "How-do. Sorry about being late, but I was in Augusta. I was fixin' to come back to Aiken anyway when I got the call." Augusta, Georgia, was about thirty minutes from Aiken across the Savannah River.

Bill was helping me learn the ropes in Aiken. He was a lanky, blond, all-American guy who was wearing a cowboy hat, blue jeans, and cowboy boots.

He also used snuff and chewed tobacco. He did ride a Harley-Davidson motorcycle, which was a positive. Bill had tested my patience from the start with his slow talking and laid back attitude. I had to remember I was here because of my mother and father and didn't plan to be here forever.

The shift lieutenant asked, "What were you up to in Augusta? Were you trying to corral a Hereford?"

"You're close. I was teaching some lassies how to two step."

"I'm sure you were quite the sight on the dance floor."

"When I'm on the dance floor, the rest of the dancers stop to watch me."

I hoped no one saw me roll my eyes.

Bill continued, "Tell me what's going on here."

The shift lieutenant proceeded to catch Bill up on the situation. We now had a group with the captain, shift lieutenant, Bill, and me.

The captain said, "Bill, you'll be the lead investigator. Jessie, you'll work with Bill on the case."

Bill asked, "How long has the forensic team been in the house?"

The shift lieutenant responded, "About an hour. I expect an update soon."

Bill looked at me and asked, "What do you think happened here?"

"If we were in Chicago, I'd think it was a hit. Since we're in South Carolina, it could be a murder suicide or maybe a robbery. Since it doesn't look like a forced entry and the alarm system was off, it looks like it could be a robbery by a friend or neighbor."

The lieutenant said, "If it was a robbery, why would they kill the couple?"

Bill answered, "That's a good question, along with a bunch of other questions that need to be answered."

The captain said, "You need to start getting answers quickly. The Lowes were a well-respected couple in the community and donated a lot of time and money to the local charities."

Bill responded, "I'm sure we'll get to the bottom of it quickly."

We stopped talking as we saw a forensic tech leaving the house. He came over to our group, and the captain asked him to give us an update.

The forensic tech responded, "As you probably already know, the two victims were shot in the head. Powder burns were on the faces of both victims. The coroner estimated the time of death at ten thirty last night. There were no weapons found, which indicated it was most likely a homicide.

The victims appeared to be sleeping when they were shot. No casings were found in the room. The blood splatter was minimal, indicating a pillow, sheet, or some other covering was used to control the splatter. There was no blood on the floor or walls. A quick look at the doors and windows didn't indicate forced entry. There were a lot of fingerprints throughout the house. There were hair and fibers in the bed, and these were collected for the lab."

I asked, "Did you find anything outside the house?"

"We didn't see anything out of the ordinary."

"Did you find anything in the rest of the house?"

"Other than fingerprints, the rest of the house didn't provide us any evidence."

The electronic geeks came out of the house and came over. The captain said "Tell us what you found."

One of the two geeks responded, "We checked the alarm system, and it was off. It has a digital recording system with cameras in the exterior and interior of the house. The recording system had also been turned off. We removed the alarm system and recording unit to take them to the lab for further analysis."

I asked, "Could you tell whether someone tampered with the system?"

Geek One responded, "No, it looks like it was operating normally. We'll know more when we check it in the lab."

I asked, "Can you tell how it was shut down?"

"We can when we get it in the lab."

The captain stated, "So we have a friend, associate, or a knowledgeable person who decided to murder this couple, assuming the murderer or murderers shut down the alarm system. Did it look like anything was stolen from the house?"

The forensic tech answered, "There appears to be nothing out of place, but there's a safe that's locked. Hopefully, there's a relative or someone else that has the combination. If not, we can get a locksmith to open it."

I asked, "Does anyone know about relatives?"

The captain answered, "I knew the Lowes from social functions but didn't know about any relatives."

Geek One said, "We took their computers and will go through them to see if we can find information on relatives."

The second forensic tech then came from the house and told us we could go in now. I stayed with Bill and we walked through the house and garage. Everything seemed to be in place except for the missing computers and alarm system. There was a safe in the office closet and also a gun safe. Neither was open. We went in the bedroom and saw the blood on the pillows.

Bill and I decided to leave and meet at the office at nine in the morning to start the investigation.

The captain said, "I think I'll be leaving too. I'm sure the media will be out in force with a double homicide. I'll have a press conference at ten tomorrow. If you have more information by then, let me know."

It was three in the morning when I headed home.

I'm Jessica Barnes. I moved to Aiken, South Carolina, last week. It was a culture shock to move to this town of twenty-five thousand people. My mother and father, Wanda and Richard, came to Aiken, where my dad began contracting at the nuclear plant, the Savannah River Site, near Aiken. Savannah River had received over $1.5 billion of Recovery Act money, so my dad was taking advantage of the opportunity. He was a retired environmental engineer, and the Recovery Act money paid him a good contracting wage and allowed Mom and Dad to move south. It gave them a chance to check out the South for a retirement home.

To my dread, my mother and father had been in a head-on collision in Aiken two weeks ago. Both my mother and dad were seriously injured and were now in the intensive care unit of Aiken Regional Hospital.

I took a leave of absence from the Chicago Police Department to be with my parents in Aiken. The Aiken County Sheriff's Department was short of investigators and agreed to hire me as an investigator temporarily after checking me out. There was a cut in pay, but the cost of living seemed much lower down here. I still had to pay for my apartment in Chicago, so I had to make my pay stretch as much as possible.

I was living in the house that my parents had rented in Aiken, so I only had to move my clothing and sparse belongings. My beat-up Ford Fusion also made the trip.

Chapter 3

Tuesday Morning—Jessie

The morning was sunny and warm in Aiken. Bill drove us out of the station and down Union Street, a divided street that had a lot of small, wood-sided homes. A railroad track was in the middle of the street. We were headed back to the Lowes' neighborhood. He turned onto Park Avenue, which had larger wood-sided homes. Our plan was to interview neighbors and visit the Lowes' house again. Next was Williamsburg Street, which had even nicer homes with brick fences. Bill stopped to let a horse-driven carriage go through a cross street. I was calling neighbors as Bill was driving. He turned on Powderhouse Road, and we went past a horse barn, horses, two race tracks, and a polo field. The town and the country were all meshed together.

The shift lieutenant had researched the Lowes while we slept and had given us a folder before we left the station. I went over the lack of information with Bill as he drove. The shift lieutenant's crew couldn't find children or relatives for the Lowes. The Lowes also didn't show up in any government database except for the IRS database. They had moved to Aiken about three years ago, the house didn't have a mortgage, and taxes were current.

The shift lieutenant had the phone company check on the 911 call. They had found the phone number to be for a throw-away phone that was no longer active. The shift lieutenant had requested the phone company to monitor the number to see if it was used again.

I found someone at home on the first call I made, and the neighbor agreed to meet us as soon as we got to the neighborhood. The neighbor lived on the right side of the Lowes. Bill drove up the winding driveway to a circular parking area in front of the house. The house looked just as spectacular as the Lowes' house. A man came to the door and introduced himself as William Bradford. We introduced ourselves, and he invited us in. William was a quite handsome man with dark hair and chiseled features. He looked like he was in his early thirties. I was giving him a once over when I saw he was doing the same to me. He was dressed in a long-sleeve shirt with Whiskey Road Race on the front. I wanted to ask him about the shirt later. He was wearing snug jeans and no shoes. I did notice he had large feet, which was good if there was a true correlation. I wasn't ready yet to invite him into my fantasies, but he was on the short list. However, his feet size suggested he didn't necessarily belong on the short list.

We followed him into a living space with a leather sofa, leather chairs, a stone fireplace, a wet bar, and a massive TV mounted on the wall. The Bears/Giants game was on.

I asked, "Is that the game Eli was hurt?"

William answered, "Yes, it's Sunday's game. I recorded it. You must be a Giants fan."

"I dink I'll pull fur my hometown team, da Chicago Bears. They're playing pretty good. I wish I was there." I hissed the S on Bears to display my Chicago accent more. I didn't pronounce my there as dere. My parents had corrected me when I started to take on the Chicago accent. I could still use the accent if I needed to.

"Are you sure you aren't from the South with that drawl?"

Bill interrupted and said, "We need to ask you some questions, Mr. Bradford."

"Give me just a second to pause the game."

William pushed a button on his remote and turned off the TV.

I asked the most important question first. "Is your wife here so we can interview both you and your wife at the same time?"

"Unfortunately, there isn't a wife to interview. I've been searching for years and am still trying to find the perfect mate."

Well, that ruled me out right away since I didn't believe I'd be anybody's perfect mate. I was sure all my dating partners in Chicago would confirm that. Maybe I'd be a substitute until the perfect mate was found.

"Excuse me and my manners. Can I get you something to drink? Maybe coffee, tea, or soda."

I said, "I'll have coffee."

I wanted to see him walk into the kitchen to scope him out more, and I hadn't had my coffee at the station or at home since I was running late.

Bill said, "I'll have coffee too."

"Do you take cream and sugar?"

I said, "Just black for me."

Bill said, "Cream and sugar for me."

William went to the kitchen, started the coffee, and returned to the living area. He moved like an athlete. I decided I would put William in my fantasies.

Bill asked, "How long have you lived here?"

"About two and a half years."

"So I reckon the Lowes lived here when you moved in?"

"That's right."

"Did you know the Lowes before you moved here?"

"No."

I finally got my mind away from my fantasies and asked the next question, "Have you spent much time with the Lowes?"

"Yes, we became close friends."

"Have you met any of their relatives or children?"

"No. In fact, I don't think they have children, and they didn't mention any relatives."

William's answers agreed with what the shift lieutenant's crew had found.

Bill asked, "Do you know where the Lowes moved from?"

"I believe they mentioned they were from New Jersey. I think they said Princeton."

I was thinking a field trip may be necessary for William and me to go to Princeton. I'd heard it was quite the vacation spot. Bill interrupted my daydreaming with another question.

"Had you seen anything suspicious or out of the ordinary with the Lowes lately?"

"No, everything seemed to be normal, and they didn't appear to be acting different."

The coffee maker beeped, and William excused himself to get the coffee. I did my best not to imagine him without the jeans and shirt in a hot-tub fantasy but couldn't help myself. I hadn't been with a man in three months.

William came back with the coffee, cream, and sugar. The cups were mugs provided by businesses or events. They weren't matching. If you had money, you didn't have to put on airs with your coffee cups. Bill added a lot of cream and a lot of sugar to his coffee. It looked like chocolate milk when he finished. I noticed William had his coffee black, as I did. That was already enough in common for a serious relationship.

Bill messed up my daydreaming again and asked, "When was the last time you saw the Lowes?"

"I went to their house last night. They invited me over for wine and to try out a new concoction Tom had cooked. It was a black bean and mushroom quesadilla. Tom was trying new vegetarian dishes, and Carol and I were his taste testers. Tom was trying to lower his cholesterol."

I asked, "Did his cholesterol problems have him depressed?"

"I don't think so. He seemed to be enthusiastic about taking on the challenge of getting his cholesterol down."

"What were the other occasions when you went over to the Lowes' house?"

"I'd go over when they invited a bunch of the neighbors over for dinner or just drinks. Other times, I'd just go over for dinner or drinks with just the three of us. Sometimes I'd cook for us, but mostly Carol or Tom would cook. I'd also go over to watch sports with them. Tom was a New York Jets fan. He had the Direct TV NFL package so he could watch all their games. We also watched golf tournaments, baseball, UFC fighting, boxing, and other stuff. College football is big here in the South, but Tom was more interested in the NFL. I also went over to talk business. Tom and I had a few business dealings together."

"What kind of business dealings?"

"We bought a few properties together. I've been buying foreclosed properties for many years, and Tom wanted to invest with me. I didn't have partners in foreclosed properties but partnered with him since we became good friends. I set up a corporation with the two of us as co-owners for the investing. My philosophy has always been to not trust my enemies in business and to trust my friends even less. I made an exception with Tom. Tom and I bought a few foreclosed properties and short sale properties in Aiken County. I also showed him how to buy properties at the Aiken County tax sale. We looked at some properties in other parts of the state but stuck to Aiken County."

Bill asked, "Do you still have properties that you own together?"

"No, we sold the last one a couple of months ago. Tom had talked about buying more without me, but I don't know if he did. I showed him how to research properties and find where they're sold. I gave him my opinion on a couple of properties, but he didn't say whether he bought them. He did buy properties at the last Aiken County tax sale, but I don't know whether the owners redeemed the properties yet."

I didn't understand anything about buying foreclosed properties and tax sale properties and decided to wait for Bill to ask the next question.

Bill said, "I think I understand foreclosed properties, but I don't have a lick of knowledge about short sales and how the tax sale works."

William said, "It's really not that complicated. It does take a lot of research, but the process is straightforward. The banks have to agree on short sales, and the counties have tax sales."

I wanted to ask for a private lesson later that evening. I thought a glass of wine while William and I sat by the fireplace would help me understand it better. We could also watch the Bears/Giants game that he recorded.

Bill asked, "How was your business relationship with Tom?"

"Good. We both made money, and Tom learned about foreclosures."

"Did Tom have a lot of money to invest?" I asked.

"I don't know much about his finances. He always had enough cash when we bought houses."

"How much did Tom need to invest?"

"In the neighborhood of a million dollars."

"Nice neighborhood." I hadn't meant to say it out loud.

Bill asked, "Do you have copies of all the corporate documents and investments?"

"I have the original documents, and Tom should have copies of all the documents. We also had a corporate checking account set up, but there's only a few hundred dollars left in it."

Bill said, "We'll need to see the original documents."

"No problem. Just let me know when."

I asked, "Did you ever have disagreements with Tom about the investments?"

"No. Tom and I always came to an agreement on what to invest in and wouldn't invest in anything that both of us didn't agree on. There were lots of foreclosed properties, so there were lots of choices."

"So why did you stop investing with Tom?"

"We invested together so he could learn and stopped when he thought he learned enough."

"It was an amicable conclusion?"

William responded with a slight grimace, "Yes, it was amicable."

I believed he was thinking we were implying that there was more to the split than he was saying.

I changed the questioning so William would relax again. "Did you and the Lowes do any traveling together?"

"Tom and I traveled in South Carolina looking at foreclosed properties. Carol went sometimes. We went to Hilton Head, Columbia, all over Aiken County, and other places in the state. Tom and I took trips to Myrtle Beach and Hilton Head for golf, and we went to Scotland last year with a group that played golf for ten days and did some sightseeing. I believe that's all the traveling we did together."

Bill asked, "Did Tom or Carol meet anybody they knew while you were traveling with them?"

"In all of my travels with them, they didn't know anybody."

I asked, "Where did the Lowes travel to when you didn't go with them?"

"The only other place was Atlanta. They said they had a house in Atlanta."

"Did you ever go with them to Atlanta?"

"No."

"Did they say what they did in Atlanta?"

"Tom said he played golf while he was there, and Carol said she went shopping. They also said they went to some events."

"Were the Lowes members of a golf course in Aiken?"

"The Lowes and I were both members of the Palmetto Golf Club."

I didn't know what the Palmetto Golf Club was, so I made a note to ask Bill later.

"Did you and Tom play at Palmetto often?"

"We played once or twice a week together. Tom may have played other times also."

"Did the Lowes have a housekeeper?" I asked.

"Yes, her name's Wandita Lopez. She also cleans my house."

"What's her phone number?"

William went to the kitchen and brought a note back with a phone number.

"When does she clean?"

"Tuesdays. She usually cleans the Lowes' house in the morning and my house in the afternoon. She'll be here about one if you want to talk to her."

Bill asked, "Does Ms. Lopez know that the Lowes were killed?"

"Yes, I called her."

"Would it be okay if we talked to Ms. Lopez at your house?"

"Sure, I'll tell her when she gets here today."

I asked, "Since you were good friends, did you watch after their property while they were out of town?"

"Yes."

"Did you have the alarm codes and keys to their house?"

"Yes."

Bill and I gave each other a look.

"Did you know how their alarm and camera system worked?"

"Yes, I helped Tom with the system after he had it installed. The system is identical to the system in this house."

Bill and I gave each other another look. We now had a neighbor who had the alarm codes, knew all about the security system, and was in business with one of the victims. This sounded like our first suspect; I needed to remove William from my fantasies. My future generations would be disappointed if I picked someone other than William to be their ancestor, but that could be the case.

I asked, "What were you doing on the night the Lowes were killed?"

"I was at the Lowes' house until about ten and then was home until I saw the police lights next door. I then went outside to see what was going on."

Bill asked, "Were you home alone?"

"Yes."

"Do you own any guns?" I asked, figuring William would be in handcuffs before we left.

"Yes."

He had an agitated look on his face. He was a smart person and knew we were now trying to rule him out as a suspect.

"Can we see them?"

"Follow me."

He got up, and we followed him into the master bedroom. The furniture in this room rivaled the furniture that was in the Lowes' house. There was a king-size poster bed, two large chests, two nightstands, and a sitting area with cushioned chairs. We followed him into the walk-in closet where there was a gun safe in the corner. William spun the combination lock and opened the safe to reveal three handguns.

I asked, "Do you have any other guns?"

"That's all that I own."

I wrote down the information for each gun so the caliber could be compared with the bullets used on the Lowes.

Bill said, "Let's go back into the living area. We have a few more questions."

We walked back into the living area and took the same seats.

I asked, "When was the last time you shot your guns?"

"It was about a month ago at the range."

"Are you planning any trips in the next few weeks?"

William knew why I was asking.

"No, I'll be around town for a while."

Bill said, "We may have more questions, so we may be calling you in the next few days."

Bill and I got up, and William walked us to the door. If I looked as tired as Bill, I probably didn't look very good. It was good that I didn't have to impress William.

Chapter 4

Tuesday Morning—William

An investigator named Jessica Barnes had called and asked me if I had time for questions about the Lowes. I told them to come right over. It was only a few minutes later that the doorbell rang. I opened the door and saw the woman in black and a man. I had seen Bill in town but hadn't met him before. The lady in black who introduced herself as Jessica was more attractive than I remembered from the other night. I hoped her attitude had improved with her appearance. I gave her the once over from head to toe and saw she was doing the same to me. I guessed it was fair for both of us to look. She was well proportioned and had an olive complexion. Her nose looked like it may have been broken and reset, which added character to her appearance. Her black hair was straight and made her look taller.

I invited them into the living area and saw that both were scoping the place out as they walked in. We sat across from each other, and I offered them something to drink. My mother always taught me to be hospitable. They accepted my offer, and I went to fix coffee.

When I returned, the questions started. Jessica found a way to ask me about my marital status, so she must be interested in me. The other questions, at first, were about the Lowes and what I knew about them. We then discussed my business relationships and personal relationships with the Lowes. They seemed surprised that I knew the alarm codes and had keys to their house. I showed them my guns and told them when I was at the range last. I became a little disturbed when the questions became accusatory. The tone of their questions indicated that they suspected I could have something to do with the Lowes' murders. They could have thought that I wasn't disclosing something. Even though it could be true, I was offended.

I had a desire to get to know Jessica in a more personal nature until the questions turned south. My intentions changed somewhat when their questions started treating me like a suspect rather than a friend of the Lowes. After they left, I put the game back on the TV and sat in my favorite chair. I'd have invited Jessica to watch the game too, but a suspect shouldn't have a personal relationship with the investigator.

I did have a trip planned to look at property at the beach and was planning to stay for a couple of days. I'd make it a day trip or would put the trip on hold just to be sure I was available for the investigators. I didn't want to do anything that would make me look more suspicious. I was sure they'd see lots of my fingerprints in the Lowes' house. My fingerprints were in the system due to my work at the Savannah River Site and an incident at one of my restaurants.

I did need to stay abreast of the investigation, so I probably would find a way to link up with Jessica. I decided I would call her soon.

Chapter 5

Tuesday Morning—Jessie

Our next interview was with the neighbors across the street. In my call to set up the interview, Mary Jones said that they had walked over last night so they knew we'd be calling. The driveway was also winding with lots of trees on the lot. It was another large house with stone and brick. Bill rang the bell, and an older couple came to the door. They introduced themselves as Mary and Ralph Jones. They invited us into the living area and offered us coffee or tea. Bill and I said we would appreciate coffee. We sat down in stuffed chairs while Mary went to the kitchen to get the coffee.

Bill asked, "Did you or Mary see anything out of the ordinary last night or in the past few days or weeks at the Lowes' house?"

The open floor plan allowed Mary to hear the question too. Both responded that they hadn't seen or heard anything. They stated that the police vehicles woke them up, and they walked across the street. Mary brought the coffee from the kitchen with cream and sugar. She must have already had it made.

Bill asked, "What do you know about the Lowes?"

Ralph answered, "They moved here about three years ago. We've been here about ten years. They're a nice couple. They invited us over many times each year for dinner or drinks along with other neighbors. They were very friendly. They also volunteered in the community."

I asked, "What did you talk about when you were with them?"

"We talked mostly about the stock market, sports, politics, and local events."

"Did they say where they moved from?"

"I believe they said they were from New Jersey. Isn't that right, Mary?"

Mary responded, "I believe they did say they were from New Jersey."

Bill asked, "Had you seen anything different in the past few weeks or months? Maybe more visitors or maybe service trucks at the Lowes' house?"

Ralph answered, "Nothing different that I saw. There are the usual FedEx trucks, UPS trucks, and lawn service trucks in the neighborhood. There're a couple of new houses being built in the back of the subdivision, so there're construction vehicles and deliveries passing through."

Mary said, "I haven't seen anything different. We're retired and home most of the time."

"Have you met any of their relatives?"

Ralph responded, "I haven't met any relatives. How about you, Mary?"

"I haven't either. They never mentioned having any either."

I asked, "Did they say where in New Jersey they were from?"

Mary responded, "I believe they said Princeton."

"Did you have keys to their house or codes to their alarm system?"

Ralph and Mary both said no.

"What do you know about William Bradford?"

Ralph answered, "He's a great guy. I play poker with him. He's almost always at the Lowes' house when we're invited over for dinner or drinks."

"Did you hear anything that made you think that William and the Lowes had disagreements?"

"No, they were always friendly and got along great." Ralph responded.

"I never heard them have any disagreement." Mary added.

We talked to Ralph and Mary for a little while longer and didn't hear anything we hadn't heard from William.

I found a few more people home when I called, but we didn't learn any new information about the Lowes. I did learn that they were a lot of retired people in Aiken who lived in this neighborhood.

When we finished with the other interviews, Bill said, "I think it's time to eat. I missed breakfast. I have a hankerin' for barbecue. Do you eat barbecue?"

I answered, "I eat everything except for most vegetables and fruit. I assume barbecue is meat."

"This barbecue is meat, and it's the best dern tootin' barbecue in the area. You can have pulled pork or barbecue chicken."

Bill drove back roads, some with no street names, and we were back on Whiskey Road. I was now only partly lost. We went south on Whiskey Road and were in the town of New Ellenton. Bill found one of the few parking places left at Carolina Barbecue. The line was out the door but moved quickly. The line flowed by patrons who were eating on picnic tables and had heaping plates of barbecue. I expected to see a lot of country bumpkins, but most were well dressed. Some of the patrons actually had vegetables on their plate.

I had my plastic plate and a real fork in my hands in a short time. I took a dab of rice and hash from the buffet line and loaded up with pulled pork barbecue. I took a little macaroni and cheese, potato salad, and slaw to add color to the plate. We paid and were handed a foam cup full of ice. Bill found a community table with two spots. There were pitchers on the table, and Bill filled my cup. It was sweet tea, so I drank it reluctantly.

I asked, "Where's the unsweet tea?"

Bill said, "It's near the nanner puddin'. You have to get your own."

"There's banana pudding?"

"Yes, nanner puddin is one of the self-serve desserts."

"We should eat here every day."

"I can't. It's granny-slappin' good, but if I ate here every day, I'd be bigger than a pig they cooked for the barbecue."

I understood after I saw him go back for a second plate and then have banana pudding.

I only had one plate but had peach cobbler and banana pudding. I couldn't eat here every day either. I couldn't afford a whole new wardrobe of bigger clothes.

We talked about the case and decided William was our best suspect and we needed someone at the station to do some research to see where the Lowes lived in Princeton and to research William.

After lunch, I called the housekeeper, and she was cleaning William's house. Wandita said William told her that we'd be calling. I let her know we'd be there in a few minutes.

We interviewed Wandita in the same room we had interviewed William.

Bill told her we were investigating the death of the Lowes. Wandita was about five feet tall with dark hair and dark eyes. She was a stout woman, probably from her hard work every day. She was wearing athletic shoes, cotton slacks, and a cotton shirt.

I asked, "How long have you worked for the Lowes?"

Wandita said nervously, "About two years."

She was sitting in a slumped position and taking short, shallow breaths.

"When was the last time you saw the Lowes?"

"Last week when I cleaned their house."

"Did you notice anything different or unusual last week?"

"No."

I could tell Wandita was nervous, and her voice was a little cracked as she answered the questions. She was rubbing her hands and rocking a little. She probably didn't know she was doing it.

"What's your schedule for cleaning their house?"

"I clean their house on Tuesday mornings."

"Do you clean for other people in the neighborhood other than William and the Lowes?"

"No."

"Were the Lowes always at home when you cleaned?"

Wandita took a short pause before answering. After a deep breath, she responded, "No, sometimes they weren't at home. They'd leave a key for me under the front door mat."

"Did you know the alarm system codes?"

Wandita hesitated again for a little while and then answered. "No, they didn't tell me the codes."

I made a quick note to ask more about the alarm codes. She didn't exactly answer the question.

"How often did you clean when they weren't home?"

"Maybe once or twice a month."

"Did they tell you where they were going when they weren't home?"

"No."

Bill asked, "Did you ever hear any arguments or shouting?"

"No. The Lowes were always nice, and they were nice to anyone who came by."

It sounded like the Lowes were the nicest people in the neighborhood.

"Did you know the people who came by?"

"Mr. Bradford was one, and there were other people. I didn't know any of them. I think some were neighbors."

Bill asked, "Did you see or hear anything strange or different that caused you concerns?"

"No. The Lowes were always nice. They always gave me money for my birthday and Christmas." She sat straighter as she answered.

"Did you ever hear anybody threaten them?"

"No, everybody that visited was nice." She was slightly more at ease as she answered. She was moving her hands through her hair now.

"Did you hear any discussion about Atlanta or property in Atlanta?"

"I may have overheard them saying they were going to Atlanta sometimes."

I asked, "Did you ever answer the phone?"

"No. I always let it go to the answering machine."

"When you were at the Lowes' house last week, are you sure you didn't notice anything different?" I probed.

"No. Everything was the same." She was still nervous as she answered.

"Did you ever have anybody else help you while you were cleaning?"

She hesitated a few seconds. "My husband helped a few times."

I asked, "Was this recent?"

"Yes. He's been laid off from work and helped me last week."

"Is he working now?"

"Yes."

"When can we talk to him?"

"He's working in Atlanta and won't be back until the weekend." She didn't look at us when she answered, so I didn't know whether to believe her.

"What's his name and cell number?"

She gave it to us, and I made a note to call him.

I decided to follow up on the alarm codes and asked, "You said the Lowes didn't give you the alarm codes, but you didn't say you didn't know them. Did you know the codes?"

"No."

She shifted in her seat and didn't look at me when she answered. I was sure she was lying.

"Did the Lowes have the codes written down anywhere in the house?"

She shifted again and pulled her hair away from her forehead. "They had a notebook in the office with all of their passwords and alarm codes."

"How did you know about the notebook?" I asked.

She took a deep breath before she answered. "I saw it on the desk a couple of times."

"Did you look in the notebook?"

"No."

"Was it on the desk last week when you cleaned?"

She answered quickly, looking at me, "I don't remember."

We asked a few more questions but didn't find out anything more. Bill gave her his card and told her we appreciated her time. Her husband was now a suspect, and Wandita could have helped him. The safe combination could be in the notebook too. Unfortunately, I didn't see a notebook with passwords and alarm codes in the house. I made a note to check again.

After our interview with Wandita, we went to the Lowes' house. The house was cordoned off at the street, and a police officer was at the end of the driveway. Bill parked behind the officer's cruiser and told the officer we were going in the house.

We walked up the stone steps to the front door. In the daylight, the house looked even bigger. We unlocked the front door. The front door looked to be mahogany although my expertise on wood was from chop sticks. The foyer looked like it had marble tile, and I did believe I could tell it was marble. There was a massive light fixture in the foyer. It went up three stories with windows way up there. Cleaning these windows would be a problem.

The foyer was wide enough to have tables, lamps, and statues. The foyer was half as big as my Chicago apartment. In fact, I believed I could put about twenty or thirty of my apartments in this house. The master bedroom was to the left off the foyer. It was just as impressive as it had been last night. A large king-size bed was at the end of the room. There were matching chests with lots of drawers and matching nightstands. The bedroom furniture looked to be cherry. There was a sitting area with a set of windows in a bay area, and a large TV was mounted on the wall so it could be viewed from the bed or sitting area. There was a lot of fingerprint residue on the surfaces, but everything else was neat. The bed had been stripped, and there was blood on the mattress.

We went in the bathroom. There was a Jacuzzi tub, a large tiled shower with four showerheads, a large granite vanity with two sinks, and a separate room with a commode and a bidet. I was surprised there weren't two commodes and two bidets. I'd like a shower like theirs. There were two showerheads up and two down. I glanced at Bill to see if he would be involved in a shower fantasy but decided against that idea right away. Bill wouldn't be in any of my fantasies. The whole bathroom was pretty much all tiled, and it looked expensive. I was sure my vinyl flooring in my Chicago bathroom was easier to clean since it didn't have grout. There wasn't a medicine cabinet, but there were some prescription drugs in two of the built-in cabinets next to the sinks. There was blood pressure medicine prescribed to Tom Lowe in one of the cabinets and the same medicine for Mary Lowe in another cabinet. I opened the bottles, and they were the same size and shape of pills. There was also cholesterol medicine in Tom's cabinet. I wrote down the names of the physicians.

There was fingerprint residue all over the bathroom, but it was otherwise tidy. There were a few items on the vanity, such as toothbrushes, deodorants, and makeup, but nothing out of the ordinary. Through the bathroom was a walk-in closet. This was another big room with lots of cabinets, shelves, and rods. The room was neat with clothes on hangers, folded on shelves, or in drawers. There was a combination of winter and summer clothes although it was winter. There was a clothes hamper but only a few items in it. The clothes in the hamper were the same size and general appearance as the rest of the clothes in the closet. The clothes were all nice quality and had expensive labels. We took the clothes from the hamper and didn't see any tears or blood stains. The closet also had the gun safe and another safe.

We then went to the living area, kitchen area, and dining room. The house was set up for entertaining, so those areas were all intertwined. The living area had a stone fireplace, leather sofas, chairs, and lots of other nice furniture and accessories. The kitchen had granite countertops, stainless steel appliances, and nice wood cabinets. It was a large kitchen with a subzero refrigerator, two dishwashers, a vegetable sink, a gas cook top, two ovens, and a built-in microwave. The cabinets were real wood as compared to the pressed wood cabinets in my parents' house.

There was a breakfast area with a glass table and chairs. The dining room had a large dining room set with twelve chairs. I could imagine the Lowes had some nice meals here.

A sunroom was located off the breakfast area. The sunroom had comfortable-looking flowery furniture and lots of windows. So far we didn't see anything that looked like a struggle occurred.

The upstairs had four bedrooms, three bathrooms, and a bonus room. The bedrooms all had nice furniture, and the bonus room had a pool table and large TV. We searched the dressers and closets but didn't see anything unusual. We went back downstairs. There was another bedroom and another bathroom to the right of the kitchen. Bill said this room was called the mother-in-law room. The mother-in-law room was set up as an office with shelving, two desks, file cabinets, and chairs. The computers were gone since the geeks took them last night. The mother-in-law obviously didn't want her room. There were golf pictures on the wall and certificates from local charities showing appreciation for the support. The first thing we looked for was the notebook with passwords and alarm codes. We looked in all the desk drawers and found it in a bottom drawer. We opened the notebook with a pen, and the notebook had alarm codes, phone numbers, and addresses. We took the notebook with us so it could be fingerprinted. I then figured we should look through the file cabinets.

I asked, already knowing the answer, "Who'll go through all the files?"

Bill responded, "We get to do that. We'll do it between our interviews."

We went to the three-car garage. There was a late-model Mercedes and a late-model Explorer. There were shelves with paint, cleaners, and other garage stuff.

Outside was a building with a lawn mower, yard equipment, and tools. It looked like the lawn mower and other tools had been used. Maybe the Lowes did their yard work. I wouldn't have thought so in this neighborhood. We walked around the house and looked for anything unusual but saw nothing. Since the front door had been open last night and the alarm system was off, whoever committed the murders must have had a key and knew the codes. The list so far included William, Wandita, and Wandita's husband.

A nice pool and a hot tub were located behind the house. There were a lot of rock walkways and steps. I felt the water, and it was warm.

I said, "They have a heated pool. Do we have time to take a swim?"

"Maybe later after it's not a crime scene."

"This would certainly be a nice place to live." I knew I probably couldn't afford the taxes on the property.

"Not on an Aiken County Investigator's pay. These folks lived in high cotton."

We walked around the rest of the house and looked for anything out of place or unusual. Nothing stuck out.

More interviews were conducted all afternoon with the same results. It seemed like the Lowes started a new life when they moved to Aiken. Bill and I called work and cell numbers and lined up two evening interviews. One was another neighbor across the street, and one was the immediate neighbors on the left side of the Lowes.

The neighbors across the street were a young couple who both worked. They had just moved to the neighborhood three months ago. They couldn't tell us anything new.

The neighbors who lived on the left side of the Lowes were a young couple who had lived there for about six years. They both worked and had small children. They too had been invited over regularly to the Lowes' house, and the Lowes bought the children presents for birthdays and Christmas. The dad had also played golf with Mr. Lowe on occasion.

As we drove to the police station, Bill and I discussed William, Wandita, and Wandita's husband. We agreed the three were the most likely suspects we had. I didn't make it by to visit my parents and certainly plan to go visit tomorrow.

Wednesday Morning—Jessie

We turned over the notebook to the forensic techs to run fingerprints. We asked that they return it quickly so that we could follow up on the information in the book. We asked for help from IT, and a young rookie was assigned. He was supposed to have excellent technology skills. His name was Jeffery Newberry. He was an inch or two shorter than me with reddish blond hair, a round face, and round, black glasses covering some of his freckles. He looked too young to be with the sheriff's office. The first chore assigned was to try to find any information about the Lowes living in

Princeton, New Jersey. We also asked him to search into William Bradford's financials and public records, as well as Wandita and her husband and the neighbors that lived around the Lowes.

The captain gave us an inspiration speech on Wednesday morning, explaining the need to solve the Lowes' case. I wasn't any more inspired than I was before the speech.

After the speech and updating the captain, we arrived at the Lowes' house about nine o'clock. We spent about two hours going through the files in their office. Bill then made calls to the immediate neighbors we hadn't interviewed. He found three neighbors who could talk this afternoon and left messages for other neighbors.

We found files for bills, warranties, insurance, investments, and other routine information. None of the information went back past three years, when they moved into this house.

There was also a file for his stock market account. An Excel spreadsheet printout in the file showed that he had about $1 million in the account. Tom was managing the account through Charles Schwab. We wrote down the phone number of the local office and would call to see if there was any personal information in his Charles Schwab account. Surely there was a document with personal information somewhere.

We looked through the medical files and saw that Tom saw two local doctors. One was a heart doctor, and one was a general practitioner. I wrote the phone numbers of the doctors. Carol also saw a couple of local doctors, and I wrote down their numbers. Tom and Carol saw the same dentist, and I wrote down the phone number.

We didn't find any obvious concerns with the investment documents where Tom and William were involved, and we didn't find any other documents where partners were involved with Tom. He had bought four tax sale properties, spending about $5,000 total on them.

I suggested we should look at the cars, and maybe the GPS system would have an address in Atlanta or New Jersey programmed into it. Bill agreed, and we decided to divide up the cars. We looked for the keys and found them in a kitchen drawer near the back door leading to the garage. We found more than we expected.

I said, "It looks like a lot of keys for a house and two cars."

Bill said, "Let's check the GPS systems in the cars and then come back and try to figure out what all the dern keys are for."

I pulled out the keys to the two cars.

"I get the Mercedes, and you get the Explorer."

We went to the garage, and I must say that I looked good in the Mercedes. It was all black, which matched my usual attire. I wondered if the captain would mind if I used the car for two or three days. The car was probably just going to sit in the garage, and this way it would serve a good purpose, improving my morale.

Bill would look better in a pickup truck than the Explorer. It seemed like half the vehicles driven down here were pickup trucks.

I started the car, and it was smooth as silk. I couldn't even tell the engine was running. The car's electronics were a lot more complicated than any car I had driven, including the police cars. Still, I figured out the menu on the built-in GPS system fairly quickly. I pulled up the favorites in the menu selection to see what favorite locations were programmed. Unfortunately, the only favorite in the menu was 225 Mulberry Drive. They did want to make sure they would find their way home. I pulled up the last selected locations and found that there weren't any selected. It looked like they always knew where they were going or deleted the locations in the GPS after they got to the location. I removed a remote control for the alarm system from the visor. The Lowes must have used it when they were leaving or returning. The garage door remote was built into the Mercedes.

Bill knocked on the driver's window. I rolled it down, and he asked, "Did you find anything that would help us out?"

"No. How about you?"

"There was nothing in the GPS. It looked like they didn't program in locations or they deleted them."

"That's the same for this GPS," I said as I got out of the car reluctantly. The leather seats in the car were very soft and could be heated and cooled. Cooled seats would be great in the South, and heated seats would be exceptional in Chicago.

I said, "Did you find a remote for the alarm system in the Explorer?"

"I didn't see one. Is it important?"

"It could be. Let's look." We looked in the Explorer and didn't find a remote for the alarm system. I would've expected another one in there.

We went back inside to check out the keys in the drawer. We laid them all out on the granite countertop and started sorting them.

I said, "Let's figure out which keys fit this house and cars so we can rule out them."

After we checked all the keys, we found that a couple of the sets had keys that didn't fit the house. In addition, the extra sets of keys matched. One of the extra sets was for the Mercedes, and one set was for the Explorer. There were also keys to another Mercedes and a Cadillac. It looked like there was also a safe deposit key on one set. Maybe there was a safety deposit box at their bank where we could find more useful information. There were also extra house keys that didn't match the Mulberry house. We figured it could be an investment house he had bought or maybe the Atlanta property.

We took an early lunch before starting our afternoon interviews. Both of us had missed breakfast again. Bill suggested Magnolia Natural Market and Café, and I agreed. Bill took a different route and drove up Banks Mill Road past the city of Aiken's ball fields, up South Boundary Avenue, which was canopied by live oak trees. It looked like we were going down a tunnel of trees. Bill turned on York Street and parked at Magnolia's. I had a tuna wrap with capers and toasted almonds. It wasn't the quantity of yesterday's barbecue but very tasty. Bill had a turkey burger.

While I was eating my wrap, I said, "Who analyzes all the physical evidence?"

Bill explained, "SLED. It's the South Carolina Law Enforcement Division, which is a state version of the FBI. They've got everything, state-of-the-art technology. They help all over the state, but they work out of Columbia."

"How does SLED get the Lowes' evidence?"

"In this case, an officer drove to SLED with the evidence. A high priority was placed on the case, but we're competing against the rest of the state."

"Now that you have time to think about it, what do you think happened?" I asked Bill.

"We usually have domestic violence cases where some family member gets himself killed and someone in the family or kinfolk are the one that kills the family member. The other murder cases involve robbery. This case looks very professional and clean and not family related or part of a robbery or spat."

"What about Wandita's husband?"

"He's probably not a professional, but he could have driven down from Atlanta and killed them. He probably got the alarm codes from the notebook. He would have the safe combinations too."

A forensic tech called while we were at lunch and told us we could pick up the notebook. He also told us he found Wandita's and Tomas's fingerprints in addition to the Lowes' fingerprints. Bill drove us back to the police station, and we picked up the notebook. Bill then drove us down to Randy and Karen Williams. I went through the notebook as Bill drove. Sure enough, alarm codes were in the book as well as the safe codes. In addition, there was a listing of property addresses with tax parcel numbers. The listings didn't include the city or town they were located. The notebook also had account numbers for utilities, phone, Internet, etc., as well as bank account numbers. The bank account numbers had initials for the banks rather than a name. I suggested to Bill that our rookie research the information in the book.

Both Randy and Karen Williams were retired and had lived in the neighborhood for seven years. We spent some time talking to the Williams and got the same information. The Williams didn't exactly know where the Lowes came from but thought they had said they were from New Jersey. They didn't know anything about children, relatives, or travels and didn't know alarm codes or have keys to the house.

We spent most of the rest of the day talking to five neighbors, all retirees and all couples. All were friendly and tried to be helpful. This was different from in Chicago where you had to threaten to take a neighbor to the police station before they answered questions.

Two more interviews were with widowers (one man and one woman). The woman was April Walcott, and the guy was Isaac Reynolds. They lived a good distance apart in the neighborhood on opposite sides of the Lowes. Neither could add anything to what we already knew. I did try to play matchmaker and asked the man in the second interview if he knew the woman we just interviewed. I told him she was a widower too and he should call her.

We called Wandita's husband, Tomas, and confirmed he was coming back to Aiken on Friday. He agreed to meet us Friday night or Saturday morning if he got back late.

It was now five o'clock, so working folks should be getting home. We could have followed the cars coming home into their driveway. Instead, we followed the cars and then called the house after they had time to get into the house. We had more interviews until about nine o'clock and then decided to stop for the day.

I called to check on my parents. The nurse said they were sleeping. This was the second day I had missed seeing them in the daytime since moving to Aiken. I drove over to the hospital to make a quick visit before I went home. Both were asleep, so I didn't stay long.

Chapter 6

Thursday Morning—Jessie

I went by the hospital before going to work and found both my parents still asleep. They were on a lot of medication that made them sleep a lot. I'd hopefully come back at lunch time and catch them awake.

I made it to the police station at eight o'clock. I usually made it to the police station in time to talk to the shift lieutenant and nightshift officers, but not today. I went by my office first to check e-mails. My office was ten feet by ten feet and was in the back of the police station. It was an interior office, so there were no windows. It probably had been the janitor's room and was converted for me. There was a typical metal desk with fake wood grain top, a file cabinet, and a bookcase. There was a desk chair and a side chair for one visitor. The computer and printer were fairly new, an improvement from Chicago.

I then went to Bill's office, and he said the captain wanted to see us. Bill got up from his chair, and I followed him to the captain's office. We took seats at an oval wood table that matched his desk and credenza. The captain was on the phone and raised a finger to tell us he'd be with us in a minute. After he hung up, he came over to the table and said, "Tell me what you know about the Lowes' murders."

Bill answered without using his redneck slang, "There isn't a lot to tell yet. No murder weapon and no evidence of a break in. The fingerprints so far appear to be from the Lowes, a neighbor, the cleaning lady, and the cleaning lady's husband. The physical evidence was sent to SLED, and we're waiting on the results. IT is still checking the electronics. The main suspect is a neighbor, William Bradford. He had the opportunity, since they had given him access to their security. No motive yet, but he used to be in business with the victim, so we'll keep digging. The house cleaner and her husband are also suspects."

"I know William Bradford. Why do you suspect him?" the captain asked.

Bill answered, "William had a business relationship buying foreclosed properties with Tom Lowe. He also had access to the Lowes' house. The motive is what we can't figure out yet."

"It'd be hard for me to believe he could commit murder, but I've been fooled by a lot of people in my career. Keep me posted as you investigate him. What are your immediate plans for the investigation?"

Bill answered, "We'll be looking more into William. We'll also look into the housekeeper and her husband. We also have a few neighbors left we'll interview. We really need to find out more about the Atlanta connection and the New Jersey connection. We'll also get into the safes today, which may help."

"What do you think the Atlanta connection is all about?"

"I'm not sure. It does seem fishy that almost all their travels were to Atlanta, and no one knew who they were seeing in Atlanta. It seems just as fishy that there're no relatives that visited them, and no one knew whether they had relatives."

"Maybe we'll get a break when SLED starts sending us results," the captain added.

"We'll check with IT today to see what they have. Maybe there's information on the computers or in the alarm system that'll give us clues."

"What can I tell the media?"

"Tell them we're still in the beginning of the investigation," Bill answered.

"I think I'll tell them we have some leads we're pursuing. You should keep me informed during the day if you have any information that's worth passing along."

I said, "Is there any way to speed up SLED?"

"I'll call this morning to see if I can get them to give us information faster," the captain answered.

The captain then said as he stood up, "Thanks for your time. Keep me posted if you have anything worth passing on."

We went back to Bill's office where Bill had started a murder board. He called the rookie, and the rookie joined us. The murder board had William Bradford, Wandita, and Wandita's husband as suspects. He had questions on the board about Atlanta and New Jersey but didn't have many more details.

Bill asked the rookie, "What have you found so far?"

"I checked the public records in Princeton, New Jersey, and couldn't find anything about a Carol and Tom Lowe. They didn't own property in their name in Mercer County, and there wasn't any data showing that they lived there. I'll keep looking."

"Are you going to look in adjoining counties?" I asked.

"I will. I've also looked into William Bradford. He owns a lot of property and some businesses and is worth quite a few millions. He's bought and sold a lot of property. There were a few properties bought and sold with Tom Lowe, and both William and Tom were on the corporate documents. The only blemish in his police record was a liquor-related misdemeanor at one of his restaurants."

"What about Tomas Lopez?" Bill asked.

"He's a different story. He has several blemishes. He was in jail for third-degree burglary. He also had several misdemeanors for disturbing the peace, simple assault and battery, drunkenness in public and public nuisance when he was younger. He's got a long sheet."

"It sounds like we'll have an interesting conversation with Mr. Lopez. He may have been busy Monday night," Bill said.

I had made copies of the pages of the notebook and handed them to Jeffery. "There are a lot of properties, and we need you to check them out. See if they match the properties bought with William Bradford and check out the other properties. There are also account numbers that you can research."

The rookie reviewed the sheets and said, "The listings only have a street address. Do you know what city they're located in?"

"That's what we need you to find out. Maybe some are in New Jersey or Atlanta," I answered.

"Oh. Okay," he said with a little embarrassment.

I handed him a listing of the immediate neighbors. "See if you can find any dirt on these people too."

"Let me get started." He left without asking if there was more.

After Jeffery left the office, Bill called the IT folks looking at the computers and security system, and I listened to a one-sided conversation. After he got off the phone, he said, "The IT folks don't see anything unusual about the security system. It wasn't tampered with and was shut down appropriately. The cameras were shut down too. It appears a remote unit was used to shut down the system like the one we found in the master bedroom. They're still checking the computers."

Bill drove us to the Palmetto Golf Club. I had researched the course the night before and found out it had started with four golf holes in 1892 when Aiken was a winter colony for the rich and famous. The land it was located on was part of the 2,100-acre Hitchcock Woods urban park, which was donated to the City of Aiken for recreational use only. The largest Chicago park is Lincoln Park, which is 1,200 acres.

I had never played golf, but the club looked like a nice place. The golf pro, Jim Wilson, was in the pro shop as well as another person, Samantha Kuhn, manning the register. Jim was an older gentleman with a weathered and wrinkled face, probably from spending most of his time outdoors. Samantha was a petite, older woman with blonde hair and a wide smile. She didn't have weathered skin, had only a few wrinkles, and wasn't wearing makeup. We introduced ourselves and asked them about Tom and Carol Lowe. They both knew the couple.

Bill asked, "Who did Tom and Carol play golf with?"

Jim answered with a heavy southern drawl, "Carol only played a few times while Tom played fairly often. Tom usually played with William Bradford as a twosome. When Tom wasn't playing with William, he usually played with one of the dog fights, played alone, or joined another group or person."

"Were there any regular playing partners other than William?"

"Not that I know of."

"Did either of you ever hear the Lowes and William argue?" I asked.

Samantha said demurely, "I heard Tom tell William he was cheating many times." She slinked back a little after saying it.

"I never heard them disagree, but I'm usually out on the course," Jim answered.

Bill asked to see the application made by Tom and Carol. Since it was a private club, members had to apply for membership, be sponsored by someone, and be approved for membership. Jim brought the application for us to look at. The sponsor on the form was William Bradford. The form had a place to fill out for a person to notify in case of emergency. Normally the contact was a relative. In this case, the Lowes had put William Bradford as the person to notify. I was hoping we'd get a phone number of a relative, but no luck.

We asked to see Tom and Carol's locker. Both had their golf clubs, golf shoes, umbrellas, and rain gear. We checked the golf bags and didn't see anything unusual.

A forensic tech was meeting us at the Lowes' house when we opened the safes, so that was our next stop. Back down Whiskey Road we went. Bill used the combination in the notebook and opened the gun safe. The forensic techs had already dusted the outside of the safes for prints and began dusting the inside of the gun safe.

While the forensic tech was checking the safe, we called the local bank to see if we could find out about a safety deposit box. The person we talked to at Security Federal stated that the Lowes didn't have a safety deposit box with them.

I said, "The Lowes could have a safety deposit box at one of the other banks. Do you want to call all the other banks in town?"

"Let's ask the captain to get someone to do it. There's probably a clerk or officer who can make time for this task. We've got the rookie pretty busy already," Bill answered.

"Do you have any idea how we can find out what house the other sets of keys fit? I'm guessing the keys are to a house or apartment in Atlanta unless the Lowes lied about their trips. The keys could be to a local foreclosure house not in the files, but it looked like all the foreclosure properties were sold," I said.

"I'd assume the keys are to a house or apartment in Atlanta too. I don't think the keys are for a foreclosure house since all of them were sold."

"I'd like to visit my parents quickly this afternoon. I haven't seen them awake all week," I said.

"You need to take time for them. We've been putting in long days." Bill knew about my parents being in the hospital. The captain had told the story to the investigation team when he explained my temporary addition to the sheriff's department.

When the forensic tech finished with the gun safe, Bill opened the other safe for the forensic tech. It was empty.

We then checked the gun safe, and there were two rifles and four handguns. The rifles were a Ruger No. 1 Varminter K1-V-BBZ and a Marlin 336XLR. The handguns were two Colt Mustang Pocketlites, a Glock 19, and a Ruger LC9. The Mustangs would be good guns for traveling since they were very light. There were earmuffs for shooting, boxes of ammunition for each weapon, gun cleaning materials, and shooting jackets. On the top shelf were bulls-eye targets that showed pretty good patterns. Mr. Lowe was an accomplished shooter.

While we waited for the forensic tech to finish, I called the doctors and dentist. Bill called Charles Schwab.

"Dr. Bedingfield's office. This is Maria. How can I help you?" the first doctor's office answered.

"This is Investigator Barnes with the Aiken County Sheriff's Department. I'd like to get copies of the medical file for Tom Lowe. Mr. Lowe was murdered this week, and his file is needed for the investigation," I said as politely as I could.

"I'm sorry, but we can't release any information without a subpoena," Maria said dutifully.

"Are there any exceptions? Especially for murder."

"Let me think. Well. No," Maria answered coyly.

I made my calls to all the doctors and dentist and got the same response. None could release any information without a subpoena. I expected that would be the answer, but this was the South and people were supposed to be nicer.

Bill called Charles Schwab and was also told a subpoena was needed. He then called the coroner and found out the coroner's report would be available this afternoon. Bill then placed a call to the captain to ask for additional help checking with all the banks to find the Lowes' safe deposit box. The captain said he would find somebody. Bill asked that he attend a four o'clock meeting in Bill's office.

The forensic tech finished with the safe, and we checked to see if anything was in a corner or in a false shelf bottom. Nothing was in the safe.

Bill asked the forensic tech, "Did you see anything helpful in the safes?"

"No. It appears that all the fingerprints in the safe are from Mary or Tom Lowe. I'll confirm it when I get back to the office."

We went back to the office, and I left to visit my parents. Bill said he'd add more information to the murder board, line up someone from IT to attend the four o'clock meeting, and get a copy of the coroner's report.

At four, Bill had the meeting in a conference room rather than his cramped office. The attendees were the rookie, the officer the captain got for us, an IT geek, and us. Bill started the meeting with a review of the coroner's report.

"The report said that both were shot with .22-caliber bullets. The time of death was approximately ten thirty at night. Blood tests showed a slight amount of alcohol in each. Since we found wine glasses in the dishwasher and William said he was visiting on the same night and drank wine, I assumed there'd be alcohol in their blood. The report also showed Tom's blood contained traces of the prescription drugs he was taking. Mary's blood analysis also showed traces of her prescription drugs."

Bill looked at IT and asked, "What have you found?"

Oscar Zerwinski was tall and lanky with a buzz cut. He answered, "The alarm system wasn't tampered with, and the system was shut down with a remote. I suspect someone shut the system down before coming in the house or was already in the house when it was shut down."

"When was the system armed on Monday night?" I asked.

"About ten. That was probably when the Lowes went to bed. There was a remote in the master bedroom that was probably used to arm the system and a different remote to disarm it shortly thereafter." Some of the information we already knew, but the team needed to hear it too.

"We found another remote for the alarm system in their Mercedes but not in the Explorer. There could be one missing. Do you know how many remotes were programmed in?" I asked.

"I'm not sure I can tell how many remotes there were, but I can tell how many remotes were used to arm and disarm the system. I'll check on that."

"Tell us about the computers," Bill said.

Oscar responded, "We're not completely through with them, but here's what we know so far. The information on the computers started when they moved here three years ago. I suspect they bought the computers then. There wasn't any information about relatives or people outside of Aiken other than professionals or online buying. We'll send over a list of all the e-mail recipients for you to go through. We'll also send over a printout of all the websites they visited and the transactions they made. It'll be a long list."

Bill and I looked at Jeffery.

"I know. I'll be getting the printout and websites too," Jeffery said.

Bill grinned. "You will. Tell us what you've found."

Jeffery cleared his throat before he spoke. "Do I need to cover what we talked about this morning?"

"No. Just since this then. I'll summarize what you told us this morning," Bill said.

"I looked more at Wandita and Tomas Lopez, and they're deep in debt. I couldn't figure out why, but their credit cards are at the max, a foreclosure was started on their house, and their cars will probably be repossessed soon. Mr. Lopez was on unemployment for about four months, which may have contributed. They should have filed bankruptcy but didn't." Jeffery paused for questions.

He continued when no one asked anything. "I checked out a few of the neighbors today, and some aren't pristine. Ralph and Mary Jones are in bankruptcy. According to the bankruptcy records, Ralph also owes a lot of people, including three ex-wives. He also made poor investments in penny stocks. Most of the funds lost in the penny stocks were Mary's money. The court has appointed a trustee to handle their finances."

I interrupted, "It looks like Ralph or Mary or both could be suspects. The rich people file bankruptcy, and the poor people don't. Interesting."

"There's more. Randy Williams has a restraining order against Ralph. Evidently, Ralph and Randy's wife were screwing around. Both are *old*." Jeffery made a face and mouthed yuck.

"Old people have sex too. Randy's wife made Ralph randy," Oscar said, smiling.

"What else?" Bill asked.

"I checked the property listings in the Aiken County records, and all the listings match except for one. I also checked the accounts, and all of them match accounts in Aiken County except for one."

"Where's the extra property located and what's the extra account?" I asked.

"I didn't have time to research either today. I will tomorrow."

"Check them against the printouts from the computer. It may help," I suggested.

"I will."

"What have you found?" Bill looked at the officer that the captain had gotten for us.

Wally Blackburn was an older guy with gray hair growing on the side of an otherwise bald head. He was wearing black reading glasses on top of a sad face with large eyes and a large, red nose. He was overweight and was slumped in his chair. He looked like he could retire any day.

Wally answered, "I was just assigned to help you late this afternoon and haven't started yet. I'll start checking with the banks in the morning."

Bill stood up and said, "It now sounds like we have at least five suspects. They are William Bradford, Wandita and Tomas Lopez, and Ralph and Mary Jones. Jeffery found out Tomas was in jail for third-degree burglary and has other lesser offenses. Tomas probably also had access to the alarm codes and safe combinations. William was at the Lowes' house, knew the alarm system well, and probably also knew the Lowes kept their safe combinations in a notebook in their office. Jessie and I opened the safes today. The Lowes had several guns in the gun safe, but most importantly the other safe was empty."

"So now we suspect it was a robbery?" Oscar asked.

I answered, "It appears the perp or perps who killed the Lowes also cleaned out the safe, assuming the safe had contents."

"How will we know whether the safe contained anything?" Oscar asked.

"Hopefully we'll find a record showing what was in the safe. If not, we'll assume something was in there," I answered.

"It makes more sense if there was something in the safe. Otherwise we don't have a motive," Bill added.

"Hopefully the notebook will list the safe contents," I said.

"I've asked for subpoenas for the Lowes' doctors, dentist, the bank, and the investment broker. I should have them tomorrow. Keep digging, and we'll solve this case soon." Bill's voice wasn't as optimistic as his words.

After Bill told everyone we would meet again tomorrow at four, he and I remained in the conference room.

Bill asked, "What do you think happened at the Lowes' house on Monday night?"

I answered, "I now suspect our perp or perps had the remote for the alarm system. It appears the motive was robbery, but the murder looks professional."

"I agree with the perp using the remote. I now believe it was a robbery, and that's the motive. We should get a subpoena for William's house, the Lopez house, and the Jones house."

I wanted to be involved when we searched William's residence. I could learn more about his personal life if I could get in his drawers.

I said, "I'm not sure we have enough evidence to search the homes yet."

"Yeah, we'd need more evidence than we have to get subpoenas. William is a likely suspect, but there's no evidence so far that would allow us to arrest him. Maybe Mary Lowe and William were having an affair, Tom found out about it, and William decided to kill them both."

"That seems unlikely since William is at least twenty years younger than Mary, and I'd think William could have about anyone in town he wanted. He wouldn't need to be with a woman twenty years older." I said this as I thought about the couple of times I had been with guys ten years younger. I'm thirty-two now and peaking sexually. Unfortunately, there's no one that could testify to that lately. I was sure that when I was ten years older, I'd be willing to be with guys twenty years younger. So the idea wasn't inconceivable but seemed unlikely in this case. Women seemed to go for younger men, but men didn't go for older women.

"Maybe she has special talents that would make a younger man want to be with her."

"What special talents would you have in mind? What talents would make you have an affair with a woman twenty years older than you?"

"I guess you didn't know my wife is near to twenty years older than me." He said this with a straight face.

"I heard you had stepchildren that were your age. I'm sure it's helpful now that your wife is on Medicare." I thought I remembered someone saying that Bill was divorced and single. I also figured Bill was in his late thirties, so I was kidding him about his age.

"So you know I'm not hitched. Since I'm single, I'd welcome an older woman taking me on as a student to teach me all of her tricks." Bill grinned.

"I don't need to know about your personal situation, but I'll be on the lookout for an older woman for you. Maybe the captain's secretary could help you out."

The captain's secretary looked to be about seventy years old.

"I think she's married. Except for that, I'd be asking her for a date." Bill raised his eyebrows.

"Enough already. Let's figure out what we need to do to solve this murder case," I said.

I did enjoy the bantering, but I didn't want to give Bill any ideas since he was single. He was certainly not my type. If he looked like William, had a house like William, was smart like William, and was rich like William, then he'd be my type. I'd certainly say that William was my type. No wonder I hadn't been happy with a guy before; I hadn't met my William.

Bill said, "I also talked to SLED this afternoon, and they'll e-mail me the information they have so far. They said it wasn't much since they had higher priorities to work on right now."

"We should talk to Ralph and Mary tomorrow, and we can talk to Tomas tomorrow," I said.

"We should have the subpoenas so we can serve them tomorrow. Hopefully we can get copies on the spot," Bill said.

"I'm going to see my parents, so I'll see you tomorrow," I said as I started for the door.

Bill said, "I may be late. The captain's secretary and I are meeting later tonight."

"Let me know, and I'll cover for you."

My mother was awake but very groggy when I went in to see her. She had a broken arm and broken leg that were in casts, several internal injuries, and a concussion. She had had three surgeries so far, and the hospital had patched her up the best they could for now. At least that was what the doctor had told me.

Mom recognized who I was and told me that she hoped I was eating right. Here she was in intensive care, and she was concerned that I was taking care of myself.

I said, "I'm doing fine, Mother. How are you feeling?"

"I'm pretty dizzy and numb all over. I think they have me on strong drugs. Otherwise, I'm doing fine." Mother was slurring her words, and her eyes were dilated.

"Is there anything I can get for you?"

"No, I don't need anything. Are you sure you're taking care of yourself?"

"I'm taking care of myself, Mom. I'm working a lot with the police department on a case."

"That's nice, sweetie," Mom said this as I saw her eyes starting to shut. She was asleep shortly after saying sweetie.

I then went to see my dad. He was close by in another intensive care room. When I went to see him, he was asleep. His injuries were more severe than Mom's, so he was still drugged to the hilt. I sat down and stayed with him for a while and held his hand. I always thought Dad would get sick from being an environmental engineer. I figured he'd have some strange environmental waste come out of the ground and attack him like in the movies.

I was leaving Dad's room when my phone rang. I didn't recognize the number but answered anyway.

"This is William Bradford, the neighbor of the Lowes."

"Yes, I remember you."

I didn't want to tell him I also knew him from my fantasies.

"I found out you're new to Aiken and thought I should offer to show you the town, starting with dinner tonight."

This was strange getting a call from William, but he would be on top of my list for my first date in Aiken. Being a prime suspect was a slight formality.

"I appreciate the offer, but I'm very busy. Maybe I'll take you up on the offer later." I wanted to leave my options open.

"If you change your mind, let me know. I'm a great tour guide."

"Thanks anyway for now."

I ended the call wondering whether I had made the right choice.

I went through a drive-through and bought a burger and fries to go. I wasn't following my mother's advice about eating right. I had lots of thoughts going through my head as I tried to sleep.

Friday Morning—Jessie

I was responding to e-mails about my open Chicago cases when Bill came into my office Friday morning.

He said, "Do you need more time to work before we talk about the day?"

"Let me finish this last sentence. It'll take just a second." I finished typing and looked at him. "I'm ready."

"We'll talk in my office."

I followed him to his office. I preferred sitting in an office with windows. I was one of the top investigators in Chicago and was well respected. In Aiken, I was relegated to a back office and had a mentor.

"Where should we start today? We have the subpoenas and could start serving them. We need to talk to Ralph and Mary again and more neighbors. We'll be talking to Tomas later." Bill stated the items he knew.

"I'd like to go back and talk to William again since Tom was accusing William of cheating when they were at the golf course. I'd also like to talk about the alarm system remote," I said.

"Call William to set up a time, and I'll call Ralph and Mary," Bill suggested.

When I called William, he answered, "Hello, this is William." It was his business voice, which was very sexy. If he wasn't our most likely suspect, I'd like to hear his business voice more.

"This is Jessica from the Aiken County Sheriff."

"Hello, Jessica. Have you changed your mind already?" He changed to his nonbusiness voice, which was even sexier.

"No, this is business. Bill, the lead investigator, and I would like to talk to you again. When's a good time?"

"Does Bill want to join us for dinner?" William asked.

"We'd like to talk to you today."

"Are you sure we can't mix business and pleasure?"

I wanted to mix business and pleasure with him but knew it was slightly inappropriate.

"We just want to ask a few more questions."

"I'm downtown now and can stop by the police station if you want. Is that okay?"

"How long will it be before you get here?"

"I'll be there in about twenty minutes," William said.

I said thanks and hit the end button on the phone. I told Bill that William would be here in about twenty minutes, and then I paused while my pulse went back to normal.

Bill said, "We're meeting with Ralph and Mary at one. Should we put William in one of the interview rooms where we can videotape his responses?"

"I don't think we should put him under the bright light and play good cop and bad cop with him yet. If we can get evidence that links him to the murders, then we'll water board him until he confesses."

I wanted to say that I'd be glad to use my special techniques involving ropes and paddles. I had other ways to get someone to tell the truth also. Bill would want to volunteer, so I didn't tell him all the things I could do to get a confession.

Bill said, "I guess we should talk to him in my office then." I got another chair out of a neighboring office for William and made sure he would be sitting close to me so I could see how he smelled. I still hadn't given up on William as the father of my children, but I wasn't quite sure I wanted to marry a murderer.

When William arrived, the front office called, and I went out to get him. He was wearing jeans and a T-shirt with Harley-Davidson on the front. Maybe he had a Harley-Davidson motorcycle and he would have something in common with Bill. Not a good thought. I just couldn't see Bill and William riding bikes together.

William sat down and looked as good as he did during the first interview. There was only a soap fragrance coming from him. Maybe he didn't use aftershave lotion or anything else that would make him smell unmanly. I was still trying to determine the soap he used when Bill said, "Thanks for coming in on short notice. We're trying to understand what we've learned so far and hope you can help us make sense of it."

Bill was more diplomatic than I was, and his statement should put William at ease. William was more likely aware that he was our prime suspect and didn't go for the bull from Bill.

I got right to the point of the interview. "We've interviewed a person that overheard Tom accusing you of cheating him. It sounds like you weren't being truthful with us earlier."

William didn't react as most people would as he looked in Bill's eyes and into my eyes. When he looked in my eyes, I lost my concentration for a few seconds. It could be time for my special interrogation techniques.

"Who was accusing me of this and what does it pertain to?"

Bill answered, "Tom was overheard at the golf course accusing you of cheating many times."

"That explains it. Tom didn't like to lose money to me and always accused me of cheating when he lost. Tom thought he should win every time even though we were playing for only a few dollars. I did let him win occasionally," William said.

"The two of you were in business together. Are you sure it wasn't business related?" Bill asked.

William remained calm but stated emphatically, "Certainly not. You're welcome to review our business dealings. They were fairly straightforward."

"Did you handle all the funds for the purchases and sales?" I asked.

"I did, and it's well documented." He sat absolutely still with no twitches or nervous movements.

I thought he was believable, but he probably was a great poker player.

Bill switched the subject and asked, "Since you were close to the Lowes, do you know where they kept the remotes for their alarm system?"

William was thoughtful for a few seconds while he sat with his hands across his chest.

"I'm sure they had remotes in their cars and at least one in the house. I helped Tom activate three remotes, but he may have bought more."

I asked, "When was the last time you rode in one of their cars?"

"It was last weekend. It was Tom's turn to drive to the golf course."

"Which car did he drive?"

"The Explorer." William answered quickly.

Bill asked, "Have you met Wandita's husband, Tomas?"

"I have. He helped Wandita clean several times."

William remained relaxed and unruffled.

"What do you know about Tomas?"

"Wandita said he'd been in a lot of trouble when he was younger but had straightened himself out when they got married."

"What kind of trouble?" Bill asked.

"I'm not sure. She said he was in jail, but I don't know the reason."

"Did you have any reason to distrust him?" I asked.

"No, I didn't."

"Did anything end up missing when he was helping Wandita clean?"

"No."

I thought William was telling the truth. I had interviewed a lot of people and could usually tell who was believable.

"Were you aware that Ralph and Mary had financial problems?" I asked.

"I was. Ralph explained their difficulties to me, and I gave him the name of a good bankruptcy lawyer. He asked to borrow money from me, but he was a bad risk."

"Do you know if he approached the Lowes to borrow money?" I asked.

"He did. Tom asked me about loaning them money, and I advised him not to."

"Do you know whether they filed for bankruptcy?" Bill asked.

"They did. It was a couple of months ago."

"Did Tom or Mary ever tell you what they kept in the home safe?"

"They didn't. We didn't talk about our assets."

I started thinking about William's assets and whether I needed to do undercover work. I wondered what covers he had on his bed. We'd need to get a search warrant for his house before I went undercover.

"Did you ever see the smaller safe open?" I asked.

"No."

"You spent a lot of time at the Lowes' house. Are you sure you're being truthful?"

"I am." William seemed somewhat offended.

We told William that we appreciated him taking the time to stop by the office and asked him to let us know if he remembered anything that would be helpful. We gave him our business cards again that had our police department office numbers and cell numbers.

William said as I was walking him to the door, "Are you sure you can't make a little time available for dinner? Consider it a welcome to Aiken dinner."

"I do appreciate the offer, but I'm quite busy."

I was tempted. Part of me was saying yes and part of me was saying no.

"I'll be at your beck and call if you need to get acclimated to Aiken."

"Thanks, William. Good-bye."

Bill was at his desk tapping his pen on his desk when I returned.

Bill said, "I don't know whether to believe him or not. He did have the opportunity to get the remote out of the Explorer, and I'm guessing he knew the Lowes had valuables in the safe. He's certainly a cool character. If I had my druthers, I'd arrest him and then find out the truth, but I can't do that."

I must have been thinking about my fantasies when I said jokingly, "We could get a woman officer to go undercover, seduce him, and get the truth."

"William would figure that out fairly quickly. He may have already slept with the officer." Bill grinned.

"We could get someone from Columbia or Augusta or maybe a SLED agent," I suggested.

"We'll need someone that's nice looking and has brains. I don't need a woman with brains, but William probably does. She can probably still live in Columbia or Augusta while we arrange a meeting for William and her," Bill said.

"Does the department have funds to set her up in an apartment and get her a nice car to drive?" I asked.

"I don't think the department has funds to set her up in a motel room for one night. The department is too poor to pay attention," Bill responded with a sly grin.

I helped shut down prostitute businesses in Chicago and now wanted to run one in Aiken. My fellow officers in Chicago had been involved in lots of undercover work. In some cases, we would have to get really close to guys.

"We'll keep that plan as a last resort," I said.

"Let's take a trip to Columbia and get the investment account information," Bill said as he got up.

I followed him to his car, and we were on the way to Columbia with a subpoena.

The trip to Columbia was almost all on the interstate. We passed the Aiken airport where I saw only small two-seater planes. The Charles Schwab office was next to the interstate. We were shown to a conference room and were joined shortly by Zachery Brown. Zachery looked to be in his twenties with slicked back hair, a black suit, a starched shirt, and a red tie. He had a slim face with narrow eyes, a thin nose, and a big, toothy smile with extremely white teeth.

"Hello. I'm Zachery Brown." He gave each of us a firm handshake.

We introduced ourselves as Zachery gave us printouts for the Lowes' account.

"As you can see, the Lowes have about a million dollars invested with us. The account is diversified with several mutual funds and types of bonds. We have managed their funds for three years."

We both looked at the printouts. I noticed they had made a reasonable return on their funds.

"How much money did the Lowes start with three years ago?" I asked.

Zachery looked at the copy of the printout he had before answering. "They started with a hundred thousand and have added funds over the past three years."

"Can we get a copy of the beneficiary form they have for the account?" I asked.

"I'd hoped you wouldn't ask since they never completed one for us. These are copies of all the documents completed by the Lowes for the account," Zachery said as he handed us a file folder.

We looked at the documents in the file folder and saw the same information we saw in the Lowes' home office.

We thanked Zachery and headed back to Aiken.

"Maybe the Lowes are in witness protection and that's why their life started again three years ago," I suggested.

"Maybe so. Do you know how to find out if someone is in witness protection? It's not something we do in Aiken County."

I called my buddies in Chicago, but they couldn't help. They promised to ask around and call me back. I'd never tried to find someone in witness protection. We had placed a few in the program when I was in Chicago. It was a shock to those placed in the program since they were relocated, had to change doctors and dentists, had to cancel their Netflix account, had to cancel their fruit of the month, etc.

Bill called the captain, and the captain didn't know of anyone in Aiken in the witness protection plan. The captain was sure he would be notified if there was someone.

"Do you think Ralph was having sex with Carol? After his affair with Karen was stopped, he may have looked for other quarry. Ralph probably still had blue pills he needed to use," I said.

"Maybe, but we probably shouldn't ask him in front of Mary."

Bill stopped at Baynham's Restaurant near the airport on the way back. I had chicken fried steak with French fries and macaroni and cheese. Bill had pot roast, green beans, and fried apples. I gorged myself.

We arrived at the Jones house just before one. Ralph met us at the door and invited us in. We sat in the same chairs as before.

I didn't see Mary and asked, "Is Mary here?"

"She's not back from her doctor's appointment. Do you want to wait for her?"

"We'll get started. We understand there's a restraining order against you. Explain that to us," Bill said.

Maybe it was good Mary was delayed.

"Karen told Randy she slept with me, so he had a temporary restraining order issued. I went over to fix a plumbing problem when Randy was out of town, Karen started telling me about her husband cheating on her, and somehow we ended up in bed. I was sleeping in another bedroom since I had lost almost all of Mary's savings, so I was easily enticed. Karen wasn't exactly innocent since she showed up at the door only wearing a loose robe and a smile."

It sounded like Karen's original intention was to get Ralph to work on her personal plumbing.

"Did you and Karen only do this once?" I asked.

Ralph slumped a little and got a guilty look on his face. "I went over a few more times. I'm not sure what Karen told Randy. I told Mary it was only the one time."

Ralph wouldn't make a good poker player, and Mary probably didn't believe him.

"Has Karen had sex with other guys in the neighborhood?" I asked.

"Karen's had sex with half the town, so probably so."

"Have you had sex with other women in the neighborhood?" I asked as I thought about Karen.

It almost looked like pride when Ralph answered, "A few others."

I turned my head and rolled my eyes. Bill looked like he had admiration for Ralph.

"Was Carol Lowe one of them?" I asked.

"No."

"Who were they?" I asked.

"Two of them are widowers. One is April Walcott, and the other is June Samuels. The third one is married. Do you need her name?"

April Walcott was the widower I was trying to hook up. No wonder she wasn't interested.

"Yes," I answered.

"She's Melissa French," he said almost in a whisper as if he wasn't telling us.

I wanted to ask how many blue pills he took a month but didn't ask. Ralph had been working on a lot of plumbing in the neighborhood.

"Are you still having sex with these women?"

"Yes," he said proudly.

I'm sure he wanted to brag that he could keep several women happy but didn't say it. Ralph was a scum bag.

Bill was grinning, so I asked, "You've been divorced three times?"

"Yes."

"What were the grounds for the divorces?" I asked, expecting infidelity as the reason for all three.

"Irreconcilable differences."

I guessed the ex-wives compromised or were bought off. He probably promised he'd pay them a lot of money, and now he was in bankruptcy.

"Tell us about the bankruptcy," Bill said.

"We made some bad investments and owed a lot of money, so *we* filed bankruptcy. A trustee is assigned to manage our financials," Ralph said.

"We understand almost all of the money invested was Mary's. Is that true?"

"Most of it was," he reluctantly agreed.

"Was she upset about the money being lost?" I asked.

"She was. I told her we'd get it back, but she didn't believe me."

I didn't either, so I agreed with Mary.

"Did you ask Tom and Carol Lowe if you could borrow money?" Bill quizzed.

"I asked Tom, but he said he didn't have funds available to loan."

"Did you know what was in the Lowes' home safe?"

"I didn't." He didn't elaborate, and I'm not sure I believed him.

"Did you talk to the Lowes about investments?" I asked.

"Sometimes."

"What did the Lowes say they invested in?" I continued.

"Tom said they invested a lot in stocks."

"Do you have remotes for your alarm system?" I asked.

"I do."

"Where do you keep them?" I asked.

"Two are in the cars, and one is in the house."

"What would you do to get Mary's money back?"

"Anything," he answered quickly.

"Even murder?"

"No, I wouldn't kill anyone."

"Would you hire someone?"

"No."

"Could you call Mary and see when she'll be home?" I urged. I thought we would grill him more in front of Mary. Bill must have thought the same since he didn't ask more questions.

Ralph called and told us Mary had decided to go visit her sister for the weekend in Charleston. So much for interviewing Mary. We told Ralph we'd continue the interview on Monday after Mary got back.

We went to the dentist's and doctors' offices, and all told us we could pick up copies of the files on Monday. We made it back to the station for the four o'clock meeting.

Bill started the meeting telling the group about our interviews and the investment documents. Bill had received a partial report from SLED and summarized it. The summary didn't have anything we didn't already know. Bill asked Oscar to go next.

"We checked the alarm system more. A different remote was used to disarm the alarm system than was used to arm the system. It appears the Lowes armed the system when they went to bed with the remote in the bedroom, and someone else disarmed it using a different remote.

"We did a lot of searches in the computer directories and didn't find any documents that gave us any addresses or phone numbers other than the ones we printed out for you. We dug deeper into the history files and didn't find any additional information. It seems we've given you all the information we can get from the computers."

"Were there any iPads or anything similar?" I asked.

"Two iPads were given to us that we need to check."

"Thanks, Oscar. Wally," Bill said.

"I called every bank and credit union in Aiken, and none of them had a safety deposit box for Tom or Mary Lowe. I even had them do a cross check against the address on Mulberry."

"Thanks, Wally. Jeffery," Bill said.

"I checked the property listing that wasn't in Aiken County, and it's in Fulton County, Georgia. The deed for the property has Thomas and Caroline Jenkins as the owners. I couldn't find a mortgage on the property, and the property was bought about four years ago. I searched for the Jenkinses in the Atlanta directories, and the address that came up was the address we have, 4212 Pebble Beach Drive. I didn't find a phone number at the same address."

Oscar had his laptop connected to the conference room projector and had 4212 Pebble Beach Drive shown on the screen with Google Earth. The house was imposing. It was a large, three-story house with stone and brick.

"Did you research Thomas and Caroline Jenkins?"

"I haven't yet. I was checking all the information on the computer printout and researching more of the neighbors."

"What about the extra account number?" I asked.

"I haven't had time to check on it either."

"Did you find anything with the computer printouts?" Bill asked.

"The notebook list correlates with the information in the computer. The notebook had account passwords, so I've been able to check credit cards and other accounts. All the addresses for the accounts are the Mulberry address, and the names on the accounts are Carol and Tom Lowe. All of their credit cards are paid monthly. I checked a few e-mails and couldn't find anybody that appears to be a relative. I still have almost all of the e-mails to go through."

Bill looked at Wally. "Can you help Jeffery with the safety deposit box and the e-mails?"

"Yes," Wally responded.

"Did you find any online purchases that were strange?" I asked.

"Not yet. Those I checked were the typical purchases, such as clothing, shoes, and office supplies."

"When can you find out more about the Jenkinses?" I asked.

"I'll do it first thing Monday morning."

I looked at Bill with annoyance.

Bill saw it and explained, "We aren't authorized for overtime, so we'll pick back up on Monday."

I was surprised since I didn't have many weekends off in Chicago but was glad I could be with my parents more.

The meeting broke up, and after everyone else left, I said to Bill, "I'd like to go to Atlanta to check the house on Pebble Beach. We have keys." I knew we couldn't break into someone's house but wanted to see what Bill's response was.

"I would too, but we can't yet. I'll contact the Fulton County or Atlanta police and lay the groundwork for getting in the house. Being on the notebook list doesn't mean the Lowes owned it."

"Maybe an unofficial trip this weekend would help," I suggested.

"No. We're not." He smiled with his tobacco-stained teeth.

"When are we interviewing Tomas?" I asked.

"Saturday morning at ten. He was getting back late tonight. He agreed to come into the station."

Mom was awake when I visited her. I hugged her and held her hand while we talked.

Mom asked, "Are you sure you're doing okay? This has to be stressful for you."

"I'm doing great, Mom. You just need to get better and stop worrying about me."

"I do worry about you—and your father too. Have you seen him today?"

"I visited him earlier, and he was asleep. I'll go see him in a short while."

"Go see him now and come back and let me know how he's getting along. I keep asking the doctors, and they only tell me he's progressing."

So I went to see Dad. He was awake but groggy. He was the most coherent so far. Dad asked me about work and the house, and I told him about both. Dad fell asleep after a short while, so I returned to Mom.

Mom said, "Tell me about your father."

"He was awake, and we talked. He's improving."

"That's good. I'm so glad."

I stayed with mom for another hour and then left.

Instead of going home, I decided to stop at a local bar to have a beer. I stopped at the Aiken Brewing Company since they had their own micro brewed beers. I'd probably get wings too. The restaurant had outside tables on the street, and all the tables were taken except one.

I went inside and took a seat at the bar. The room had fifteen-foot ceilings, brick walls, and heart pine flooring. The stainless steel beer tanks were located in the front windows. The bartender was a nice gentleman who looked to be in his early thirties and was quite handsome. He handed me a Thoroughbred Red. This was only my third time in the bar, and the bartender already remembered what I drank. He'd probably get a bigger tip. I also placed an order for half-dozen hot wings. The Thoroughbred Red was an Irish style red beer that had a lot of malt and had only a minor amount of hops. This was a beer that went well with any food.

This was the first restaurant I visited when I came to Aiken. It reminded me of a Chicago pub with the tables outside and the compact bar area. In Chicago, many of the bars were long and compact so that most patrons had to stand up. There weren't a lot of tables in the Chicago pubs. This gave more room for patrons and more sales.

After only a few visits to the Aiken Brewing Company, I was already seeing the same patrons. The regulars must drink the same each time since the bartender, Austin, had the regulars' drinks ready when they came through the door.

Austin asked, "Still thinking about my earlier offer to go out? I get off at two and could get you off by two fifteen."

I almost spewed my beer on him. "It's a great offer, and I'll keep thinking about it."

"There're grain bags in the basement that are quite comfortable. Chris can attest to it." He winked. Maybe he was winking at Chris.

"Another outstanding offer, but I'll pass for today."

Sitting beside me was an older, handsome gentleman who I guessed was Chris. He was reading the *New Yorker* magazine, so I asked him if he was from New York. He said he was now from Aiken and grew up in Atlanta.

I asked, "Why are you reading the *New Yorker* magazine?"

"I buy the magazine for the pictures." That made me smile since there were hardly any pictures in it.

"I can think of a lot of magazines with better pictures, and you don't have to read long articles like in the *New Yorker*."

"I have a *Reader's Digest* in my fanny pack that I loan to people who don't like long articles."

I grinned. "Do you have a digest version of the *New Yorker*?"

"No, but I can give you a synopsis of each article if you have time."

"I'll just wait until it comes out on CD. By the way, my name is Jessie."

"My name is Christopher. It's a pleasure to meet you."

"How long has the Aiken Brewing Company been here?" I asked.

"About five years; it's a laundry for mob money."

"A what?" I asked, confused.

"Mob money was used to build it, and their money runs through it," he clarified.

"Is this a fact or a rumor?" I questioned.

"It's a strong rumor."

I couldn't believe a small town like this had mob involvement.

Christopher was one of many characters I saw as I continued to chat while I drank beer and ate wings. There were a couple of young women wearing their riding pants and riding boots. A cold beer after a horse ride sounds like a great day for me. Both had their manes tied back in a ponytail. Their attire included Gucci pants, which would likely cost me a month's salary. Two older, shorter guys were talking about having to get up early to ride the thoroughbreds tomorrow. Both sounded like they might have a hangover in the early morning. They were drinking the beer with the most alcohol. They were likely riders in horse races in their youth. Their faces were weathered, and their hands looked strong and worn. An older couple was discussing the wife's plans for Botox treatments. The more the gentleman drank, the more agreeable he became. The woman looked fine to me without Botox. There were two couples dressed in their finery. I overheard them talking about going to the play tonight. I left immediately after my beer and wings were gone.

I decided to stop on the way home at Walmart to get a book. I decided to get one of the *Harry Potter* books. Some of my friends swore that the J. K. Rowling books were great. I guess I'd find out what my friends were talking about if I actually read a book. I picked *Harry Potter and the Philosopher's*

Stone as my book. It was the first *Harry Potter* book, so it could inspire me to read more.

Chapter 7

Friday Morning—William

I left the police station after my interview with Jessica and Bill. If they were straight with me, they didn't have a lot to go on to solve the Lowes' murders. They could have been pulling my leg, but I didn't think so. They asked some questions about Ralph, Mary, Wandita, and Wandita's husband, so they were digging.

I still thought it in my best interest to get close to Jessica, so I was laying the groundwork when I called her. I'm sure she'll eventually fall prey to my charm. Or she'll feel sorry for me after I start begging.

I'd have dropped a tidbit or two to help with the investigation, but I wasn't sure I should. It already felt like they were suspecting me of the murders, so I thought I'd be incriminating myself if I gave them information to help them out. Maybe I'd find out a way to help without incriminating myself.

I could let Jessica come to my house and punish me until I cracked. There were several methods I was thinking of. It'd be a conflict of interest for her to get involved with me but would be a way for me to keep abreast of the investigation. I did feel like there was a connection between us. I could usually tell if there might be a potential relationship. Sometimes I was wrong, but I enjoyed finding it out. I talked like I was a womanizer, but I really wasn't. I was usually too busy for a lasting relationship.

I wasn't honest with Jessica and Bill when I told them I didn't know about the Lowes' past. I knew they had a house in Atlanta and the names on the deed. I was sure Jessica and Bill could use this information since the names on the deed weren't Tom and Mary Lowe. Maybe they could find out without my help. I would like Jessica obligated to me so she would shower me with appreciation or just shower with me after a night of nonstop sex.

After I left the police station, I went downtown to meet a building owner on Laurens Street. I had planned to open a meat and two vegetables restaurant. I had been working with the owner for a few weeks and was now down to the last details. I wanted to buy the building for the restaurant, but the owner didn't want to sell the property.

This restaurant would be my third restaurant downtown. The last two had been very successful, so I expected this one to be successful too. At least I'd have a place to have a nice breakfast. I probably wouldn't be a regular since I usually ate a light breakfast.

I worked out more details for the lease. I was trying to do a triple net lease, which I believed would save me money in the long run. I stopped for a beer at the Aiken Brewing Company before I went home. I went to the bar, and the bartender gave me my regular beer. I went home after my beer to do more work and get ready for the next day.

Chapter 8

Saturday Morning—Jessie

It was early Saturday, and I went to the hospital. There was a different shift on duty. I had met these nurses when they worked an evening shift recently, and they remembered me. I went to visit my mother first, and she was awake. She remembered that I was there the night before, so that was good.

Mom asked in a groggy voice, "What's going on in our Chicago neighborhood?"

I caught Mom up on everything I knew. Mom asked a lot of questions, and I didn't know the answers. I'd have to do a better job of getting all the news and gossip from their neighborhood in Chicago. Mom must have been feeling somewhat better since she was getting back to her nosy self. When I was growing up, it felt like Mom knew what I was doing immediately after I did it. Everybody knew to keep my mom informed, and Mom returned the favor.

Mom gave me a look and said, "It only takes a few calls and a few minutes to find out what's going on. Maybe you can find time."

I knew it didn't take a few calls since Mom would spend hours on the phone learning all the happenings in the neighborhood.

"I'll try to call."

We chatted more as I waited for the doctor to do rounds. I excused myself to visit Dad, but he was asleep. I came back to Mom's intensive care room and waited for the doctor.

Mom fell asleep, and I decided to take out my book. J. K. Rowling seemed to be a pretty good writer, but I couldn't compare her with anybody since I wasn't a reader. I was reading for about thirty minutes when the doctor came in. I introduced myself, and he did the same. He looked at the charts for my mom and had the nurse wake her up. The doctor did some checks on Mom and asked her about her pains. I walked outside the door just before the doctor came out.

He stopped when he came out of the room and said, "Your mother is recovering fine, and she'll probably be moved to a regular room in a few days."

"How about my dad?"

"Your dad had more injuries, and it'll take longer for his recovery. He'll probably be in intensive care for at least another week or two."

I asked a few more questions and then thanked the doctor and went back into my mom's room. The doctor's news on both Mom and Dad was encouraging. A lot had changed in a week. Mom was back asleep, so I decided to stay and read. Before you knew it, I'd be joining a quilting group.

The book kept me occupied for a couple of hours when a nurse came in and said that my dad was awake. I went over to see him. His actions still showed that he was under the influence of drugs, but he seemed to be more coherent than he had been.

Dad asked, "How are you holding up?"

"Fine."

"How's the house?"

"The house is okay."

He asked about the news from Chicago and whether I had found a southern gentleman. I caught him up on all that I knew, and he asked more questions. I ignored the southern gentleman question. Dad was always a detailed person. I told him I started reading a book, but he wouldn't believe me. I had to get it out of my purse and show him the bookmark to convince him. It was nice to see Dad getting back to his old self. He'd usually kid me more, but it was nice anyway.

Dad and I talked for a long time until he started getting sleepy. I then went back to my mom's room, and she was asleep.

It was about nine thirty, so I left for the police station. Bill and Tomas were already in an interview room. I entered as Bill was telling Tomas that the interview was being recorded. Tomas was stout like his wife and had black hair and a round face with dark eyes. He was clean shaven and was wearing jeans and a pullover jacket. He was taking deep breaths when Bill started the interview.

"State your name and age," Bill said.

"Tomas Rodriquez Lopez. I'm thirty-three years old," Tomas said shakily.

"We saw that you have a sheet on you with several incidents. Tell us about them."

"I was a little wild when I was younger and before I met Wandita. The guys I hung around with weren't the best, and we drank and caused trouble."

"Didn't you have some jail time for burglary?"

"I did. It was stupid. I gave a girl some expensive jewelry when I was flush. She was a *crema*. A rich girl who was probably slumming. When we were high one day, I went into the *crema's* house and got the jewelry. My *abogángster*—I mean my lawyer told me to plead guilty since I'd probably get more time if I didn't."

"Have you stolen anything since?" I asked.

"No." He looked at the wall when he answered weakly.

"Do you still get high?" I asked, not knowing whether he used drugs, alcohol, or both.

I have a beer or two but nothing else.

"Have you been unemployed lately?" Bill asked.

"*Si*, I work on new home construction, and homes weren't being built."

"But you're working now," Bill added.

"*Si*, in Atlanta on new homes. I started this week."

"Did you help Wandita clean Tom and Carol Lowe's house?" I asked.

Tomas was now rocking his legs and upper body. He answered between deep breaths and grimaces, "*Si*."

"Did you help clean the office in their house?"

"*Si*." He looked at the wall when he answered.

"Did you see a notebook with alarm codes and account numbers in the office?"

"Wandita showed it to me when we were cleaning once. She pointed it out since she couldn't believe the rich folks left it out."

"Did you look at it?"

"Just to move it while we cleaned," he answered quickly. Almost too quickly.

I was sure he was perspiring now.

"We understand you have financial problems. A possible foreclosure and repossessions," Bill stated.

"We can fix them now that I'm working." He sounded positive.

"Where were you Monday night?" I looked him in the eyes while asking.

He didn't look me in the eyes when he answered, "In Atlanta."

"Where in Atlanta?"

"In my motel room." He was now looking at the ceiling.

"Who can confirm you were in Atlanta?"

"No one. I had a room by myself." He was wringing his hands now.

"Do you have a credit card?" I asked.

"No."

"How do you buy gas?"

"Cash."

I was hoping to check if he bought gas on Monday night.

"Do you own a gun?" I asked.

"No."

"Have you had a gun in the past?"

"Yes, Wandita made me get rid of them when we were married."

"Were they handguns?" I asked.

"*Si.*"

"Were you aware the Lowes were killed with a handgun?"

"*Si.*"

"It'd be easy for you to get a gun in Atlanta, drive to Aiken, kill and rob the Lowes, and make it back to Atlanta to work the next morning. Wouldn't it?" I sharpened my tone.

"It wasn't me. I swear to it."

"We think you could have done it," I said.

"It wasn't me."

I continued to pressure him with more questions but didn't get a confession. We got the name of the motel he was staying at on Monday night and the company's name he was working for in Atlanta.

Bill and I talked after the interview.

Bill said, "I can't rule Tomas out yet. He certainly could have come to Aiken from Atlanta and killed them. He had access to everything he needed. We'll ask the Atlanta police to go to the motel and ask his employer if he was on time for work Tuesday."

"We could search their house."

"I think we should. We'll request a search warrant on Monday," Bill agreed.

There was no sense of urgency in the South.

"We'll start Monday with an interview with Mary," Bill said.

We talked a while longer, and I followed Bill to the parking lot. He was riding his Harley today. He didn't put on a helmet and road off.

I decided to go home for a while. I had laundry to do and house cleaning. My wardrobe didn't require any ironing if I took the clothes straight out of the dryer and put them on hangers. So that was what I did. I then had all my clothes ready for the next week.

Dad was asleep when I went back to the hospital, and Mom was awake and talkative.

Mom asked before I sat down, "Did you pay the bills?"

"Yes, I paid the bills."

"Are you sure? I started paying some of them online."

"I paid them too."

"Do you have enough food in the house?"

She was the bill payer for the family and reminded me to put all the bills in the mail right away. I usually waited until the bills were almost due before paying them. Mom's philosophy was to pay bills when they arrived. Of course, it helped if there was money in the bank when the bill arrived.

It was a great Saturday so far with my time spent with Mom and Dad. I stayed about two hours and then decided to go work out. I had started working out with one of the local martial arts instructor and would stop by to see when he was available. The instructor was also the owner of a dojo, and his name was Choi Hong Hi. Choi was from Korea and studied martial arts in Korea. When I stopped by, he told me he had an advanced class planned shortly in his dojo and invited me to join in. I took him up on the offer and changed into my *karategi*. I put on my black obi. I had visited several places in Aiken before coming to this dojo. I thought some of the other places in town were like a McDojo. My technique was Shotokan, which was the same technique that Jean-Claude Van Damme and Wesley Snipes did.

The dojo was doing *kumite* or sparring, which would give me a good workout. There were only five black belts in the class. There were only four if you counted the instructor. We did *kata* first. We then did stretching to get ready for the *kumite*. I was paired up with a guy in his late twenties who was athletic, two inches taller than me, muscular, and had a black belt. His name was Ron. The *kumite* to start the evening was to practice strikes without actually hitting your opponent. Good self-discipline was obtained by stopping your blows just short. Occasionally, you ended up hitting your opponent when he didn't move like you thought he would.

Ron and I started out slowly so we could figure out how the other person moved. Ron had good moves and was very agile. As we continued to spar, I continued to test him more. He was getting a little frustrated since I was blocking all of his blows and countering with my own blows. His speed and reaction time were slower than mine, which was to my advantage. It was a good workout with Ron.

We switched partners, and I was paired up with Jim. Jim was an inch taller than Ron, not as muscular, and was a little quicker. We started out slowly and then picked up the pace. Although a little more difficult, I blocked Jim's blows and countered with my own. I also had Jim frustrated by the end of our session.

Next was Robert, who was Ron's height and size but was a little slower in speed. He had already seen me with Ron and Jim and started out with a lot of pace at first. This surprised me, but I caught up quickly and made sure Robert had a good workout. I worked on my defense and didn't try a lot of strikes. Robert was starting to tire by the end of our session.

Paul was next, and he was about three inches taller than me, athletic, and had more speed than the other three. He was obviously the best of the group. I found out later that he had won *kumite* tournaments for his age group. Paul and I got a good workout sparring. I was still quicker than him and blocked almost all of his blows. I countered with a lot of blows and frustrated him with my attacks. I could tell that he was actually trying to hit me as we neared the end of our sparring time.

Paul and I bowed as we ended our *kumite*. This was the first time I had worked out with the students. Choi and I had done *kumite* when the dojo was closed. Choi was impressed that I was almost up to his level.

When the class was over, Choi asked if I would do a little *kumite* with him as a demonstration to the class. I agreed although the four other black belts had tired me out. Choi and I had sparred enough already that we almost had a dance. Part of sparring was to understand the opponent's strengths and weaknesses.

Choi and I started out slowly and eventually got to almost full speed. We had about the same quickness and reaction time, but he had more strength. I had more agility, which helped me. We both blocked a lot of blows and countered with our own. We did throws as well and allowed each other to get back up. Eventually, Choi took me to the mat, and I was too tired to continue. I obviously needed more road and gym time. I bowed to Choi and thanked him for the workout and allowing me to join the class.

We talked after class, and he offered me a part-time job helping with classes. Choi had gotten a good reputation in town, and his business was continuing to grow.

He said, "The pay isn't the greatest, but you can have access to the dojo for workouts and to spar with me. I need more workouts like we had."

I said, "I'll think about it. It's a tempting offer."

I was polite but knew that I'd make a poor teacher. I didn't have a lot of patience, and it came across when I tried to train someone.

"Several of the instructors in the area also get together to spar on Sundays. This week we're meeting here at one o'clock. If you want, I'll ask the group if they wouldn't mind if you joined us."

"Thanks, I'd like that."

"I'll introduce you as my new instructor if you want."

"Let's wait on that introduction."

I headed back to the house for a shower. I knew my muscles would hurt tomorrow.

After my shower, it was still early in the evening, so I decided to go downtown to have a beer and food. I finally found a parking spot across the street from the Aiken Brewing Company and walked across the street. Aiken's main downtown street was Laurens Street. The street had two lanes of traffic going in each direction and had diagonal parking on both sides going each way. There were fountains and flowers in the intersections and shrubbery, flowers, and trees in the median. I was told that there was a botanist for the city who had many awards for his work. I was impressed, but a potted plant would impress me. This was certainly a green city.

I went into the Aiken Brewing Company, and the nice-looking bartender handed me a Thoroughbred Red. It was in a frosted glass and was very cold. I typically liked my good beers at room temperature so I could enjoy the flavors. With a domestic beer, a cold glass was better since there wasn't much flavor. Since the bartender was cute, I wouldn't correct him and would continue letting him serve me frozen glasses.

There was one seat at the bar, and I grabbed it. There was a mug sitting on the bar where the chair was, so I made a hand motion to the guy sitting in the next chair. He told me the guy that had been sitting there was gone. I hopped up on the barstool and made myself comfortable. The bar was busy. I looked around to see if I spied my *New Yorker* magazine guy, but he wasn't here. My backup plan was to take *Harry Potter* out and start reading. My friends would think I had gone off the deep end if they saw me reading a book in a bar. They would be telling stories, comparing guys they had met, telling lies, telling jokes, and kidding each other all evening. I would just watch since I was so shy. I did miss my friends in Chicago.

The guy next to me was working on the newspaper crossword puzzle, and it looked like he had already completed the cryptogram. Knowing that I shouldn't interrupt his deep thought, I finally asked, "Have you seen Christopher tonight?"

I thought I caught him by surprise. He seemed like he didn't really hear my question since he looked at me with a quizzical face and said, "What?"

"Have you seen Christopher tonight?"

"Who?"

On second thought, it probably was the beer and not my surprising him that was making him confused.

"The guy who reads the *New Yorker* magazine."

"No."

"Have you seen anybody that I know tonight?"

I figured I'd confuse him more as a way of amusing myself. It was fun harassing the yokels.

"I'm not sure who you know, lady."

"I know lots of people in town. Just tell me who's been here, and I'll tell you whether I know them."

"There've been lots of people here. I don't even know them all."

"What do the people look like that you don't know?"

The guy finally put cash on the bar and walked out. Austin had been listening to our conversation and said, "You should have been easier on him. He's been here for the whole happy hour. Happy hour is over, so he'd be leaving anytime."

"They're just happy hour customers?" I asked.

"We have a lot of customers that come in for happy hour and then leave as soon as it's over."

I looked around and saw that the bar had emptied out.

"I was serious about a date. Will you be in town long?"

"I'll be here for a little while."

"Where are you from?"

"Chicago."

"Welcome to Aiken."

"Thanks and can I ask for a favor?"

"Sure."

"Can I get my future beers in an unfrozen glass?"

"I'll try to remember."

He then saw more patrons come in the door and started pouring their drinks. I was sure he'd remember to give me an unfrozen glass the next time.

Since it was a little after seven o'clock, happy hour must have ended at seven. No one had sat down in the crossword puzzle guy's chair. There was a guy on the other side of me, but he was chatting with a woman in the next chair. I decided to order food. The other choice was to read my book. I got Austin's attention and make a motion with my hand, pointing at my mouth. He asked if I wanted half a dozen hot wings again. I nodded.

As I was ordering my food, Christopher, the *New Yorker* magazine guy, came in and sat next to me. He asked, "Is your date late again?"

I said, "I think I'm being stood up."

"Your date could be the one that just passed out in the alley behind the building."

"No, my dates usually wait until we're together to pass out."

"He must have gotten an early start tonight."

"Would you mind keeping me company until he wakes up?"

"I just received the latest *New Yorker* today, and I'm not sure I can keep my hands off of it."

"I could understand that if it was a *Playboy* magazine but not the *New Yorker.*"

"Have you read the *New Yorker?*"

"I just look at the pictures."

"That answer sounds familiar."

"I did bring a book to read in case you didn't show up tonight."

"I can't believe I forgot. I don't have many dates since I got married."

"You're married and still coming on to me so strong."

"We're actually separated, so it's okay."

I showed a small frown on my face. "I'm sorry to hear that."

"She's in Washington State, and I'm in South Carolina."

"I get it. You're separated physically but not really separated."

I figured out it was a joke.

"My wife is an emergency room physician. She's trying to get a job here in South Carolina."

"How often do you get to see her?"

"She works long hours for a month and then comes down here to stay for a month. She's working now, so I'm on my own for a while."

Austin had already placed Christopher's mug in front of him while we were talking.

"What's the deal with the mugs?"

"The mugs are for mug club members. We pay an annual fee and get to drink beer from our own mugs. The price for a mug of beer is the same as your sixteen-ounce glass. However, I think this year's mugs aren't really twenty-four ounces."

"That sounds like a good deal. I may decide to join the mug club."

Christopher did the hand-to-mouth movement when Austin walked by, and Austin asked if he wanted half a dozen hot wings. Christopher nodded. You didn't need to talk to order food in this establishment.

"What do you do for a living?"

"I work at the Savannah River Plant. I work on budgets in the site financial group."

"That sounds exciting."

He heard my lack of sincerity.

"It's much more exciting than you think. Some days I get giddy knowing I'm going to work on a new budget. I even get lightheaded."

"I can think of a million other better ways to get giddy. I'd probably also get lightheaded right before I passed out from working on a budget. I don't even like balancing my checkbook."

My wings arrived, and Austin sat them in front of me. They had celery on top and had ranch and blue cheese dressings on the side.

"I'll loan you wings if you'll pay me back."

"That sounds like a good deal."

Christopher picked a wing from the plate and motioned for Austin to bring him a plate.

Austin acknowledged and got a plate and napkins.

Christopher asked me what work I did. I told him about my temporary assignment at the Aiken County Police Department and about my parents' accident. I told him that my father was down here to work at Savannah River Plant as part of the Recovery Act funds that the site got.

"The Recovery Act funds have been great for the area but made my job more difficult since the work being done isn't very organized."

"So the Recovery Act funds haven't made you giddy."

"No. Not giddy or lightheaded."

Austin came over and said to Christopher, "Have you been riding any?"

I was thinking he was talking about motorcycles since I had just seen Bill riding his motorcycle today.

"I've been riding some. I'm trying to stay in shape for a biathlon coming up. Have you been riding?"

Austin said, "I've been riding more lately."

He then saw another customer making a hand motion and went to provide a beverage to the patron.

I said, "I assume you're talking about bicycling rather than motorcycles."

"Yes, we're speaking of bicycling. Austin did a lot of running, and I got him interested in bicycling. I haven't gotten him to do a biathlon or triathlon yet."

"What's the difference between a biathlon and a triathlon?"

I remembered the Iron Man triathlon held in Hawaii each year. I also remembered a biathlon in the Olympics involving skiing and shooting.

"A biathlon is actually an Olympic sport, but it has been adapted to mean two of the parts of a triathlon. The race can be swimming and running or swimming and bicycling. I'm getting ready for one that's swimming and bicycling. Do you do any cycling?"

"I haven't done any since I was a kid. I do ride a stationary bike in the gym and run to keep in shape."

I pointed at my beer, and another one came. When it was time for my check, I acted like I was writing a check, and Austin gave me my bill.

Chapter 9

Sunday Morning—Jessie

On Sunday morning, I decided to take a short run downtown. While I was running, I could see all the businesses and get to know Aiken better. I parked the car at the library. I read the historical sign at the library while I was stretching and found out it started out as Institute Hill. Institute Hill was the Aiken Academy that was started in 1890. I ran past the Willcox Hotel and Hitchcock Woods. I thought about running through Hitchcock Woods but decided to run on Laurens Street. As I passed the Aiken Brewing Company, it looked like there was a fire in the building since the windows were smoky. I stopped to investigate and saw a couple of people inside. I pulled on the front door and saw that it was steam rather than smoke.

I saw a guy at the bar and asked him, "What's going on in here?"

He said, "We're making beer."

"What kind are you making? By the way, my name is Jessie."

"My name is Rodney. It's nice to meet you. We're making a stout today."

"It's nice to meet you too. I drink the Thoroughbred Red. It's one of the best beers I remember having."

"That's a good choice. I like the pale ales. We make several varieties of pale ales, and I like them all."

"What's the secret to making a good beer?"

"A recipe, roasted grains, hops, and yeast is all that's needed. A brewer who can follow the recipe is also important."

"Are you the brewer?"

"Actually, we have several brewers. I'm here to work on the monthly reports and figure out what we need to brew next."

"How do you figure that out?"

"I look at the beer consumption for the week, look at the tank levels to see what beer is available, and project what is needed next."

"So what do you need to make next?"

"It looks like we need to make a pale ale next and then a red. We'll make sure we have a red on tap for you."

"I won't stay in town unless there's a red on tap. I also may leave if Austin the bartender no longer works here. I had to explain to Austin that my beer needs to be served in a room-temperature glass and not a frozen glass."

"I've told them to get rid of the frozen glasses, but they won't listen to me. Would you like to see inside the brewery?"

"I'd love too."

Rodney got off his barstool, and I followed him over to the brewery door. The door was open, and steam was coming out the door. I looked in and saw William pouring something into one of the tanks.

William looked at me and said, "Hey, Jessica. Are you the new assistant that Rodney hired to help me? You look like you're dressed for the job."

I was wearing my running shorts and running shirt, so I didn't have a lot of clothes on. William was unshaven and had the rugged look. It actually fit him well although the beard would be scratchy on my tender skin. I paused for a few seconds to imagine his beard on my skin and cringed. I played along with William.

"Yes, I'm the assistant. Rodney actually told me to wear my Hooters uniform, but it had stains from a busy night."

William looked down at my chest and said, "Nothing personal, but I don't think you could have passed the nose test at Hooters."

"Are you saying my nose is too big?"

Rodney said, "I think he's talking about the boob test. When you walk up to a wall, your boobs need to hit the wall before your nose."

"Then he's saying my nose is too big."

"I guess you can take it that way too. You and William must know each other."

I said, "We have a professional relationship."

"I think William can afford to pay for your professional services. You look like you could be good at your profession." He said this as he looked from my head to my feet.

William said, "She does house calls too. She came over this week."

Rodney asked, "Do you work for a service or are you an independent contractor?"

"I work for an agency in Chicago. I'm establishing a new office in Aiken."

William asked, "So what brings you down here? It doesn't look like you're working unless you do have a side job."

"I was running by, and it looked like there was smoke inside, so I came in to check the building."

Rodney said, "Would you still like to see how to make beer? William isn't a real brewer, so I'll have to do the tour."

"That's because you won't give me my brewer's certificate. Maybe you can convince him to certify me as a brewer."

"William is just the owner, and he refused to complete my brewer training program."

"I bought the equipment, put the system together, and brewed over fifty times, and he wants me to complete his program."

I said, "It sounds like you still need training, so I agree with Rodney."

Rodney then showed me the process from the hot liquor tank, the mash tun, the kettle, the control panel, the fermenters, the serving tanks, the carbon dioxide tank, and the chiller. He showed me the wort in the kettle and explained how it'd turn into beer after it was moved to the fermenters and yeast was added. There was a lot of equipment installed in the two front rooms of the restaurant to make beer. I was impressed with the beer and now with the process.

I asked, "How long does it take to make a beer?"

"It takes about two weeks to make the ales. It'd take longer if we made a lager."

"What's the difference?"

"An ale is like the red beer you drink while a lager is a Budweiser. A lager is made with different yeast and needs to stay in the fermenter longer."

I knew this was the short answer but didn't want a longer explanation.

"So I can drink the stout being made today in two weeks."

"You could if it gets transferred into a serving tank in two weeks."

"So William actually owns this place?"

"He does."

"Why is he brewing if he owns the place?"

"He likes to brew sometimes. He also helps in the kitchen sometimes, helps wait tables, and helps the bartenders sometimes."

"That sounds like an owner that's involved in his business."

"The staff like him since he stays involved."

We walked out to the bar where William was drinking water. He looked like he'd been sweating.

I asked William, "Does your sweat get added to the beer?"

"It's the secret ingredient that Rodney doesn't have in his recipe."

A beeping sound came from the brewery, and William said, "I need to go back to work. You can join me if you want."

I followed him into the brewery, and he added hops to the kettle, turned valves, and turned on a pump. "I'll be whirl pooling for about five minutes and then start the transfer."

"What's whirl pooling? Rodney didn't mention that."

"The wort is whirl pooled to get all of the hops in the center of the dish at the bottom of the kettle."

"I don't understand."

"If you stay around for a while, I'll show you when we can look in the kettle."

"I'd like that."

I had a lot of exercise sparring yesterday, so I'd have a short run today. I also knew I'd be going to the dojo for sparring later. However, I wasn't sure that I should be hanging around with William since he was one of our prime suspects.

William explained that he had added the last hops just before whirl pooling. The last hops added were the bittering hops. I nodded like I knew what he was saying. He then explained how he had sanitized the transfer hose, moved yeast into the fermenter being used, had set up the transfer pump, and attached the oxygen line.

"What do you need oxygen for?"

"The oxygen is to help the yeast start fermenting. We want the yeast to start working as soon as possible."

The beeping went off again, and William started working. He turned off a pump, did other things with piping, and started another pump. He moved me out of the way as he went over to a fermenter. He moved valves and then came back to the kettle. He opened another valve and looked at a gauge. I moved further out of his way as he worked. He finally stopped moving around, so I assumed everything was working okay.

"We're transferring beer. Look in the sight glass and you can see the wort going to the fermenter."

I looked in a site glass and saw beer with a lot of bubbles moving.

"Why is it so bubbly?"

"That's the oxygen being added to the wort."

"I need a drink."

William went to the bar, took two glasses from behind the bar, added ice, and used the soda gun to add water. He handed me a glass and drank all the water in his glass. He then refilled his glass and took a seat at the bar.

Rodney said, "Do I need to take over in the brewery or can you manage?"

William said, "Are you trying to embarrass me in front of this lovely lady?"

"You usually don't need any help embarrassing yourself with a lady."

I said, "I thought we already established that I wasn't a lady."

Rodney said, "If we can now teach her to brew beer, your business will mushroom. Can you imagine a professional woman who can also brew beer? That would be a great combination. I can imagine a brothel where you can watch a hooker make beer before you have her in bed. That sounds like my fantasy."

"I prefer to be called an escort. I do like the idea of having a brothel and a brewery. That sounds like a business model that'll work."

William said, "I'll call to find investors tomorrow or maybe we could change this place into a brothel."

William got up from his stool and went back into the brewery. I followed him to see what he did. William looked at the gauge and adjusted a valve. He checked the kettle.

I asked, "Is everything going okay?"

"It's going well. I'm sure it'll be a great stout."

"How often do you brew?"

"I try to find time to brew every few months. I enjoy making beer and need to do it occasionally so I remember how."

"Is Rodney here in case you forget?"

"Did Rodney ask you to say that?"

"No, I was just wondering since it seems complicated."

"So you're saying you don't think I can handle something complicated."

"No, that's not what I mean. You and Rodney sure do like to instigate trouble."

"There are many other people that think the same thing, but we don't understand why."

Rodney overheard us talking and said, "William is a troublemaker but not me."

William said, "You're always scheming and plotting something mischievous. You're definitely more of a troublemaker than me."

William heard a noise change in the brewery and turned to check the kettle level. He then started closing valves and working around the kettle. In a short while, he went over to the fermenter and changed valves. He went back to the kettle and checked it again.

"Come up here and I'll show you why we whirl pool."

I went up to look in the kettle and saw a mushy mass in the center of the bottom of the kettle.

"The pile of stuff in the bottom is the hops. The whirl pooling keeps the hops in the kettle so that they don't get in the fermenter."

"I see the pile of stuff."

I didn't quite understand what he meant.

"I'll be doing a lot of cleaning and spraying. You'll probably get wet and dirty if you stay in the brewery."

"I certainly don't want you to get me wet."

Rodney piped in again, "It sounds like you struck out again, William."

"It's great to have friends."

"It's time for me to leave anyway. I need to finish my run."

"What are you doing later today?"

Rodney said, "Are you going for strike two?"

I said, "I'm busy most of the day." I knew I was going to the dojo and then to see my parents.

"Can I call you later? Maybe we could do a late lunch."

"I may be busy, but call me later."

I told them good-bye and headed out to finish my run. I ran back the way I came and ran into Hitchcock Woods. I went from civilization to the forest. There were trails to run on, but the rest was a natural forest. I saw deer, squirrels, and birds as I ran. I was tired when I returned to my car.

Chapter 10

Sunday Morning—William

When she left the brewpub, Rodney asked, "How do you know her?"

"She's an investigator with the Aiken County Police Department and interviewed me about my neighbors' deaths."

"I read about the murders in the newspaper. Those were your neighbors?"

"They were my neighbors and my friends."

"She's an attractive investigator and would be perfect for you."

"I'd like to get to know her better."

"Ten bucks that she'll be too busy to see you today."

"How about ten bucks and my brewing certificate?"

"Just the ten bucks. No training, no certificate."

"It's a bet."

I went back to the brewery to finish the cleanup and to make sure everything was set up with the fermenter and the brewery was ready for the next brew session. I was sure Rodney would double check behind me since I didn't brew very often.

After finishing the session, I headed home to clean up from my workout in the brewery. I only left a little of my sweat in the beer. As I was leaving, I saw Rodney going into the brewery to check behind me.

Since the brew session started at six, and it was now twelve thirty, I was getting hungry. I decided to call Jessica and see if she could meet for lunch. I gave her a call on my cell phone.

The phone rang, and she answered, "Hello."

"Hello. Is this Jessica?"

"Yes, is this William?"

"This is William, and I was calling to see if you'd join me for lunch."

I figured the direct approach would be the best.

"I'm on my way to the dojo for sparring and can't make it to lunch."

I didn't expect that answer and hesitated for a few seconds before responding.

"Maybe you can call me later after you spar at the dojo."

"I'll see how I feel after my beatings at the dojo."

"I'm sure you can hold your own."

I was actually serious and not trying to make points. I also wanted to win the bet with Rodney.

"I might be able to keep up, but I'll be with the martial arts instructors who are getting together to spar."

"You must be good if you're invited to join the instructors."

"The instructors may not let me play with them today. I may just be a spectator."

"I hope they let you play with them. If you're physically able, call me after and I can help you get over your injuries."

After I said it, I decided that it was a little stronger come on than I should have done.

"I'll see how I feel before committing."

"That's all that I can ask."

Jessica said, "Good-bye."

I said good-bye and thought about my chances. I hoped she decided to call. After my shower and shave, I fixed myself a sandwich for lunch and sat down in my office to catch up on the news and do research. When I brewed, I skipped the morning shower and shave, knowing I'd need them after. I hoped the unshaven look didn't scare Jessica this morning. I was planning to play a little golf at the Palmetto Golf Course in the afternoon but decided to forgo the golf to see if Jessica had time for me.

The afternoon flowed by as I engrossed myself in research on properties, caught up on the news, and looked into a car business. I had dipped my big toe into the salvage vehicle business and was trying to learn how to make money doing it.

I was still working when the cell phone rang. I thought it may be Jessica, but it was Rodney.

Rodney said, "Did I win my ten dollars?"

"She said she may call later."

"I need lunch money for tomorrow so call me to let me know when I can come over to get my ten dollars."

He hung up as soon as he said it so that I didn't have time for a retort.

The phone rang again, and I figured it was Rodney calling because he needed to rib me more. It was actually Jessica.

I said, "Hello, Jessica."

I decided to program her number in the cell phone just in case.

"You can call me Jessie. That's what my friends call me."

This showed promise.

"How was the sparring? Did you leave anybody standing?"

"It was sparring where you hold your punches. None of the instructors can afford to be out of commission. It was still a good workout, and there are bruises from blocking punches and from the throws. I'll hurt tomorrow."

I didn't want to come across corny again, so I took the high road.

"Would you like to have a relaxing dinner later?"

"I have an errand to run after I go home to clean up. I'll call if I have time for dinner."

It sounded like I was being let down easy, but there could be a small chance for success. I wasn't ready to give ten dollars to Rodney, but it wasn't out of the question.

"Call me if you can make time."

I hung up the phone and thought that I now sounded desperate. I had gone from one extreme to the other.

Chapter 11

Sunday Afternoon—Jessie

I finished my sparring session at the dojo and was tired. After yesterday's sparring, the run in the morning, and sparring, I was feeling my age. I was also out of shape since I hadn't spent enough time running and working out in the gym. I could blame it on the hectic times with my parents, but the truth was that I didn't take the time.

I decided to go home, clean up, and go see my parents again. I felt guilty that I had taken time for myself.

I also decided to call William to let him know I'd be busy. I was torn between my job and getting involved with William. I was trying to justify it as work related.

The phone rang, and he said, "Hello, Jessica."

This meant he had programmed my number into his phone. I hoped this wasn't the first step of a stalker.

I said, "You can call me Jessie. That's what my friends call me."

Maybe this was the wrong thing to say. It made us sound like friends already.

"How was the sparring? Did you leave anybody standing?"

"It was just sparring without the hitting but did include throws."

"Would you like to have a relaxing dinner later?"

"I have an errand to run after I go home to clean up. I'll call if I have time for dinner."

My errand was to visit my parents, but I didn't want to tell William that. Just in case he was a murderer, maybe he'd just kill me and not kill my whole family.

My parents were both awake when I arrived but fell asleep shortly thereafter. The medications had kicked in. I now had choices. One was to stay and read my book. The second was to go home for the evening. The third was to call William and take him up on his dinner offer. I debated for a while and decided to call William. Maybe I'd get information out of him to help with the case. William could also fix my lack of a man problem, but that might be asking too much. I'd make sure the evening stayed professional.

I called William, and he answered his phone, "Hello, Jessie." I heard the hesitation in his voice.

"Hi, William. I've decided to take you up on your offer of dinner."

"Where would you like to go for dinner? Do you have a favorite?"

"I only go to Aiken Brewing Company and do fast food. Since Aiken Brewing Company is closed, I guess we'll go to a fast-food joint."

"I was thinking of going a little more upscale. What would you say about Mexican food?"

"That sounds good. Do they have beer?"

"I believe they do. The restaurant is on Pine Log Road beside the credit union. It's Maria's."

"I know where Pine Log Road is, but where's the credit union?"

"Turn on Pine Log Road on the McDonald's side of Whiskey Road, and Maria's is on the right just before the SRP Credit Union. There are several businesses in a strip mall. When can you be there?"

"I'll be there in about twenty minutes."

I was guessing since I didn't know how long it'd take me to get there.

He told me he'd see me there and hung up.

I did find the place and it did take about twenty minutes from the hospital. William was already there and had two beers on the table. They were Coronas with limes. There were also chips and salsa and a cheese dip on the table. We did our polite hellos, and he raised his beer for a toast to health, prosperity, and a long friendship. I liked the toast and hoped it came true for me. He could have changed the long to lustful. I started immediately on the chips, salsa, and cheese dip.

He said, "Are you aware that Corona is actually a German beer?"

"I didn't know that."

"During World War II, German brewers left Germany and came to Mexico and started breweries. Corona was a German recipe."

"I'm on my way to being a beer expert with my class this morning and this information."

"You'll need to know this when you open your brothel brewery."

"I'm hungry. Are you ready to order?" I said.

"I'm ready."

I looked at the menu and decided on a taco salad. William ordered a burrito. I was usually filled up on chips before my food arrived, so I didn't eat much. This would be different since I had a good workout today.

"How was your day?" I asked.

"It was tiring but enjoyable. How was your day?"

"The same."

"What brought you to Aiken? You don't seem to be the exact fit for the Aiken County Police Department."

"I'm on loan to Aiken County."

"Did the county bring you in for the Lowes' murder case?"

"No, I was already here before the case."

My beer was already empty, and William's bottle was almost empty. The waiter asked if we wanted another beer, and we both said yes. I'd drink the second one slower.

"So what brought you to Aiken?" he asked.

"It was for personal reasons."

William nodded as if he understood. He was probably thinking of a dozen personal reasons that brought me here.

"Tell me more about you."

"There isn't much to tell. I grew up in Southwest Virginia, went to school at a community college and Virginia Tech, came down here to work the Savannah River Site, and have done some investing while I worked. I left Savannah River a few years ago."

"I'm sure there are more details than that."

"It's your turn to tell a few details."

"There's also not much to tell. I grew up in Chicago. I went to a small college, went to work for the city as a police officer, and made investigator."

"I guess that's all I need to know about you. So how many children do you want to have?"

I played along with his charade.

"I'd like three children, two girls and one boy. They should be about two years apart."

"I understand girls are more trouble than boys, and the weddings cost more."

"My mind is made up."

"When are we going to start having these children? The biological clock is ticking."

"I'll look at my schedule next week, and I'll pencil in a time to work on children."

"I'll leave my calendar open all week so that our calendars don't conflict."

After a little more conversation, our food arrived. I started eating quickly. I looked up, and William was eating a lot more slowly so I forced myself to slow down. My impatience carried over to my eating. We didn't talk while we were eating the first few bites of food. I finally broke the silence and asked William how long he had owned the Aiken Brewing Company. He said he started it up about three years ago. I asked him how he decided to open the restaurant, and he said the idea started out as a sports bar and blossomed into Aiken Brewing Company.

"What happened to the sports bar?"

"The sports bar is upstairs. The building has a separate outside entrance, and an entrance is located at the rear of the kitchen."

"So it's hidden from the public."

"No, the place stays busy, so a lot of people definitely know about it."

"I'll have to go upstairs the next time I visit."

"You can be my guest."

"Thanks, I'd like that. I like sports bars."

"What sports do you like?"

"I like pro football, especially da Bears, UFC fighting, and baseball if it's da Cubs. I'll also watch other sports on TV. What about you?"

"I watch most sports but like football, UFC fighting, and the Braves."

William changed the subject and asked, "What have you learned about the Lowes? They were such good friends, and I miss them."

Maybe this was why he wanted me to have dinner.

"We're still following up on a lot of leads. We haven't concluded anything yet."

"I'd be grateful if you let me know what you find out," he said with a pitiful voice.

"I will." I thought a little white lie wouldn't hurt.

We talked more about sports, Aiken Brewing Company, making beer, and Aiken. When my food and beer were gone, I told William I had to go. I wanted to go home and write down all the things that we needed to do for the Lowes' case. I didn't think going home with William tonight would be on the list. William probably just wanted to add me to his list of conquests.

William said, "Thanks for coming out. Can we do it again?"

"Sure."

I was still torn between work and a relationship with William. William could be using me to find out more about the case. We could be using each other. I offered to pay half, but William insisted on paying. I left and went home.

William could be using me, but so far I liked being used.

Chapter 12

Monday Morning—Jessie

On Monday morning, I stopped and got three dozen donuts. A dozen would be for the morning meeting the captain wanted, and I left two dozen in the break room. The captain wanted to be briefed on the murder case, and Bill called the team together in case the captain had questions. The meeting was at eight thirty, and I was in the conference room a few minutes early. The coffee in the police station was hit or miss based on who was making the coffee. Today was a good day. I brought a carafe of coffee into the conference room to go with the donuts.

At eight thirty, Bill began with a summary of where we were on the case and the suspects we had. He went on to explain the assignments each person had.

The captain asked, "When can I expect an arrest?"

"By the end of the week," Bill answered.

"Who do you think will be arrested?"

"I'm not sure about that yet. I'll let you know."

"What's the motive?"

"Money. It has to be the money."

"Where can I help?" the captain asked.

"We still don't have everything from SLED, and we'll probably need subpoenas soon."

"Subpoenas for what?"

"We may want to search the Bradford home, the Jones home, and the Lopez home," Bill responded.

"I'd suggest you narrow the choice to one," the captain said, more like an order.

When the captain left, Bill addressed the group and rephrased the captain's message. "We need to narrow our list down. We'll be interviewing Mary Jones this morning, and she'll probably confess. Just in case she doesn't, find me the perp."

Mary Jones had agreed to come to the police station at nine. Bill had arranged an interview room.

"We'll be taping this interview," Bill told Mary after she sat down.

"Okay," Mary said weakly.

Mary looked tired and weary. Her makeup didn't cover the bags under her eyes, and it appeared tears had made runs in her makeup.

"We appreciate you meeting with us this morning," Bill said.

She didn't respond but sat quietly.

"We wanted to talk to Ralph and you about the temporary restraining order and the bankruptcy."

Mary started crying, and Bill fetched a box of tissues.

"We need to discuss this with you," Bill said in a soothing voice.

I wanted to tell Mary to get over it and that she married a scum bag. Bill showed more patience than I would have.

After a few minutes, Mary said she was fine.

"Tell us about the restraining order," I said.

She told us about the restraining order that was issued recently.

"Ralph is being served with divorce papers today," Mary added, sitting up straighter in her chair.

"Was Ralph involved with other women?" I asked.

"I'm sure there was. Ralph moved to a bedroom on the other end of the house a year ago."

"Do you think he was involved with Carol Lowe?"

"I don't think so, but I don' know." She shook her head in disgust and sighed.

"Did you still get along?" Bill asked.

"Yes. We played cards or scrabble or watched TV together each evening. He cooked, did laundry, and cleaned. He was a great cook. I'll miss that."

"I know this is personal, but why did you stop sleeping together?" Bill politely asked.

"I snore very loud, and it bothered Ralph. He slept in the other room only part-time, but it became permanent after my hysterectomy and other surgical complications."

Bill didn't ask about the medical complications, and I didn't either.

"What about the bankruptcy?" I asked.

"Ralph made some very poor investment decisions and lost all of my savings. He thought he could get rich quickly."

She gritted her teeth and said, "Damn it," under her breath.

"Did he consult you about the investment decisions?"

"No, I let him take over the accounts. I thought he had a lot of savings too, but it turns out he didn't. I understand why now."

We discussed the financial accounts more, and then I asked, "Can you confirm Ralph was in the house last Monday night when the Lowes were killed?"

"I wouldn't know. He woke me up and told me to walk over to the Lowes' house with him. I asked him why, and he said there were police cars over there."

"So you don't know if he was in your house at ten thirty?" I asked the question a little differently.

"No, I went to bed at nine thirty and went right to sleep."

"Did Ralph go over to the Lowes' house other than for dinners and parties?" I asked.

"Sometimes he helped them with home repairs. He was great at fixing things, and Tom wasn't."

"When was the last time he helped them?" I asked.

"I believe it was a few days before they were killed."

"Did Ralph ever suggest he wanted to steal to replace the lost savings?"

Mary seemed to be telling the truth, but I was in a dilemma. Was she lying to set Ralph up or was she truthful? I'd personally like to have Ralph rot in prison if he cheated and lost my savings. Mary was most likely nicer than me.

"If you're implying Ralph would kill the Lowes and steal from them, I know he wouldn't do that. He's never suggested stealing from anyone either."

"Did he tell you he would replace your savings?" I took a different approach.

"He did after I yelled and screamed at him for being such a fool."

"And you believed he would?"

"No, I know he's an idiot now. He was so good to me after my husband died. He cooked great meals for me, spent time with me, took me on wonderful trips, and was such a nice friend." Mary had a more peaceful look on her face now.

"Did he say how he was going to pay you back?"

"He said he would go back to work. He owned a dry cleaning business that he sold when he retired. I don't know what work he would do to earn all the money he lost." Mary rolled her eyes and took a deep breath.

We finished Mary's interview and then went to Bill's office.

Bill asked, "What did we learn?"

"We learned that either Ralph or Mary could be our killers. Both had access, and money could be the motive," I answered.

"Mary may be divorcing Ralph since she already has the Lowes' money," Bill said.

"Ralph seems more likely since he did repairs at the Lowes' house and could have the remote and copies of the keys," I said.

"Maybe, but I can't rule out Mary."

"Me neither."

Bill's phone rang, and it was the Fulton County sheriff. Bill put us on speaker phone.

After the introductions, Kevin Collins, the Fulton County sheriff's deputy, said, "We didn't find anyone home at the Pebble Beach Drive house, so we interviewed neighbors. The neighbors said that Caroline and Thomas Jenkins lived in the house and they were only there part of each month. They said they hadn't seen them for a couple of weeks."

"Can you show the neighbors pictures we send you?" I asked.

"Sure. Send them to my e-mail address." Kevin gave us his e-mail address.

When Bill logged on to his e-mail, he saw that SLED had sent additional pages for their report. Bill printed it out as he sent the pictures of Carol and Tom Lowe.

The additional pages included more details of the bullet trajectories, the blood splatter, photographs of the scene while the Lowes were still in the bed, and the fiber analysis. None of the analysis pointed a finger at any of our suspects.

We took an early lunch. Bill went to Betsy's on the Corner for a deli sandwich, and I went to visit my parents. The hospital nurses greeted me when I arrived. One nurse told me that my father was awake, so I went to see him first. My dad was groggy and still looked half asleep.

Dad asked, "How's my little girl?"

"Fine, Daddy." I was getting emotional and had wet eyes. He hadn't called me his little girl in a long time.

"How's your mother?"

"She's getting better. What's the doctor telling you?" I knew but wanted to see what the doctor told him.

"It sounds like I'll be in intensive care for a while."

We conversed for about ten minutes before he started going to sleep again. It was nice to see him awake. It was tough to see him in bed and not able to get around. He was always quite active.

I then went to see my mother, and she was awake also. She asked me how I had being holding up. I expected her to apologize for having me come to South Carolina. Sure enough, I must be psychic since the next words from my mother were those.

She said, "I'm sorry you've had to go to so much trouble for your father and me. I hope this hasn't been too much burden on you."

"It hasn't been a problem for me to come to South Carolina. It's more like a vacation for me to get away from the rat race in Chicago."

I wondered if she could tell I was lying.

I talked to my mother for a while to see if she needed anything before I left. I planned to be back in the morning to hopefully catch the doctor during the rounds. I could be patient when I was going through documents or files to find clues for a case, but reading a book was different. Maybe I needed to get an iPod and listen to a book on CD. That way I didn't have to actually read.

As I was leaving the hospital, my cell phone rang. The call was from William. I had programmed him into my phone as well.

I said, "Hello, William."

"Hi, Jessie. Sorry I couldn't wait on the forty-eight-hour rule, but I could hear your biological clock ticking from my house."

"I'm thinking I'll need to get my biological clock fixed."

"Do you mean fixed like you'd fix a cat or dog?"

"No. Not that kind of fixed."

"Good, I have your battery of tests scheduled this afternoon to make sure you have all the right qualities needed to carry on the Bradford name."

"That's the sweetest proposal I've ever received. Do I have to pass the battery of tests before I get a ring?"

"Just one test."

"What test would that be?"

"A fertility test."

"I can see where that would be necessary to carry on the Bradford name. I was, however, thinking of keeping my name and passing my name to the children. I'm an only child, and I need to carry on my name."

"I think our children would like Bradford as a last name rather than Barnes. I think we should discuss this over dinner."

"Yes, we can talk over dinner, but I may have to toss in work questions."

"We'll need to do work questions before the alcohol. I tend to have loose lips after a drink or two. I'll call you later to give you the location and time."

He then hung up the phone. He must have wanted to hang up before I changed my mind.

Since we still needed answers to find the perp, the chances of getting answers from William helped make the decision to have dinner with him. I didn't think I should tell Bill or he'd veto it. If I was a male investigator, I would have been told to think with the head above the waist and other words of wisdom. I was sure there were similar sayings for women.

When I returned from the hospital with a burger stain on my shirt, Bill was in his office. Driving and eating ruins several shirts a month.

He said, "The Fulton County deputy called. They took the photos of Tom and Mary Lowe out to the Pebble Beach Drive, and the neighbors identified the Lowes as Caroline and Thomas Jenkins. They'll process a subpoena to get in the house. We'll meet them there at ten in the morning."

"We need to take the extra house keys and the notebook," I said.

"I agree."

We went back to the Lowes' house, got the keys, and went through files again to see if we missed anything. We also reviewed the SLED report again.

Bill called the captain and let him know we'd be going to Atlanta tomorrow.

William called about two, and I stepped outside to talk to him. He told me where to meet him for dinner.

It was now four o'clock, and we met with the others in the conference room.

Bill summarized our day and our plans to go to Atlanta tomorrow and then asked Oscar to go first.

"We went through the cell phones but didn't find anything that stood out. We made a printout from the cell phones for you." Oscar handed the printout to Bill, and Bill handed it to Jeffery.

Jeffery was next. "We found the extra account. It's a checking account at Atlanta Trust. It's in Thomas and Caroline Jenkins's name. We also found out the Jenkinses have a safety deposit box at Atlanta Trust."

Jeffery paused so he and Wally could bask in the appreciation.

Jeffery continued after his moment, "We went through most of the computer printout and didn't find anything important. We did find another neighbor who was a felon. He's Thad Cornwall. He was a lawyer who helped an embezzler hide several million dollars and took his cut. Thad's wife divorced him, so his house is vacant on Mulberry."

I made a note to talk to Thad, although it didn't sound like he was involved.

"Did you find any online orders shipped to Atlanta or billed to Atlanta?" I asked.

"No, I thought we would, but no."

Wally added, "I looked for any connection to Atlanta and couldn't find any. All the online orders were delivered to the Aiken address. The Atlanta Trust account does have the Pebble Beach Drive address."

We discussed each suspect with everyone telling us who they thought did it. The choices included all the suspects.

Bill and I agreed to meet at six thirty tomorrow morning for our trip to Atlanta.

Chapter 13

Monday Afternoon—William

I knew the rules for dating were to wait two days before calling so that you didn't seem too desperate. I called the next day and bantered with her a little, and she agreed to meet me for dinner. It was too early to invite her to my house for dinner, so I decided to take her to Travinia, an Italian restaurant. I hadn't been there yet but always liked to try out the competition. I called Jessie back at three o'clock.

The phone rang several times before she answered, "Hello, William."

"Hello, Jessie. Can you still come out and play later?"

I heard wind noise, so she must have walked outside to talk to me.

"Is the game still planned?"

"I'm planning a battle of wits. Do you have what it takes to compete?"

"I'm the city champion in Chicago."

"A repeat of the War of Northern Aggression. We can probably sell tickets. How about seven o'clock at Travinia for the kickoff."

"Seven o'clock is fine. Where is Travinia?"

"Turn on the Wendy's side of Whiskey Road at Pine Log Road, and Travinia is in the strip mall behind the Goodwill store."

"I'll find it and see you at seven o'clock."

I was definitely looking forward to time with Jessie. She had a quick wit that entertained me and kept me on my toes. I was debating whether to tell her about the Lowes' house in Atlanta. I probably wouldn't admit to the breaking and entering. Technically it wasn't breaking and entering since

I borrowed a set of keys from the Lowes' house. I figured the alarm codes were probably the same, and they were.

I went by the Aiken Brewing Company and spent a little time there before I went to Travinia. I didn't see Rodney to collect my ten dollars. I arrived a few minutes early and got a table for two. I wasn't sure whether Jessie drank wine, so I waited to order drinks. I did order a bruschetta appetizer hoping that this would be acceptable. She arrived promptly at seven.

I said, "Hi, Jessie. I was thinking of ordering a bottle of wine but didn't know whether you drink wine."

"Hello, William. I do drink wine."

"Is pinot grigio okay?"

"Any wine is okay with the exception of the street brands."

The waitress came by, and I ordered a bottle of pinot grigio, a white wine that would go with most foods. I usually drank without regard for the food pairings.

"How was your day, dear?"

"It was a horrific day. The traffic jams were awful, and the gangs were out wreaking havoc today. I'm surprised I survived the day."

"So you had a boring day?"

"It was boring. I need a day in Chicago to get my blood flowing again."

"You were working on the Lowes' case today?"

"Yes, Bill and I were following up on stuff today."

"The Lowes were good friends, so I hope you can find out who murdered them."

"Before we start with the alcohol, do you remember anything that would help with the case? You were the closest friend to the Lowes, so I was hoping you may know something that could help. It may be something that you don't think is important, but it may be important to us."

"I've racked my brain and can't remember anything other than what I've told you. If I think of anything, I'll call you."

When I figured out how to help without hurting myself, I would.

"Bill and I really need any help we can get. We may request a reward for any information."

"I hope you get information to help solve the case."

The wine came, and the waitress let me smell the cork, and then she poured me a smidgen. I gave the okay to the wine, and she filled our glasses. I toasted to health, happiness, and a lasting friendship.

Jessie said, "That's enough about work. How was your day?"

"I couldn't keep my mind on anything today, knowing I was going to see you tonight."

"So you had a boring day."

"I was actually working on projects today."

"So what are the new projects?"

"I have a new restaurant going in downtown, and I've started buying salvaged vehicles."

"What restaurant are you doing?"

"I'm in the final stages of starting up a meat and veggie restaurant in what was a Chinese restaurant. One of my previous chefs is going to be involved to ensure I do it right. I'm also starting to buy salvaged vehicles and fixing them for resale."

"Why do you need another restaurant?"

"Aiken is growing, and a new and different restaurant is needed downtown. It's my duty to provide it."

"So you're doing it to make money."

"Basically, yes."

"And what about the salvaged vehicles?"

"I'm an environmentalist and don't want these vehicles to pollute the earth in a junkyard."

"So you're doing it for the money."

"Naturally."

"Do you do anything that's not for profit?"

"I've done many things not to make a profit. However, it was usually was done to promote something that would make a profit."

"I figured as much. It sounds like life is a business to you."

"Not all of life is a business. Tonight isn't a business but a very nice pleasure."

It was actually partly business since I wanted to keep tabs on the Lowes' case.

"I'd need a dinner and a movie before I'd do any business with you."

I handed her the *Aiken Standard*, our local daily newspaper, with the newspaper folded to the movie section.

"You can pick the movie."

"You're a troublemaker. I bet you always stayed in trouble when you were growing up."

"I don't think I've fully grown up yet."

The appetizer came, and the waitress told us about the specials. Jessie picked lasagna, and I ordered the same.

"Now it's time for you to tell me more about yourself. Where do your parents live? What else do you do for entertainment other than beating up instructors at a dojo? Where do you want us to go on our honeymoon?"

"I'm an only child. My parents are in Aiken. I work on my martial arts, work out in the gym, watch football, watch UFC fighting, like card games, like to travel but don't get to, and just started reading a book. As far as my honeymoon, I'd like to go to Paris. However, I haven't been anywhere outside the United States, so anywhere in Europe would do."

"That settles it. I need not know any more. I'll book our tickets to Paris. When can you leave?"

"Let me solve these murders and tie up a couple of other loose ends, and I'll be available after that."

"I'll go ahead and book flights for Sunday. That should give you plenty of time."

"I'll let you know my frequent flyer numbers so I can get my points. Now it's your turn. How many sisters and brothers do you have? Where do your parents live? What do you do for entertainment? Where do you want to go on your honeymoon?"

"I have three brothers and one sister. My parents live in Cedar Bluff, Virginia. I enjoy golf, tennis, any card game, traveling, and investing. I'd like to go to a resort where we can spend lots of time together for our honeymoon."

Jessie said, "So you'll be in a resort while I'm in Paris."

"Did you want to take our honeymoon together?"

"Not necessarily. As long as you pay for the trip, we don't have to go together."

"What about the honeymoon sex?"

"If I get to go to Paris, there won't be time for sex."

"I guess we can just go to Vegas to get married. One of my desires is to be married by an Elvis impersonator. Maybe I can get honeymoon sex in Vegas."

"I like to gamble, so there probably won't be time in Vegas for sex. And I'm not getting married by an Elvis impersonator."

"I guess the engagement is off if there isn't a possibility of using an Elvis impersonator."

The waitress came and took away our appetizer plates. She then served us our main courses and filled our wine glasses. She asked if we needed anything else, and we said no. This was a relief for me since I had dated women that always asked for something extra or different. The food wasn't cooked right; the sauce was wrong; they didn't want their dressing on the salad; etc. Jessie might still turn into a drama queen, but it didn't look like it.

Neither of us wanted dessert, and neither of us wanted more to drink after the wine.

I said, "I certainly enjoyed myself tonight. You were great company."

She said, "Thanks for inviting me out. I had a great time too."

I now debated whether to ask her to come to my house for an after-dinner drink. I finally decided to try a different ploy to get her over to my house.

"I'm having people over on Tuesday night for a poker game. One of our regulars isn't coming, so you can sit in if you want. We only play for dollars, so it isn't expensive. I'll stake you if we split your winnings."

She hesitated and finally answered, "I may be able to come over. A poker game would be a lot of fun. It'd be a good investment for you. I should be back from Atlanta in time."

"Fair enough. Let me know your decision. Why are you going to Atlanta?"

"The Lowes have a house in Atlanta, so we're checking it out tomorrow."

I was glad they found the house without my help. I could've told them, but now I didn't have to.

I paid the check, and we said our good-byes. I leaned over to kiss her, and she pushed me away and shook my hand. I should have taken her to the movies too. I hoped she could come to the poker game. I knew the other guys would like her.

The more time I spent with Jessie, the more I liked her. She was witty, smart, great looking, not a drama queen, easy to talk to, fun to be with, and on and on. She was certainly getting under my skin. I hoped she wasn't playing me to get more information about the Lowes' case.

Chapter 14

Monday Evening/Tuesday Morning—Jessie

It was a great evening with William. He was intelligent, had a great wit, was good to banter with, was handsome, and was just fun to be with. There had to be faults that he was hiding from me. I was an investigator, so I'd find them. I wouldn't be happy if he was playing me just to stay close to the Lowes' investigation, or maybe I would.

I went home and went to sleep thinking of William. I was thinking I'd go to the poker game. I hadn't played poker since I left Chicago.

I met Bill at the police station at six thirty, and we headed to Atlanta. I had all the keys from the Lowes' house and the notebook with the Aiken alarm codes and safe combinations. I hoped they worked in Atlanta. Bill and I talked about the case on the way when I wasn't daydreaming about William. I'm sure Bill was daydreaming of some lassie in Augusta or parts unknown. I didn't look for any visual effects.

I did get desperate and said, "Did you have a good weekend off?"

"I took my two kids to see their grandmother in Charlotte. We went to Carowinds on Saturday and rode on the lake on Sunday."

I knew Bill had kids since he had pictures of them on his desk and wall. I also knew Carowinds was an amusement park like Six Flags.

"Nice. Did they have a good time?"

"They did. My mother was glad to see them. She's sixty but still rode all the roller coasters with them, even the ones that flipped you upside down."

"Are you close to your mother?"

"Sure am. Our whole family is close."

We talked about his brothers and sisters and where they were. They were raised on a large farm, which two of his brothers now ran. Bill didn't want to be a farmer and went into law enforcement.

Bill asked about the crime rate in Chicago, and I tried to relate the significant differences between Aiken and Chicago. I told him I'd be investigating several murders if I was still in Chicago.

We were early getting to the Pebble Beach house. We entered a very upscale neighborhood with a guard at the entrance. Bill showed the guard his badge, and the guard let us in. We parked on the street. There weren't any other vehicles on the street. It was probably a homeowners association rule that cars couldn't be parked in the street. The home was massive like the house in Aiken, but the lot was significantly smaller, with houses built close by. Land must have been more expensive in Atlanta. The house was brick and stone with massive front doors. A large chandelier was in a large window above the front doors. A metal fence separated the front yard from the backyard. Planters were on the front porch, and the plants were alive and green. The yard looked like it was recently cut, and there were flowers in the pots on the steps. Maybe they had a caretaker when they weren't here.

The Fulton County deputy showed up first, and we made introductions.

Kevin Collins, the deputy, said, "Two investigators are meeting us here shortly. They were assigned since it's a murder investigation. They have the subpoena."

Bill asked Kevin about his work with the Fulton County sheriff. I listened occasionally as they quizzed each other about their work, families, and hobbies.

The investigators showed up about ten minutes later, and we made introductions again. The two investigators were Charlie Allgood and Cynthia Williams. Charlie was an older guy with gray hair and lots of wrinkles on his face. He was about five feet eight with droopy eyes, a large nose, and a large mouth. Cynthia appeared to be in her sixties, had black hair, large dark eyes, a smaller nose, and large mouth. Both had a scowling look on their faces.

Charlie said, "Catch us up on what happened to the Jenkinses."

Bill went through the details of the murders, what we learned about the Lowes, and how we found the house in Atlanta.

Cynthia asked about our suspects, and Bill told them about our possible perps.

The investigators then took our keys and the alarm codes from the house in Aiken. Both worked. Bill and I were allowed to go in with the investigators. The house looked similar to the house in Aiken. There were no family pictures on the walls or tables in the living areas. I suspected we wouldn't find any more about the Lowes here. None of us touched anything. I had this funny feeling that William had been in this house already.

When we went in the office, the office had two desks with computers. There were file cabinets with lots of files similar to the Aiken house. There were two safes in the master bedroom closet, similar to the ones in Aiken. We walked through the whole house and didn't find anything else that caught our eye.

Charlie said, "We need to let the crime scene folks go through the house. They'll be here this afternoon, so we can meet you back here tomorrow morning."

"What about their bank account and safety deposit box at Atlanta First? Did you get a subpoena for them?" I asked.

"Not yet. We wanted to look through the house first," Charlie answered.

"Can you have one tomorrow?" I asked.

"We'll wait until we look at the house more to verify the Jenkinses were the two that were killed."

"Kevin showed the picture to the neighbors to verify that," I said.

"We'll decide when to get the other subpoenas," Charlie said in a matter-of-fact tone.

I stayed quiet although I wanted to grab Charlie and throw him on the ground and knock some sense into him.

Bill and I decided to go back to Aiken and come back tomorrow about noon. We talked on the way back, and Bill thought the Lowes or Jenkinses were probably involved in corporate espionage or were foreign spies. I didn't have an opinion.

We stopped for lunch at a Subway. I actually had vegetables on my sub. After lunch, I took a short nap while Bill drove.

At the four o'clock meeting, Bill informed the group of our adventure and reviewed additional information provided by SLED. The SLED information was more detailed but nothing new. He then asked the others about their day's activities.

Oscar spoke first. "We checked the two iPads and found the same information that we found on the computers. The one exception was two iTunes accounts, but that was it. Jeffery has everything we found. We did computer searches for different addresses and phone numbers but found nothing new."

Jeffery was next, and he handed Bill a printout from two lawsuits. "Our research today found a neighbor that had a lawsuit with another neighbor about a property line. The lawsuit has been going on for two years. A fence was built a couple of inches on the other person's property. Both of the neighbors are lawyers. We also found the divorce filing by Mary Jones. Adultery was the grounds for the divorce. We looked more in New Jersey and didn't find property owned by Thomas and Caroline Jenkins or Tom and Carol Lowe in several counties around Princeton. There were some potential candidates, but they either still lived around Princeton or weren't the right age. We researched more e-mails, and none of them were linked to people in Atlanta or relatives as best we could determine. We still have more data to look at."

Wally said, "We also researched the Jenkinses. They bought the Pebble Beach house with cash three and a half years ago. We can't find anything that shows where they moved from. We also can't find any tax returns filed by them."

After the meeting, Bill and I decided to leave around eight thirty for the trip to Atlanta on Wednesday.

I stopped to see my parents after I left the station.

My father was asleep when I arrived, and my mother was awake and alert. She told me that the doctors had reduced her medications and she'd be moved out of intensive care on Wednesday morning. She also said that her physical therapy would start on Wednesday.

She said, "I'm not looking forward to the physical therapy. I know it's going to be painful."

I said, "I'm sure it won't be too bad. You always said that you could handle anything after childbirth."

"I think this will be different than childbirth. At least I knew what was going to happen in childbirth. I don't know what to expect with physical therapy."

"When you get into your room, I can take you down to see Dad. I know you'll like that."

"I haven't seen your dad since the accident. It'll be great to see him."

"I'll try to be here when you get moved to your room."

"When will your dad get moved out of intensive care?"

"I haven't been told a time yet."

"I asked the doctor this morning, but he wouldn't tell me. I thought he may have told you." She continued, "Tell me how you're getting along down here. I know this is a culture shock for you."

"I've had a couple of dates in the past few days. I've met a great guy, and he has invited me out to dinner the last two nights."

"That makes me so happy that you're dating down here. I've been worrying about you."

"You have enough to worry about without worrying about me."

"You're still my baby, and I want you to be happy. Maybe you can marry someone and you can quit that dangerous job with the police department."

"I still plan to work with the police department even after I get married."

"You should think of your mother when you make such a decision."

It was time to go now that the conversation had started to be about me and not her. Mom was definitely getting back to normal.

I told Mom I had to go back to work and left her room. I went over to see Dad and found him awake. I told him about Mom moving tomorrow and the physical therapy. Dad said he was looking forward to moving out of intensive care and taking physical therapy. Dad didn't ask me about my personal life, and when he started looking tired, I told him I had to go to work.

I was driving to a fast-food restaurant as I was deciding whether to go to the poker game tonight. I was enjoying my time with William, but this would be three days in a row. Even when I was in Chicago, I never saw a guy three nights in a row. I finally decided that tonight wouldn't really be a date since it was a poker game and there would be other guys there.

The phone rang only once when I called William. He said, "I'm glad you called. I'm sitting here looking at baby names and thinking Paris would be good name for our first child."

"Why Paris?"

"I thought we should name our firstborn after the city where we consummate the child."

"Can you be serious for a minute? I wanted to make sure you didn't embarrass me tonight at the poker game."

"If I'm a good boy, what's my reward? Do I get a special treat?"

"Your treat will be that I won't bring an extra-sharp knife tonight and cut off your manhood."

"I guess I should go down to the sperm bank and make a donation today. I hope they have new magazines this time. The pages were sticking together in the ones I looked at last time."

"You're being crude. Try to control yourself tonight."

"It sounds like you may be joining the game tonight."

"Yes. I'll be there, and I expect to take home most of the money."

"It starts at seven o'clock. If you'd like, you can come at six thirty and help me set up."

I said, "I'll come early if you behave. I hope this poker game isn't a ruse to get me to your house. If I'm the only other poker player, I won't stay."

"You're so distrusting. I was saving the ruse for Wednesday night."

"I'll see you at six thirty."

I rang the doorbell, and William came to the door.

"Welcome home, honey."

"Thanks, I need a drink."

"What would you like, sweetheart?"

"A beer please."

"How was your trip to Atlanta?" he asked.

"The house in Atlanta was similar to the house here. We didn't get to look for anything since the forensic guys hadn't checked it yet."

William probably knew this already. Maybe we'd find William's fingerprints in the Atlanta house.

"Will you be going back?"

"Yes, tomorrow."

I followed him into the kitchen, and he opened the refrigerator and showed me a nice selection of beers.

"You can help yourself. The poker guys know to come in and help themselves."

"So what can I do to help you get ready for the game?"

"I just wanted time with you before the other guys get here."

As he was talking, he was moving closer. I had a beer in my hand, so I had only one hand to protect myself. My resistance was weak, as I didn't work hard to push him away. He probably knew I could hurt him if I wanted to. He placed his arms around me and pulled me close to him. I sat my beer down, and we stood there for a minute just holding each other. William did sway a little but did nothing else. It felt good in his arms. In Chicago, I'd be ready to kick the guy in the crotch when his hands started wandering. William did loosen his grip a little only to kiss me on the forehead, then my cheek, and finally on my lips. The first kiss was a light kiss, the second was still a light kiss, and the third, the fourth, the fifth, and the sixth kisses were still light. My lips started parting a little in expectation of a firmer kiss. The seventh kiss was harder and lasted longer. My lips parted as I pressed back on his kiss. We both tilted our heads as we became more involved in the kissing. We started touching tongues. He rubbed my back, and I rubbed his as we heated up the room. We started a long French kiss when I heard the doorbell. William broke our embrace and asked if I heard something. I told him I thought it was the doorbell. The doorbell rang again. Was I saved by the bell?

He said, "I guess one of the poker players is here."

"Is there really a poker game?"

"If I could cancel it, I would."

He walked away a little wobbly while I held on to the counter. I took a long drink of beer to cool off. I was sure it was just lust and not anything more serious. I didn't need more serious.

When William came back, Ralph was following William. William introduced me to Ralph, and Ralph said that we had already met. Ralph knew the routine and went to the refrigerator and got himself a beer. I saw Ralph looking around the refrigerator door, checking me out. *That horny old bastard better not hit on me or I'll deck him.* William had food on the island countertop where I was just pushed up against. Ralph picked up a clear glass plate and started filling his plate. William looked at me, and I wiped the cold beer bottle across my forehead.

Ralph said as he stared at my breasts, "William has the best food for our poker games."

I looked, and there were warmers with hot food and cold food in chilled containers. It looked like a feast rather than the chips and nuts I was used to when our Chicago group got together for a poker game.

William said to Ralph, "I try to make you feel like a guest."

"I don't eat dinner when William has the poker game. I just have my dinner here."

It looked like it'd be enough for dinner with chicken fingers, meatballs, bratwursts, pigs in a blanket, potato salad, coleslaw, and pasta salad. There were also the chips, nuts, and dip. I planned to have dinner here too. The doorbell rang again, and it was another neighbor. William introduced us, and William was told that we had already met. The neighbor then picked up a plate and started fixing his dinner. I'd be surprised if anyone missed William's poker game with the food and drink.

William asked me, "Do you know everyone in the neighborhood?"

"I worked this street before I got a corner downtown."

The doorbell rang again, and it was John, the neighbor who lived on the other side of the Lowes. William introduced us, and John told William we had already met.

The doorbell rang again, and two guys followed William in. They were Art and Samuel. I didn't know either, so William did get to introduce me this time.

Art and Samuel knew the routine and got their beers and food. All of us were drinking beer tonight. William also had a beer. I was on my second beer since I needed to cool off.

I asked William, "What happened to the guy that didn't show up? It looks like everybody likes coming here for the food."

"I told him the poker game was canceled, so there was room for you."

"That's mean."

"Actually, he's out of town and couldn't come."

"That's better."

William announced that we would shuffle up and deal at seven o'clock. It was about five minutes to seven now. I took another chicken finger and dipped it in honey mustard sauce. I was guessing William had these cooked at the Aiken Brewing Company. I'd ask later.

I saw the guys start wandering toward the back of the house. I waited for William to follow them and went with him. I entered a large game room with a pool table and card table. The card table had green felt, cup holders, and looked like it was made from oak. There were seven chairs around the table with poker chips already in front of each seat.

It was now obvious that William did have everything ready for the evening and just used it as a ploy to get me there early. Now it was time to get down to business. It was time for the boys to give up some cash to me.

William explained to me that the poker game was dealer's choice. This would definitely not be to my advantage since I'd probably not know their redneck poker games. William then told me that the cost was fifty dollars for the poker chips and that he had paid for me. Everybody else had already put in their fifty dollars. We drew for high card, and Ralph was the first dealer. I sat next to William, on his right. I'd have preferred to be on his left so I'd be after him for the betting.

Ralph took it easy with the first game and called seven-card stud. This helped me start learning how everybody played. Some of the guys would play tight, and some loose. I held my own as everybody dealt one time. There were some weird games from little squeeze where kings were wild, follow the queen where the card dealt after the queen was wild, and others just as wild. There were games where there was just a high winner or just a low winner. There were also games where there was a high winner and a low winner. I had a great time with the guys, had a beer or three, and was taking money from the guys.

William was the hardest to read at the table. Sometimes he played tight, and sometimes he played loose. I also couldn't tell when William was bluffing. Sometimes he looked like he had a tell by taking a quick glance away. I now knew he could be lying to us in the interviews and we wouldn't know it. I would definitely sit on his left next time to give me a little advantage.

When ten o'clock came, William announced that it'd be the last round. It was still early for a poker game to stop, but it was a weekday, and some of us had to work tomorrow. The last game was called roll-your-own where everybody kept their cards face down and rolled them up until their cards beat the previous hand. I didn't have a pair, which eliminated me early.

We cashed out the pot, and I won twenty dollars. William won about thirty dollars. Everybody thanked William as they left. I stayed to help William clean up. The food was almost completely gone. We finished in about thirty minutes, and I picked up my purse to leave. William came over with his arms out to give me a hug. I gave him a quick hug and said that I needed to go.

"Can we pick up where we were before the guys interrupted us?"

"I think I should go home. It's been a long day."

I gave him a peck on the cheek and backed to the front door. I knew what my heart and my loins were telling me, but William was a suspect.

The phone rang on my way home, and it was William.

"I'm lying in bed and can't stop thinking of you. Maybe we could have phone sex to help me sleep."

"I think you should take Tylenol PM to help you sleep. I have a headache."

I didn't really have a headache. I didn't know whether a headache was a good reason for not having phone sex, but it sounded good.

"I just spent hours playing poker with you and know you're lying. Maybe you should just come back here and help me go to sleep."

"You must want the poor man's sleeping medicine instead of Tylenol PM."

"I won't take advantage of you if you come back."

"I just played poker with you and know now that you could be lying."

"Maybe just a little phone sex then."

"Good night, William. Call me tomorrow."

"Good night, love of my life."

Wednesday Morning—Jessie

On Wednesday morning, I went to the hospital and found that I was too late. Mom had already been moved out of intensive care. I found her, and she had a shared room. The other woman was asleep, but Mom was awake and alert when I came in. She looked better every day.

She said, "You missed my move."

"I'm sorry, Mom."

"The nurses took care of me. Now tell me what's going on with you. What about this guy you're seeing? When can I meet him?"

"I'm not sure I want you to scare this one away. I may keep him."

"I've always just wanted to make sure the guys you dated were good enough for you."

"You interrogated them and made them nervous." I grinned.

"I don't think any of them I met were right for you."

"Maybe you'll meet this guy sometime."

I knew when I said it that it shouldn't be said. Mom would now aggravate me every time I came in here.

"Have the nurses taken you down to see Dad yet?"

"No. Not yet."

"Let me see if the nurses will let me."

I went out to the nurses' station and asked if I could take Mom down to see Dad in intensive care. They told me that an orderly was scheduled to come up at two o'clock to help take her down to see Dad. I asked about her physical therapy, and the nurse said it'd start this afternoon. I went back and told Mom and stayed a little longer with her. I was hoping that mom and I'd get to go together to see Dad. I told her I was going down to see him.

Dad was awake and having breakfast. He offered me some, but I said no. He had trouble eating because of his injuries. I told him Mom would be down later, and a smile came on his face. I then saw tears in his eyes. I said good-bye and left for the police station.

William must have known when I left the hospital because he called just as I was leaving.

I said, "How are you, William?"

"I'm dying from a broken heart and lack of sleep."

"Did you not take your pills to help you sleep?"

"I took my pills, but my fantasies about you kept me awake."

I started to ask if they involved a hot tub, shower, and sun porch but didn't.

"Should I ask about the fantasies?"

"No, you shouldn't ask. It'd be much better if I described them to you in person with visual aids."

"Why did you really call?" I humored him.

"I have an evening planned for you with dinner and a movie."

"Don't you think four days in a row is too much?"

"I don't think hundreds of days in a row would be too much."

"Only hundreds?"

"Maybe thousands."

"And where is this dinner and movie?" I quizzed.

"It would be at my house."

"Is this a sleep over?"

"It could be if you want it to be."

"So I may need to bring a change of clothes?"

"I thought you wore the same clothes every day."

"I do change clothes sometimes. I have a lot of the same clothes. I'll think about the dinner and a movie and let you know later."

Well, this was it. Should I decide to possibly throw my career away for William? I was sure it wouldn't be that bad. Maybe I'd only be shipped back to Chicago with my tail between my legs. I wished there was an easy answer. There was an easy answer, but I didn't like it. I'd decide later today.

When I got to the station, Bill was outside at his Impala on his phone. I thought I heard him confirming a date for tonight. Maybe we'd both get lucky.

We talked more about the Lowes' case, his kids, and my parents as we rode to Atlanta.

After a quick lunch at McDonald's, we met the detectives at the Pebble Beach house. There was a different guard at the neighborhood entrance, so we showed our badges again. This guard was questioning why we were in his neighborhood when Charlie and Cynthia showed and told him to let us in.

Bill parked in the street, and Cynthia parked their car in the driveway of the house. Except for the fingerprint residue and some disarray, the house was as we saw it yesterday.

I said, "I'd like to look in the safes first."

Both Charlie and Cynthia looked at me with disdain before Charlie said, "We can check the safes first." It was obvious they were in charge here in Atlanta, and we weren't.

Cynthia took the combinations we brought and opened the gun safe. The safe had several guns similar to the guns found in Aiken. Cynthia then opened the smaller safe, and it was empty just like the Aiken safe. Charlie had arranged for the crime scene techs to come back at one to check the safes after they were opened.

I looked at the clothes inside the master closet, and they were similar to the clothes in Aiken. The Lowes used a different name in Atlanta but wore the same clothes. The dresser drawers also revealed similar attire as I saw in Aiken.

We followed Charlie to the office and saw imprints on the desks where the computers had been. We'd have to wait on the forensic techs in Atlanta to check the computers. We were invited to help go through the files, and so we did.

After an hour of looking, Charlie stepped outside to make phone calls.

Cynthia asked, "What did you find in the files in Aiken?"

"We found similar things. There were files for utilities, credit cards, and insurance. The Aiken files had medical and investment files, so it appears they only saw doctors in Aiken and only had one Charles Schwab account," Bill answered. "We didn't find any information on relatives."

"We had the Jenkinses checked out and couldn't find relatives either, but it seems like the Jenkinses only came into existence about three and a half years ago when they moved into this house. We checked our witness protection files and didn't find them."

"They could have a third identity too," I said.

"The notebook with the alarm codes and safe combinations was in Aiken. Has either of you seen a notebook?" I asked.

Both said no.

"We should check the spare keys to see if there are keys to a third house," I added.

Cynthia followed us into the kitchen, and we looked in a cabinet drawer almost in the exact location as the drawer in Aiken. There were spare keys and the car keys. We checked the back door, and all of the keys fit. No extra keys for a third house were in the drawer. There also wasn't a safety deposit key. The Lowes must have kept the only key with them.

"What was found on the alarm system?" I asked. I had noticed that the Atlanta system didn't include video. The Lowes must have had video added to their system in Aiken.

"Charlie is calling about it now."

When Charlie came back, Cynthia asked him, "What did you find out?"

"The alarm system was shut off for about two hours early Tuesday morning a week ago. We'll need to check and see if any of the neighbors saw someone at the house. Deputy Collins and his partner will start going door to door this afternoon."

I asked, "When will you have subpoenas for the bank and safety deposit box?"

Charlie gave me a short stare before answering, "Later today or tomorrow morning."

"We'd like to go with you to the bank," I said.

Charlie looked at Cynthia and rolled his eyes before answering, "I'll let you know when we plan to go."

I suspected they probably wouldn't let me go, but I asked.

We decided to head back to Aiken. Bill had a date, and I had plans for William. Bill called Oscar and Jeffery while we were driving back, and they had nothing new. We got back in Aiken about six o'clock. I stopped by to see my parents for a few minutes before going to see William.

Dad said, "Your mother came to see me today. It was wonderful."

I said, "That's great. I knew she was planning to visit."

"Isn't it nice that she's out of intensive care?"

"It is. She improved a lot in the last week."

Dad looked more energized. Seeing Mom should inspire him to get well quicker. After seeing Dad, I went to see Mom. She was sitting up watching *Jeopardy* on TV. My mom and dad always watched *Jeopardy* every night before the accident. You'd think they'd be trivia experts; in fact, they were pretty good at it. They could answer a lot more questions than I could. They had the advantage since they read books and watched a lot of TV. I was usually working late every night in Chicago and didn't get to watch TV.

"I went to visit with your father for a little while today. It was great to see him," she said with more joy in her voice than I'd heard since the accident.

"I'm sorry I wasn't here."

"The orderly took good care of me. Your father was in good spirits, but he was hurt worse than me. He told me he'd made a lot of progress but …" She trailed off as she must have pictured how Dad looked.

"Dad will be fine. He just needs a little more time to get better," I reassured her.

"The orderly said he'd take me down tomorrow too. Can you be here when I go?"

"I don't know. I'll try."

Mom grilled me on William, and after dodging her questions as best I could, I left her with Alex Trebec.

Chapter 15

Wednesday Night—William

Jessie had agreed to come over for dinner and a movie. It was our fourth night in a row. I'd never seen a woman four nights in a row in Aiken. Now I had a dilemma. I could tell Jessie more about the Lowes or not. I was concerned that our budding relationship may wilt if she knew I was involved.

At seven thirty, Jessie showed up at the house. She didn't have an overnight bag, so that was discouraging. I invited her in and wanted to make advances right away. I figured I'd either scare her off or get myself hurt if I was too forward. I did give her a kiss, and it was on the lips.

I said, "Can I get you something to drink?"

"The rules are different tonight since it isn't poker night."

"Please get your own drink, my dearest Jessie."

"Can I get you something?"

"I'll have what you have. After you get our drinks, please follow me. We're having dinner in the sunroom."

Jessie got two beers out of the refrigerator and followed me to the sunroom. I had the brewpub cook a meal for us, and it had arrived about ten minutes before. I thought it'd be best to eat while it was hot and before I became hot. I had them prepare racks of lamb, asparagus, twice baked potatoes, and mixed green salad and had them bring a couple of slices of chocolate cake. If Jessie didn't like it, I had TV dinners I could heat up. I took the covers off the plates, and Jessie said, "Yum." I assumed she ate lamb. I held the chair for Jessie and lit the candles.

"This looks great. You can cook too."

"The brewpub cooked for us tonight."

The meal was indeed great, and Jessie and I bantered and talked about sports and politics. I purposely didn't get into personal stuff. If I had a shot at getting her to stay the night, I wanted to make sure I didn't push on personal stuff.

She did like asparagus or pretended to and definitely liked the chocolate cake, so the meal was a hit. Jessie helped me clear the table and put the dishes into the dishwasher.

After, I asked Jessie to get us another beer and follow me to the movie room. I had one of the bedrooms set up as a small movie theater with reclining seats and a large TV. There was raised seating so that ten people could watch movies. I rented the movie *The Proposal* so that it'd be entertaining and not have violence. I suspected Jessie would also watch action movies with violence and would ask the next time.

I started the movie and got popcorn from the popcorn popper I had in the room. It was a commercial popper, and I had it set on a timer. I put butter over the popcorn and grabbed a handful of napkins.

I watched as Jessie shifted until she was settled in the chair. I also shifted to get my most comfortable position. After the movie started, I put my arm around Jessie, and she moved closer to me. About halfway through the movie, I made a move. I leaned over and kissed Jessie, and she kissed me back. I figured that I did choose the right movie. We continued to kiss for ten minutes or more. I was losing track of time. I began to let my hands wander and didn't get karate chopped, so I continued. She was starting to move her hands under my shirt, so I figured I could do the same.

We continued the petting and kissing. I reached over and picked her up and carried her out of the room. I struggled as I carried her through the doorways. I thought I only hit her head twice. I laid her gently on my bed, and we picked up where we had left off in the movie room. Since there were no buttons on her shirt, I pulled it off over her head. I had a shirt that buttoned, and Jessie was undoing the buttons. We kept removing clothes until we were in the au naturel. I continued to caress her for a couple of minutes before I rolled on top of her.

We were joined together and moving together until we both finished together. Our first time could be called a quickie. I rolled off of her after finishing and was catching my breath. Jessie then rolled on top of me and said, "You sure know how to spoil a movie."

"This was worth a second day of rental."

"You say the most romantic things."

I started to say something when Jessie started kissing on me. She then started kissing my ears and all over my face. She kissed my neck and my chest, stopping at each of my nipples. I could only lay still, though I did move with a shutter when she moved down to William, Jr. and the twins. It was only a few minutes before Junior came to full alert. Jessie then slid back up my body and sat on top of me. After a few minutes, I flipped her over on her back and continued what she started. After a few minutes, she flipped me over and got back on top. I was thinking this was now a contest. After a few minutes, I tried to flip her over and found that I couldn't flip her. A few more minutes passed, and she let me flip her. Now she knew who was in charge, and she knew it wasn't me. I finished again and rolled off. This time she didn't roll over and didn't try to entice me again. After several minutes, I suggested we take a shower and finish watching the movie.

I had a walk-in shower with multiple shower heads. We showered together and washed each other. I shampooed Jessie's hair and washed her all over with my soapy hands. I did stop to concentrate on parts of her body. Jessie then did me. Her hands did extended stops as she soaped me up. I then gave her a gentle massage on her neck and back. She had knots in her neck, which I worked out. She returned the favor, and I was surprised at her strength. We continued to make sure each other was clean before we got out of the shower. I handed Jessie a large cotton towel. While I was drying off, I went back into the bedroom and turned down the bed. The rest of the movie was going to be a mystery tonight. When Jessie came into the bedroom, I was lying in bed naked. She didn't say a word and crawled over me to the other side of the bed. My side of the bed was closest to the bathroom, so she passed another test.

It was my turn to kiss Jessie all over, so I began at the top of her head and worked my way down. I finally had her shuttering as I moved down to her private area. I slid back up, and we began our jousting to see who would be on top. I let her stay on top. I finished for the third time and knew I was spent. She rolled off me, and we were both breathing hard.

I didn't remember falling asleep but woke up about two in the morning when Jessie's foot touched me. Jessie was still asleep, so I got up. I went in the movie room and turned off the TV, the DVD player, and the popcorn popper. I went to the kitchen and got a glass of water. Jessie drained all my fluids, so I needed to replenish them. I took an extra glass of water to the bedroom in case Jessie was awake. As I got back in bed, she did wake up. I offered her a glass of water, and she drank the whole glass in one motion. She had other talents. I gave her a light kiss but not enough to give her the message that I was ready again. We cuddled and went back to sleep. At five, I woke again and remembered Jessie was there. I rolled over and kissed her again with different intentions this time. As she was waking up, I rolled on top of her and started taking advantage of the situation. Before I could feel like I was in control, I was flipped on my back. That was a short-lived feeling of being in charge. Jessie let me be on top some, and we continued until she used me up again. In a few minutes, I was back asleep.

Chapter 16

Thursday Morning—Jessie

I couldn't believe I let it happen although I was glad it did. It was now six o'clock in the morning, and I had spent the night with William. It was a great night, but I was concerned about the professional consequences. I'd ask William to continue to keep our relationship private. William and I finished a morning session, and he went back to sleep.

At six thirty, I woke William up and asked if we could take a shower together again. We showered and repeated the same routine as last night. This could be habit forming. This time when I finished toweling off, William wasn't in the bed naked. There was a robe lying on the bed, and I put it on. I heard William in the kitchen and went to find him. He hugged and kissed me when I came into the kitchen. I reached down to grab his privates, and he moved away.

He said, "Junior and the twins need a rest."

I said, "That's their names?"

"It's on their birth certificates."

"If I can have coffee, I'll leave the boys alone."

"The coffee is almost ready. Would you like food?"

"Can I have a couple of eggs and toast?"

"Have a seat in the breakfast area. Today's newspaper is there for you."

"I sure am hungry this morning. I don't know why."

"I don't either."

I was reading the newspaper as William brought me coffee. An article was included in the newspaper about the Lowes' case. The article stated that the police hadn't generated any leads and the case was at a standstill. William brought me eggs and toast. He also brought over a plate with fried ham. I took a piece of ham even though I didn't request it.

William sat down opposite me at the breakfast table. This would be a nice life to have breakfast each morning this way, especially after a night like last night.

I told William about the article.

My phone buzzed, and I read the text from Bill. The captain wanted a status meeting this morning.

I dressed and was at the office at about eight o'clock and went straight to Bill's office. Bill got up when I went in, and I followed him to the captain's office. We took our usual seats around the captain's table. The captain had also invited the chief of police. I hadn't spent much time with the chief of police.

The captain told the chief the details he knew, and Bill filled in the few details that the captain missed. Bill must have told the captain all about our Atlanta trips since the captain included the Atlanta trip details in his details provided to the chief.

The captain asked, "What's next?"

I looked at Bill, and he answered, "We're waiting on subpoenas for the Atlanta bank account and the safety deposit box."

"How can I help?" the chief of police asked.

"The investigators in Atlanta assured us they'd get the subpoenas this morning."

"I'm getting pressure from the mayor to get this case solved," the chief said with a growl.

"We want to solve it as much as the mayor," Bill responded with a subservient voice.

The chief of police left, and the captain gave us another pep talk.

Investigator Charlie Allgood called Bill at nine and told him they were picking up the contents of the safety deposit box and printouts of the bank account at noon. I could tell Bill was pissed as he was talking to Allgood.

"We're going to Atlanta," he said as he stood up and walked out before I could ask any questions.

"What's going on?" I asked when we were in the car.

"The Atlanta investigators offered to e-mail me copies of the bank account information and the contents of the safety deposit box. They told me I didn't need to be involved anymore. It's still my case." He was fuming.

I expected a string of profanities, but they didn't come.

We made it to the bank just before noon and waited in the lobby. Charlie and Cynthia showed up and looked surprised to see us.

Charlie said to Bill, "You shouldn't have come down." It was more like an order than a suggestion.

"We needed to," Bill said.

The bank manager met us and gave Charlie a printout of the bank account. Charlie didn't offer it to us. The bank manager then escorted us to the safety deposit box. Cynthia gave him the key we found in Aiken, and it worked. The bank manager then placed the box on a table for us. I should say for Charlie and Cynthia. We looked as they opened the box. The contents were only passports and cash. Charlie placed the passports and cash in a plastic evidence bag without opening them. I would have opened them with a pen or knife to see the names. They probably would have too except they wanted to prove who was in charge.

We followed them to their police station. It was a modern, heavily glassed structure with lots of landscaping and trees. Charlie's office had a full window facing the trees and greenery. He had a large wooden desk with a table and chairs for visitors. His desk was larger than the Aiken captain's desk or my captain's desk in Chicago.

The evidence bag was opened, and the passports slid on the table. Cynthia took a knife from her belt and opened each one so she could see the names and addresses. Charlie and I wrote them down as Cynthia read the information. The Lowes each had a passport with the Mulberry address. The Jenkinses each had a passport with the Pebble Beach address. Two other passports had been in the safety deposit box. One was for Rudolph Lewinski, and the other was for Eugenia Lewinski. The address on each was 232 Almond Street, Newark, New Jersey 07114.

Charlie and Bill began looking at the bank account printout as Cynthia took the passports to forensics for fingerprints.

I e-mailed Jeffery and asked him to start immediately researching Rudolph and Eugenia Lewinski at 232 Almond Street in Newark. I googled Rudolph Lewinski on my cell phone, and there was a Newark newspaper article from three and half years ago about Rudolph. A picture of Rudolph was on the front page of the newspaper with a story about a CPA and his wife who had disappeared. The story related how Rudolph had possible connections to the mob and his demise may have been because of his association with them.

I showed Bill the article first, and then he showed Charlie and Cynthia.

"What's your take, Jessie? You know more about the mob than we do," Bill said. "Jessie's an investigator in Chicago on temporary loan to Aiken," Bill added for Charlie's and Cynthia's benefit.

Neither Charlie nor Cynthia seemed impressed.

"Since they didn't appear to be in the witness protection program, I'd say they decided to relieve the mob of funds. If so, they've hidden the money trail well unless they had all the funds in their safes."

Cynthia said, "We didn't find any money in the safe."

Bill added, "We didn't find money in the Aiken safe either."

"Whoever killed the Lowes also took everything out of the safes," I said.

"So who killed the Lowes?" Charlie asked.

"Someone that was hired by the mob or someone in the mob. I don't think we'll ever know. There were probably two people involved. One was in Aiken, and one was in Atlanta," I answered.

The one person I knew that could have done it was William. The problem I had with William was the time the alarm system was disarmed at the Pebble Beach house. I remembered him at the scene Monday night, and he was available for an interview early Monday morning. Maybe a second person was helping William. The other problem I had was that Tom and Carol were his friends.

"Why did they wait three and a half years?" Bill asked.

"Maybe the mob couldn't find the money trail either," I responded.

"So they found the money and then killed them?" Charlie asked.

"Either they found it or gave up on finding it. I'd say they found it," I answered.

"How did they find it?" Bill asked.

I thought about William and the $1 million needed for the foreclosures six months ago. It'd probably come to Bill later. My phone buzzed with a text.

"I'm not sure," I answered as I looked at a text from Jeffery. I showed Bill.

"I had Jeffery research Rudolph, and it appears Rudolph may have absconded with forty million from the mob," I said.

"So you don't think Ralph, Mary, Tomas, or William killed the Lowes?" Bill asked.

"I don't." I thought William may have had something to do with it, but I wasn't ready to say it.

"Where do you think the forty million is located?" Cynthia asked.

"I'd bet the Jenkins passport will tell us." I wanted to add that we should check for a trip six months ago but didn't.

Charlie said, "We'll check the passport, and we'll find the money."

I knew they wouldn't find the $40 million even if they found where it had been hidden. The money was back with the mob.

"I hope you do," I said.

The four of us discussed the case while we had lunch in the deli in the police station. Bill and I headed back to Aiken after lunch. We had a copy of the bank printout, and Charlie promised to e-mail copies of all the passport pages later today. Bill called Oscar and Jeffery and told them we'd meet at eight thirty on Friday morning.

I stopped to visit my parents for a short time, and then I went to William's house at eight. William met me at the door with a glass of wine and a tray of cheese, salami, and crackers. I had stopped to get my drive-through burger but welcomed a snack. I figured I'd be getting exercise soon.

William said, "Welcome home, honey. How was your day?"

"Slow and boring. We went to Atlanta again."

"Three days in a row. You must have found some important clues."

I decided to tell him and see his reaction. I'd then ask him questions to see if he glanced away as he answered. I was assuming he did have a tell.

"We found passports for the Lowes, Thomas and Caroline Jenkins, and Rudolph and Eugenia Lewinski in a safe deposit box."

I paused to see if William would react. He didn't, and he didn't say anything.

"Rudolph Lewinski was a CPA in Newark, New Jersey, and was supposedly involved with the mob."

William still didn't change his expression and kept looking at me. I looked to see if he did something as simple as swallowing, but he didn't.

"The rumor is Rudolph took forty million from the mob. Now we know why they lived under a different name in Aiken and Atlanta."

There was no change in expression from William.

"Did you ever think that Tom had been involved with the mob?" I asked.

"No. I didn't." He looked me in the eye as he answered. He didn't glance away and didn't show an indication he was lying.

"Did you know that the Lowes were the Jenkinses?"

"I didn't. Is this an official interview?" he said without showing any change in expression.

"It's a personal interview. I need to know."

"Keep asking then."

"Did you know that Tom Lowe or Thomas Jenkins was Rudolph Lewinski?"

"No." He stared me in the eyes and didn't blink.

"Have you ever worked for the mob?" I asked.

"No." He appeared to be truthful.

"Did you help the mob find the forty million?"

"No."

"Did you know where the forty million was located?"

"No."

"Did you find out where Tom got the million dollars for the foreclosures?"

"No." He wasn't expanding on his answers and was telling the truth as far as I could tell.

"Have you ever been in Tom's house in Atlanta?"

"No."

"Have you been in their safes?"

"No." He wasn't adding any humor to his answers, which was a little different. I did expect a few retorts.

"Did you give anyone the combination to the safes?"

"No."

"Did you give anyone a remote for the alarm system?"

"No." He was as calm as when I came through the door. He sipped his wine and ate a piece of salami as he waited for my next question.

"Did you have any involvement with the murders of Tom and Mary Lowe?"

"No."

"Do you swear you're telling the truth? I can't be involved with you otherwise."

"I swear I'm telling the truth."

"Good." I kissed him, and he kissed back.

We went into the living area and sat cuddled together, drinking wine and eating the cheese and salami. After a few minutes, William made his move and started kissing and fondling me. I didn't resist and checked his manhood. After a few minutes, William led me to the bedroom. Although I usually had trouble sleeping in a different bed, I slept great in William's bed and woke up refreshed. William woke up around seven and started nuzzling me. I woke up as he was on top of me kissing my neck and ear. I pushed him off and told him I had to get ready for work.

William said as he was fondling me, "I have to leave town for a couple of days for business."

"Where are you going?" I asked, wanting to go with him.

"New York City. Would you like to go?"

He probably knew I wouldn't go, but he was polite to ask.

"No. I can't. Call me as soon as you get back," I said too desperately.

"The minute I get back I'll call. I'll even call you from New York."

Friday Morning—Jessie

Bill and I met with Oscar, Jeffery, and Wally at eight thirty. Bill told them about the Atlanta bank account and the safety deposit box. Jeffery handed out copies of what he and Wally had found about Rudolph Lewinski. Bill made copies of the bank account printout and passports and gave them to Jeffery.

"More for Wally and me to do?" Jeffery asked.

"Yes, do a thorough search of the bank account and the passports. Look hard at where they traveled, especially for places forty million could be hidden," Bill said.

Jeffery said, "We didn't find anything useful in the Aiken bank records, but maybe we can in the Atlanta bank records."

"Do you think the forty million was found?" Oscar asked.

"Jessie thinks it was found by the mob, and I tend to agree," Bill answered.

"What about Ralph, Mary, Tomas, and William? Are we through with them?" Jeffery asked.

"Concentrate on Ralph Lewinski. The others are still considered suspects for now," Bill answered.

"Are you going to ask for search warrants?" Jeffery asked.

"Not for now. But it's still possible we'll need one," Bill said.

All got the message that Bill now believed that the mob was involved and not our other suspects.

We met with the captain before lunch. The captain had scheduled a press conference at two and wanted Bill and me to attend and answer questions. He handed us a press release that had been prepared and asked us to review it. The press release discussed Tom Lowe, the other names he used, his possible involvement with the mob, the possibility of $40 million being taken, and the probability of the mob being involved with the murders.

"Review the press release and let me know of corrections or embellishments that are needed," the captain stated.

Bill and I took our copies and left to do our review and get ready for the press conference.

Chapter 17

Friday Night—William

I was in the limo on my way to have dinner when I returned Jessie's call.

Jessie answered, "Hello, William."

"Hi, Jessie. How was your day?"

"It was interesting. We had a press conference that accused the mob of killing the Lowes. It was big news for Aiken."

"Did you get the local yokels stirred up?" I repeated what I first heard her say at the Lowes' home.

"They were outraged that a mob hit could happen in Aiken."

"I'm sure they were."

"When will you be back?" She actually sounded like she missed me already.

"A day or two." I said, "I've got to go. Good-bye, sweetheart." The limo was at the restaurant.

Jessie said, "Good-bye."

She didn't return the sweetheart or any other endearment.

A room had been reserved for the dinner, and my seat was at the end of the table beside the head of the family. The room was extravagant with walnut paneling, crystal chandeliers, a mahogany table and chairs, porcelain china, silver cutlery, and Egyptian cotton napkins. A large flower arrangement was on the table when I came in but was removed to allow everyone to see each other. I was the last to arrive. I assume other business was conducted prior to my arrival. Salads were being served, and I accepted wine from the server in my large crystal wine glass. I also requested water, and it was poured in another crystal glass.

"A toast," the head of the family said. "Here's to the successful conclusion to the Lewinski matter."

"*Salutare*." All spoke in unison, and I spoke it with them.

"We're gathered to honor William, who completed an assignment unlike others he has performed for us," the head of the family continued.

I was sure that everyone in the room knew the outcome of the Lewinski situation.

"For this task, William spent years obtaining the information we needed to access and obtain the funds stolen by Lewinski. The other tasks he provided for us have been more quickly accomplished."

The head of the family was selective with his words, but the wait staff knew their fate if they discussed anything they heard at the family dinners.

"I invited William here tonight not to just honor him but to request that he tell us how he accomplished this important family task. William assured me he could handle this assignment, and my patience was rewarded. William."

I hadn't attended or spoken at a family dinner before but started my quick summary.

"When the boss asked me to do this, I was reluctant since it wasn't my typical forte."

"Call me Frank tonight. You've earned it," the head of the family said.

"I told Frank …" I was stopped by the laughter. Anyone else in the room wouldn't be allowed to call him Frank.

I continued, "When Rudolph Lewinski moved to Aiken after he stayed a short time in Atlanta, I purchased a house next to his and befriended him and his wife, went to the same social functions, and let him win at golf occasionally. Rudolph and Eugenia liked Aiken since they were big fish in a small pond unlike Atlanta. They were invited to all major social events since they were very generous."

The boss interrupted, "Rudolph was very generous with our money. I've also learned over the years that William is a shrewd businessman, and he actually bought a foreclosure next to Rudolph Lewinski."

I smiled as I continued, "Rudolph had safes in both the Aiken home and Atlanta home. I checked both safes and found cash and jewelry but not the forty million. The cash in each safe was about ten thousand and was probably emergency traveling money. I also got in the safety deposit box later and saw that it only contained passports and a little cash."

The boss interrupted again, "William knew the contents of the safes within weeks, but he and I weren't satisfied until we found the forty million."

The boss should have been telling the story rather than me.

I looked at the boss, and he patted me on the shoulder and said, "Continue."

"I followed Rudolph on his trips, but he never went near the money. I knew he was getting short on his liquid cash when I enticed him to invest in foreclosures. I had been bragging about the profits until the ex-CPA couldn't resist. Rudolph must have felt safe after three years and took a trip to withdraw a million for the foreclosures we were buying."

The boss touched my shoulder, so I stopped talking. He wanted to speak.

"William, if you believe this redneck, makes a lot of money with foreclosures. I've tried to convince him to use our money, but he has refused. I'm sure we could convince him if he wasn't so helpful in other areas."

Everyone at the table laughed.

The salads were being taken away and the entrees served. I only ate a couple bites of my salad. My wine glass was topped off.

I continued when the laughter subsided. "I followed Rudolph when he went to get the million, and he led me to the bank where he had the money."

The boss touched me again, so I stopped talking.

"William did his part to find the money, and we need to recognize Benny for getting access to the account. It cost a few bucks, but it was well worth it." The boss looked at me again, which was a sign for me to continue.

The entrees were being served, and I now had a parmesan crusted New York strip with fresh vegetables and garlic mashed potatoes. The aroma was overpowering, and I was hungry. I decided to finish my story quickly unless I was interrupted.

"I supplied the alarm remote for Aiken, the alarm code for Atlanta, and the safe combinations but wouldn't agree to snuff out Rudolph and Eugenia."

The boss interjected again, "William would have been the perfect choice for the assignment, but he actually liked Rudolph and Eugenia."

"I was surprised on the night Rudolph and Eugenia were killed. I didn't want to be told when it was going to happen."

The boss added, "William wouldn't be very good in our family. He doesn't like to kill people he knows."

"It's a personal issue I'm working through," I said as the table laughed.

The Don stood up and said, "In appreciation for your efforts, you can select any jewelry from Eugenia's collection."

One of the Caporegime held an open briefcase next to me that was loaded with jewelry.

"I can't accept. It'd be too personal." I held up my hands. I did think about how one of Eugenia's diamond necklaces would look on Jessie.

"Would you also like to refuse the million-dollar finder's fee?" the Don asked.

"Money isn't personal, so I can accept it."

The same Caporegime handed me another briefcase, and I set it beside my chair. I'd slowly funnel the money through the restaurants and other businesses until it ended up in my bank accounts.

The Don pulled me up out of my chair so I was standing up beside him. "Another toast to William who helped us recover the forty million and the additional five million the Lowes had accumulated in the account, not counting the jewelry."

"*Salutare*."

The dinner was great, and I was ushered out while everyone else stayed. They probably didn't finish their business before I arrived. I had a fleeting thought that they may be discussing eliminating loose ends with the Lewinskis. One would be me. I figured I was safe though.

The limo was outside waiting for me, and I was driven back to the hotel.

"Do you need me more this evening?" the limo driver asked as he was letting me out.

I thought for a few seconds before answering. I did know a few women in New York who might have been willing to meet me for a late drink.

"No, I won't," I answered as I handed him a fifty-dollar tip. I was feeling generous tonight.

After putting my briefcase in my room, I went to the hotel bar and ordered a beer. It was craft brewed beer from upper state New York. I thought about the Lowes and felt some sympathy but also thought about their greediness. Rudolph was paid well by the mob and had a successful CPA firm. I thought about tomorrow and my plans. I'd have a late breakfast after working out. I'd then go to an afternoon play and then an evening play. I could call the women I knew in New York to accompany me but didn't think I would. I thought about Jessie. I looked forward to getting back to Aiken to see her.

Chapter 18

Friday Evening/Saturday/Sunday—Jessie

I spent Friday evening with my parents. Mom was awake and alert most of the time and quizzed me about William, my job, and my time in Aiken.

"Tell me more about William," Mom said several times during the evening.

"He's a great guy." I wanted to say he's a guy I'll probably never see again now that the Lowes' case is settled as far as the Aiken County Sheriff's Department is concerned. I was probably being used for William to keep tabs on the case.

"Did you say he was out of town?"

"Yes, he went to New York." I was guessing that was where he actually went. I thought about checking with the airlines to make sure but didn't.

"Why didn't he ask you to go?" Mom was relentless.

"I told him I couldn't go."

William returned my call while I was visiting Mom, and we had a quick conversation.

"Was that William?" Mom asked as soon as I hung up.

"Yes. He was busy, so he couldn't talk."

I used my excuse to go see Dad to get away from the interrogation. Dad was asleep, so I went home. I couldn't take more questions from Mom about William. I was reminded several times that she needed grandchildren and William would be a perfect father.

On Saturday, I took Mom down to see Dad two times. Dad was staying awake longer, and our visits were extended. I took time to do laundry and clean the house. William didn't call on Saturday.

On Sunday, I repeated Saturday except for doing the laundry and cleaning the house. William didn't call again, and I decided to not call him. I figured it was over between us just when it was heating up. I'd waited all my life for Mr. Right, and he turned out to be someone that wanted to use me. I thought I'd get on eHarmony.com or Match.com tonight.

Chapter 19

Monday Morning—Jessie

It was Monday morning, and I was called by the Aiken County sheriff's dispatcher to meet Bill at the sheriff's offices. I was already dressed and about to leave for the office. On my drive, I thought about William not calling since I saw him Friday morning. Bill was waiting when I arrived.

"What's going on?" I asked.

"There's a murder in Burnettown."

"Where's Burnettown?"

"It's a mill town in the valley. It's just a few miles from Aiken."

"What happened?"

"I don't know. We'll find out when we get there."

"I thought the sheriff just handled the county outside the cities and towns."

"Since Burnettown is an incorporated town with a police department, we'll ask our captain and the Burnettown captain how we'll be involved. In the past, the Burnettown captain has requested us to lead the investigation since Burnettown doesn't have investigators. Burnettown has a population of about twenty-five hundred, and the police department has a small staff."

Bill drove down Jefferson Davis Highway and turned just past a Reid's grocery store. Bill said that he'd get his crickets and worms for fishing from Reid's grocery store. There was machine that dispensed them just like a coke machine. I was reminded often that I was in the South.

Bill drove across the dam for Langley Pond. I read a sign as we crossed the dam that said Langley Pond was in the *Guinness Book of World Records* as the largest pond. The pond looked like a lake to me, but I wasn't a pond expert.

Bill drove into a paved driveway surrounded by a long, red brick fence. Bill parked the car at the end of the long, curved driveway in a parking area that circled a fountain. By the number of cars and emergency vehicles, we must have been the last ones to arrive. The house was what I envisioned for a southern home, with large columns and an impressive entrance.

I asked when we got out of the car, "Why do these southern houses have all the windows and outcroppings?"

"These older homes needed circulation for cooling, so they had a lot of windows. These houses were also built off the ground to allow circulation under the house. The brick foundation must have been installed after air-conditioning. The chimneys were always on exterior walls. The outcroppings are pediments, gables, dormers, and balustrades. There are also weaver's windows on the top floor. There could also be a witch window."

I said, "Thanks. That's more than I needed to know." I shouldn't have asked since I didn't want or need to know about southern architecture.

Bill and I walked up the wide, wood, curved, railed steps onto a porch that wrapped around the large house. I heard creaking under my feet as I walked across loose boards on the porch. The hinges squeaked as Bill opened the wood screen door and entered a foyer with high ceilings and massive paintings on the walls. They were bigger than life.

Bill said he'd find someone to tell us what had happened. I waited in the foyer. My cell phone rang, and I answered it without looking at the phone display. I usually screened calls and didn't answer calls from some people. I'd let them leave a message and call them back when I felt like it.

William Bradford said, "Hello, gorgeous. How is my favorite investigator?"

I said in my coldest and most formal voice, "Hello, William. I'm fine."

"I'm back in Aiken and thought we could have dinner tonight."

"I'm busy tonight. I'll let you know when I'm available."

"I'm sorry for leaving, but it was important business that I had to take care of. I'll make it up to you. I do my best apologies over a nice dinner and wine."

"I'm working on a new murder case and don't know what my schedule will be. I'll let you know."

I wasn't planning to call, and the new murder case gave me a good reason for not having dinner with him. A nice dinner and wine, and I'd be back on my back. It was a good thought however.

"Tell me about the case. I may be able to help."

"I'll let you know if I need your help. We just arrived at the scene."

"Who was murdered?"

"I'm not at liberty to discuss that. Good-bye, William." I used my cold and formal voice again. I pushed the end button while I reminded myself to look at the display before answering.

As I ended the call, Bill came back with the responding officer. He was a Burnettown officer and his name was Jim Abbey. Jim looked about twenty. He didn't look like he was even shaving. He was about five feet nine with blond hair, a round face with a wide mouth, a medium nose, and blue eyes. I'd ask Bill later, but it looked like this could be his first job as a cop. His uniform also looked brand-new.

We followed Jim upstairs, and Bill asked him who was murdered.

"It was Mr. Burnette." Jim swallowed hard while answering. He seemed nervous.

I was thinking that the town could be named after Mr. Burnette, but I'd ask later.

Jim pointed at the master bedroom door but didn't look in. He was starting to get a little pale. He must have remembered what he saw earlier. On the bed in the master bedroom was an older man lying on his back. He was fully clothed including his shoes. We could see the bullet hole on his temple and dried blood on the side of his face and on the pillow and sheet.

We walked back outside so Jim wouldn't pass out.

"I understand you were the first one on the scene," Bill said.

Jim was nervous as he said, "Yes. I arrived about 9:25 a.m. and met the housekeeper, Ms. Sanchez, at the front door. Ms. Sanchez told me Mr. Burnette was in the master bedroom upstairs, and she thought he was dead. I went to the master bedroom and found Mr. Burnette in his bed, and he was dead. I'd never seen someone shot before. It appeared he had been shot in the head and had been dead for a while. After calling it in, I came back downstairs to wait on the coroner, my captain, and Aiken County deputies. Ms. Sanchez told me that she had gone to the second floor to the master bedroom to get the sheets for the laundry. When she got to the master bedroom, Mr. Burnette was on the bed with a lot of blood at his head. She said that she went back downstairs and called 911."

I asked, "Where's Ms. Sanchez now?"

Jim said, "She's in my car. She's very disturbed about the whole thing, and I am too."

I walked away from Bill while he was on the phone and looked around the property. In front of a separate garage with four garage doors was an older Toyota. I figured this must be Ms. Sanchez's car. The yard had lots of plants and flowers that made my parents' yard look like it needed a lot of work. From the house, I wasn't able to see anybody else's house through the forest of pine trees. I did see Jim Abbey talking to an older Burnettown police officer and guessed it was the Burnettown captain.

Bill walked over to me and told me our captain was on the way. If I was in Chicago, I'd have taken over, but I'd wait for the captain since I wasn't in Chicago. I meandered over to Ms. Sanchez, who was in the police car, and started asking her questions. She was happy to have someone to talk to, so she answered my questions readily. Unfortunately, she didn't know anything that was helpful. She cleaned on Monday and Thursday. She didn't know any of Mr. Burnette's friends or family. She had started working two weeks ago. I walked back over to Bill as I saw our captain's car arrive.

The Burnettown captain came over about the same time, and I was introduced. The others knew each other. Our captain asked the Burnettown captain if he wanted us to lead the investigation, and the Burnettown captain said yes.

Our captain said, "Bill, you'll be the lead on the investigation, and Jessie will assist you. The Aiken County Sheriff's Office will support you with whatever you need, and I'm sure the Burnettown police will support you as needed. Who can tell me what happened here?"

The Burnettown captain went through an explanation that was related to him from Jim Kelly. The captain also told facts about Mr. Burnette. Paul Burnette was a relative of the Burnette that Burnettown was named after. Mr. Burnette had owned a lot of land and properties in Burnettown and was well respected in the community. He also had businesses in the area. The captain didn't know what businesses he was still involved in. According to the captain, he was about sixty-five years old and had sold his business interests and properties after his wife died about three years ago. Mr. Burnette had also become more reclusive since his wife died.

I asked, "Have you had any 911 calls or other problems at the Burnette house?"

The Burnettown captain answered, "No, I can't recall any 911 calls or any other reason for us to come out here."

"Do you know if he has any relatives in town?"

"No, but you can check with the town clerk, Mrs. Fields. She's been the town clerk for thirty years and knows everybody."

Bill said, "Thanks, we'll talk to her."

We walked over to Ms. Sanchez and asked her to step out of the car. Ms. Sanchez politely answered the same questions I had asked. On the days she worked, on Monday and Thursday, she worked about four hours, cleaning the house and washing laundry. She started laundry first so that the clothes would be dry before she left. One of the first things she did was change the sheets on the master bedroom bed so she could wash them. Since she had worked for the two weeks, there hadn't been any other bedroom used that required the sheets to be changed. She said that she swept, mopped, dusted, took out the garbage, and cleaned the kitchen and bathrooms. She said the house stayed pretty clean compared to other houses she did. Mr. Burnette washed his own dishes and kept the kitchen, bathrooms, and house clean. She said that for other houses she cleaned, the owners didn't clean at all since they had a housekeeper.

"Have you seen anything unusual at the Burnette house lately?" Bill asked.

"No."

"Who was the last housekeeper?" I asked.

"I don't know. I responded to an ad on Craigslist to get the job."

"Was Mr. Burnette home when you cleaned?"

"Mr. Burnette was home every time I cleaned. He would stay in his office downstairs. I didn't have to clean the office, but Mr. Burnette would bring out the trash. Mr. Burnette would come to the kitchen about eleven thirty, fix himself a sandwich for lunch, and get a soda from the refrigerator. Mr. Burnette always asked me if he could fix me a sandwich, and I always said no."

"Where did you go after cleaning Mr. Burnette's house?"

"I have another big house in Aiken to clean on Monday and Thursday afternoons."

"Did you see any visitors while you were cleaning?"

"No. There weren't any visitors."

Ms. Sanchez gave us her cell phone number and address, and Bill told her she was free to go after giving her his business card.

The coroner came out of the house, and a group of us walked over to him. He said the victim was shot twice in the head and appeared to be deceased for about ten hours, putting the time of death at about eleven last night.

I asked, "Did there appear to be a struggle by the victim?"

The coroner said, "It looked like the victim was asleep when he was shot. The autopsy should be able to tell us more."

This murder was similar to the first murder I investigated in Aiken where two victims were shot while they were asleep. William was initially a suspect in that case, so I'd now find time to see if he was really in New York last night. The two cases could be connected. I wondered if the Lowes knew this victim.

The coroner answered more questions from the group. I hoped the forensic techs would provide clues that would point directly to a suspect. Maybe the killer left his wallet or the weapon with fingerprints.

One of the forensic techs came out next and said the house had lots of fingerprints, but there wasn't any evidence of break in, and there didn't appear to be any struggle by the victim. He said they had collected a lot of trace evidence, which would be processed by SLED.

The tech went on to say that the only blood found was from the victim. There were no weapons found in the house. The garage was checked, and there were a lot of fingerprints found on the vehicles, and they would be processed. They didn't find any footprints or other items outside the house. The tech said that we could go in the house again shortly. It was now about eleven o'clock.

I asked, "Was there an alarm system for the house?"

"Yes, and it was turned on. Our electronic techs will be checking the system as well as the cell phone and PC from the office."

"Did you see any evidence of tampering with the alarm system, and is there a video surveillance system?"

"The alarm system didn't appear to be tampered with, and we didn't see a video surveillance system. Sometimes there's one that's hidden, but we didn't find one." The tech then said, "I'm going back in to help and will let you know when you can come in."

A few minutes later, a gurney came out with the victim's body. The victim was loaded into an ambulance for transporting to the morgue.

An hour later with my impatience peaking, we went into the house. My hope was that this wait would result in a revelation. However, the only indication that something was amiss was the blood on the sheets in the master bedroom. Other than that, the house looked orderly, and there were no signs of foul play. There was fingerprint powder throughout the house.

Bill and I spent two hours touring the house and discussing the logistics of what happened. It was apparent to both of us that the person or persons who committed the murder were probably in the house waiting or had a key to the house and had a code for the alarm system. There were two vehicles in the garage. One was a twelve-passenger van with an expanded metal cage between the front seats and the backseats. The other vehicle was a Ford F150 truck.

We spent most of the time in Mr. Burnette's office. There were files and documents on the desk and a wall of bookshelves full of books. The books ranged from mysteries to do-it-yourself books. We divided up and browsed through the files and documents. The files were organized alphabetically, and the tabs were organized and spaced. Nothing jumped out at us, such as a threatening letter, copies of blackmail checks, or incriminating photos. It looked like we needed to go through all the documents in more detail later. There was also a gun safe in the office that we needed to have opened. It was a large safe about five feet tall.

Bill said, "I reckon I'm getting plumb hungry. It's time we ate lunch, and then we can get up with the neighbors."

I was beginning to think that Bill talked southern redneck just for my amusement.

I said, "Lunch sounds great."

"I have a hankerin' for pizza. Let's hit the road for Buck's Pizza."

We had lunch at Buck's Pizza. The choices in Burnettown for lunch were limited, and pizza did sound good. We had a large pepperoni pizza and shared the cost.

Chapter 20

Monday Afternoon—Jessie

After lunch, Bill and I went to see the neighbor next door. We walked up wooden steps with shaky wooden rails to a small porch that just had enough room for the two rocking chairs. This house was a stark contrast to the Burnette house. Bill knocked on the screen door, and a very old lady using a cane came to the door. The main door to the house was already open, and I could see her face through the screen.

She was having trouble hearing us, so we repeated our names quite loudly. After we showed her our IDs, she introduced herself as Ann Thomas and invited us in. She told us she'd be back in a couple of minutes.

I looked around and saw that the house was decorated with faded lace curtains, and the furniture was old and worn. I sat down in a chair and kept sinking. I finally stopped just before hitting the floor. Bill sat on the sofa and was more upright.

When she came back, she sat on the sofa with Bill. She apologized for leaving us and asked us what we needed. Bill raised his voice and told her we were investigating the murder of Mr. Burnette.

Ann said, "You don't have to talk so loud. I now have my hearing aids in."

Bill said, "I'm sorry, Ms. Ann. What I was saying was that we're investigating the murder of Mr. Burnette, and we have a few questions."

"I heard about the murder and saw all the police cars going over there this morning. What happened to him?"

"I can't really tell you anything yet. We do have a few questions for you in hopes you can help us find out who murdered Mr. Burnette. Did you know him?"

"I knew him. We dated in high school. He ended up marrying someone else, and I ended up with my loser husband."

"So you knew Mrs. Burnette too?" I asked.

"I did. We became best friends. I told her about my lousy husband, and she told me how perfect Paul was."

"Paul is Mr. Burnette."

"Yes. Paul broke my heart when I was young. I remember when he took me to the senior prom. He was the class president, and I was his date. I gave him my virginity that night. I was already planning my future with him. I was wearing a light blue gown with lace on the sleeves and bodice."

Ann was motioning across her chest where the lace was. I was rolling my eyes.

Ann went on, "The dress was low cut and made my breasts look bigger. I bought it with babysitting money. I wanted to impress Paul, and I did. He couldn't keep his hands off of me that night. All the guys were staring at me. I was a great dancer too and was twirling all over the dance floor. I told Paul I'd put out that night. Paul couldn't wait until the dance was over, so we went out to his car about an hour after the dance started. He had my dress pushed up, and I was no longer a virgin. I knew when I started putting out that we'd be together forever."

I started tapping my pen on the table, waiting for Ann to stop. Bill put his hand over mine to stop the tapping.

Ann didn't slow down. "After the prom, a bunch of us went camping near the lake. I had sex with Paul four more times that night. I was sore for a week, but that didn't stop us. We had sex almost every day until he left for college. His parents had given him a car, and we tried to wear out the backseat."

"Why didn't you get married?" Bill asked with a caring voice.

I gave Bill a stern look since I didn't want to hear more about Ann's sex life when she was in high school.

"Paul went to the University of South Carolina, and I went to work at the mill. That's what happened. Evelyn went to the university too, and he dumped me for her."

I was thinking that Ann was our first suspect. She could have waited all these years and finally taken revenge on him. The anger could have built up for the past forty some years.

"How often did you see Evelyn and Paul?" I asked.

"I was over there once or twice a week when Evelyn was alive. Since Evelyn died, I haven't gone over at all."

"Have you seen Paul around town?" Bill asked.

"Occasionally, and we spoke to each other. I don't get out much anymore."

She was calmer since she told her story about her lost love. I was sure lots of other people had heard the same story.

I asked, "Did you see any other vehicles or any other people going into Mr. Burnette's house the past few days?"

"Paul didn't have a lot of visitors."

"What about yesterday?"

"There may have been a white van yesterday, but I'm not quite sure. Sometimes I get the days mixed up."

"What time did you see the van?"

"I believe it was in the evening while I was sitting on the porch—or was it when I was cleaning the front window? It's too cold in the morning to sit on the porch. My granddaughter was coming over to check on me, so I may have been cleaning the window while I watched for her. She's going to sell some of my treasures at her yard sale next Saturday, and I was showing her my stash. She said she may sell some of the items on eBay after she does some research. She's a smart granddaughter and knows all about the electronic gadgets. She loaned me a cell phone, but I told her to take it back."

I started tapping again, and Bill stopped me. I was so low in the chair that my elbows were at head level.

"How often does your granddaughter come over?"

"About twice a week."

Ann gave us her granddaughter's name and phone number.

Bill asked, "Do you know if Mr. Burnette has anybody that would want to murder him?"

"No, everybody I know liked Paul, and I can't think of anyone who would want to hurt him."

I asked, "Did you hear any gunshots?"

"No. I only put in my hearing aids when I have company."

"Can you tell us about the make and model of the van or could you tell what state the tag was from?"

"Lord no. It was a big, white van, and I couldn't even see the tag. It comes and goes pretty often, but I never thought to look at the tag."

"Did the van have any writing on the side?"

"I'm pretty sure it was a plain white van."

Bill said, "Thanks for your time, Ms. Ann. Here's my card. If you think of anything else, please call us."

"I'll help anyway I can. Paul was a fine gentleman even though he didn't marry me."

I tried to get up out of the chair and struggled. I rocked three times before I finally got out.

Ann saw me struggle and said, "That was my last husband, Kevin's, chair. He was a rather large man and wore the chair out. I should get rid of it, but it reminds me of him. He was my sweetest husband. I married my first husband six months after Paul dumped me. He was a few years older than me and worked at the mill. He was better than Paul in bed. He died while we were having sex. My second husband wasn't very good in bed, but he wanted to adopt my children. He died in bed too. Kevin was the best. He was sweet and well endowed. I wish I knew him when I was young."

Bill and I left Ann in her thoughts about her husbands and went to the neighbor on the other side. The Ms. Ann stuff sounded weird. If Bill called me Ms. Jessie, I'd deck him.

The other neighbor was another older woman. She was Mary Anne. Mary Anne already had her hearing aids in so she could answer our questions as soon as she invited us in. Her house was similar to Ann's house with an old-fashioned décor. I tested the chair before I sat down, and it was okay. Bill sat on the sofa with Mary Anne.

Mary Anne had visited Mrs. Burnette when she was alive but hadn't visited Mr. Burnette since. She didn't see many vehicles going in and out of Mr. Burnette's property and didn't know makes and models. She didn't see the van yesterday but had seen a white van lots in the past. She didn't hear any gunshots and went to bed about nine thirty without her hearing aids.

Seeing these two women had me thinking about my elderly times when I'd be wearing hearing aids. It made me quiver. It also made me want to have sex with William while I could still enjoy it. I needed some good stories about sex so I could tell them when I got old. I sure didn't have any from Chicago.

When we were inside Bill's car, Bill turned to me and said, "We learned that the victim was a likeable guy and only had a few visitors. We also learned that the victim has old ladies for neighbors who don't know vehicles."

I said, "I do believe Ms. Ann may be my prime suspect so far. I think we should have her house searched for weapons. I thought she was leading us on a wild goose chase until we talked to Ms. Mary Anne."

"I'll ask the captain if we can get a warrant. Maybe we should have her house staked out."

The neighbor directly across the street was another older woman. She was in a wheelchair when she came to the door. Her name was Carol. Carol invited us in after the introductions and we showed her our IDs. When asked about last night, she didn't have any more information than Ann and Mary Anne. Carol said she too went to bed early and didn't hear anything or see any vehicles yesterday or last night.

"Does Mr. Burnette get many visitors?" I asked.

Carol answered, "Not anymore. There were a lot of dump trucks at his house a few years ago, and there was a lot of comings and goings. Since then, there hasn't been much."

Bill gave Carol his card, and we left. We decided to go see the town clerk, Mrs. Fields, next.

The town offices were in a one-story brick building in the center of town, not far from the victim's house. This was true for any business or residence since the town was small. Mrs. Fields had three other persons waiting to see her when we arrived. All three were there to pay for speeding tickets. Bill told me while we were waiting that Burnettown issued a lot of speeding tickets. The town limits crossed Jefferson Davis Highway, and the speed limit was reduced to forty-five miles per hour on the four-lane road. Burnettown took advantage of this and caught a lot of speeders. Bill went on to say that Burnettown didn't always respond to 911 calls because their officers concentrated on traffic patrol. He said that 911 calls were handled mostly by the Aiken County sheriff's deputies. They must have made an exception for Mr. Burnette since he was a well-respected resident.

When it was our turn with Mrs. Fields, she said she had been expecting us. Two other people came in after us, so Mrs. Fields went to the rear door of the office and asked someone to come up front to help out. It was Jim Abbey. Mrs. Fields then invited us to go down the hall to a meeting room.

The meeting room had a coffee pot, and she offered us coffee. I took mine black while Bill took his with lots of cream and sugar.

Bill said, "Can you please tell us about Mr. Burnette?"

Mrs. Fields answered, "Mr. Burnette lived in Burnettown almost his whole life. He did go away to get a business degree from the University of South Carolina and then came back to help his father with the various businesses they were involved with. After Mr. Burnette's father died, Mr. Burnette moved into his father's home. This was about thirty years ago. They were involved in construction, home building, remodeling, lumber, and real estate. They had a couple of businesses in town but sold them after Evelyn died. I believe they had a hardware store, and Evelyn had a dress shop. Mr. and Mrs. Burnette didn't have any children. Mr. Burnette had been a deacon at the Baptist church, was involved with the civic clubs, was on the city council, and was mayor for a number of years. After his wife died, he hasn't been active in much of anything. I've only seen him at church a couple of times since his wife died. I don't believe he's involved in a lot of businesses anymore."

I asked, "Do you know whether he has a business in his home?"

"No, he doesn't have a business license for that. I would know if he did."

"He had Ms. Sanchez as a housekeeper for the past two weeks. Do you know who the housekeeper was before Ms. Sanchez?"

"It was Mrs. Rodriquez. She lives on Dell Street with her husband and children. Mrs. Rodriquez stopped working for Mr. Burnette because she was having a baby. She had the baby last week, and I'm sure she and the baby are now home. She worked for Mr. Burnette for about two years."

Bill asked, "Do you know of anybody who would want to hurt Mr. Burnette?"

"No. He was such a nice gentleman."

I asked, "Do you know who he was involved with in his businesses?"

"As I mentioned, I don't know of any businesses he was involved in recently. In the past, it was always just him and his father that had the businesses. He had employees but hasn't had any in many years as far as I know."

"Do you know any of his friends' names?"

"A lot of his friends have died or moved away. There are still two in town that I can recall. There's Joe Jackson who lives on First Street and Allen Jones who lives on Randolph Street. They can probably tell you about others."

"Can you think of anything else that may be helpful to us?"

"I can't think of anything, but I'll call if I do."

Mrs. Rodriquez lived in a small house with a porch across the front. The house was white with wood siding and had a cinderblock foundation. Bill knocked on the door, and it was several minutes before Mrs. Rodriquez came to the door. Bill introduced us, and we showed her our IDs. She invited us in, and we sat down on modern furniture. I tested the chair again. The house was tidy with everything clean.

Bill said, "We're here to ask about Mr. Burnette. He was killed last night, and we'd like to ask you some questions."

Mrs. Rodriquez said, "Oh gracious. Mr. Burnette was such a fine gentleman. Who would want to kill him?"

"That's what we're trying to find out. We hope you can help us."

"How can I help? Poor Mr. Burnette. He was so nice."

"You can tell us about your time while working for him."

"There isn't a lot to tell. I cleaned his house on Monday and Thursday mornings. I would get there around eight or nine o'clock and leave about twelve or one. I did his laundry and cleaned his house. It wasn't difficult since he kept the house pretty clean himself."

I asked, "Did you see many other people while you were cleaning?"

"Sometimes someone would stop by while I was there. Sometimes they would talk outside, but most of the time they would meet in his office."

"Who were these men? Do you remember any names?"

"No, I don't remember. I was always working, and Mr. Burnette would always answer the door when they came."

"Have you seen any of these men around town?"

"No, the only time I've seen them was at Mr. Burnette's house."

"Did you hear any of these men threaten Mr. Burnette or did they have arguments?"

"No, they all seemed nice and always talked quietly."

Bill said, "Ms. Sanchez is doing the cleaning now, and she said that she didn't have to clean the office. Did you have to clean the office?"

"Mr. Burnette was always working in his office when I cleaned, and I didn't clean his office. He'd leave the trash can at the door for me to empty. Mr. Burnette was such a nice man. It's sad to hear he was murdered."

"Do you remember anything strange or unusual that happened?"

"No, it was always the same, and Mr. Burnette was such a nice person to work for. When I told him I was quitting for a while because I was pregnant, he said I could come back to work whenever I wanted. He said he would inform the new person about it. He even gave me a thousand dollars when I left."

We asked Mrs. Rodriquez a few more questions but didn't find out anything new. Bill gave her his card, and we left. We decided to head back to the office to start a murder book and decide on the plans for tomorrow.

On the way, the dispatcher came across the radio asking us to respond to a fire. The dispatcher gave us directions, and Bill responded that he knew where it was. Bill made a U-turn and drove on a couple of country roads and then turned on a gravel road. There wasn't a marker or mailbox, but he knew where it was based on the dispatcher's directions. After about a mile on the gravel road, there was a house that had burned down. It was in an open area surrounded by scrub oaks and pine trees. An eight-foot-tall chain-link fence surrounded the house about fifty feet on each side. There was razor wire on top. Bill stopped just outside the gate.

A fireman was spraying water on the areas that were still smoldering. The fire truck was parked next to the house. I wondered as I got out of the car why we were called to a house fire.

The captain and shift lieutenant were there, and we walked over to them.

The captain said, "A house fire was called in about nine this morning when smoke was seen. There wasn't much left of the house when the Aiken County Fire Department arrived. When they walked through the house, they saw five corpses. Investigator Robinson will be handling the investigation, but I thought you should see it. The house is close enough to Burnettown that the cases could be related."

Investigator Robinson was Michael Robinson. He was lean and tall and was wearing jeans and a department-issued shirt with Aiken County Sheriff on the front. He had a trim nose, a small mouth, and eyes close together. Dark brown hair was showing underneath his hat. His office was next to Bill's office in the station.

"Do you know who died in the fire?" Bill asked.

"No, there were five cars here when the fire department arrived." He pointed to five late-model cars parked near the fence on both sides of the gate. "We ran the tags, and they belong to three men from Columbia and two from Augusta. I'll start calling the families shortly to see if the men were supposed to be here."

"When did the house fire start?" I asked.

"Sometime last night. I haven't heard a time yet."

Shortly after we got back to the office, William called, and I decided to answer it.

"You answered my call twice in a row. I feel honored."

"It's your lucky day."

"I've felt lucky every day I've known you. How about dinner tonight?"

This made my heart flutter a bit as I recalled our last meeting at his house.

"I'll be working for a little while. I'll call you after I'm done."

"I'll be waiting patiently. Try to have energy left for me."

"Bye, William." I pressed the end button. I knew what he wanted me to have energy for, but it wasn't my intention to fall for his advances—or was it?

I went to Bill's office, and he was still on the computer. I knocked on the door to let him know I was there. He raised his head and acknowledged me with a nod. I took this as a sign to sit down and wait. Instead, I made a hand signal about coffee. He nodded, so I left to get us coffee.

I gave Bill his coffee as he hung up the phone.

We decided that tomorrow we'd visit Joe Jackson and Allen Jones, who were the friends mentioned by Mrs. Fields, go see more neighbors, and go back to the victim's home to look through the files in the office. We decided to have Jeffery do research into all the businesses and properties that the victim was involved with to see if there were partners. Bill said he'd work this out.

I said, "Have Jeffery also research the construction work at the vic's house a few years ago. We'll need Jeffery's help to find a life insurance policy and a will if we can't find them at the house."

Our discussion of the facts pointed to someone who knew the vic well. We decided to meet in the morning at eight. I called William as I left.

William answered, "Hey there, the love of my life."

"Hi, William," I said with a cool voice.

"I believe you called me to tell me what time I should have dinner ready."

"I was thinking dinner would be in a restaurant."

"I'm sorry to disappoint you, but I've been slaving hard in the kitchen all afternoon," he said with a very sexy voice.

My pulse quickened a bit. It was probably from the caffeine.

"What time is dinner?"

"Seven thirty."

"Seven thirty is fine. Bye."

Chapter 21

Monday Night—Jessie

I rang the doorbell at William's house at 7:35, and he came to the door. He pulled me against him and kissed me on the forehead. He stroked my back, massaged my shoulders, and gave me this gooey feeling. He didn't say anything, and I was feeling too good to say anything. He tugged on the back of my hair and tilted my head. I had my eyes closed, and my lips were apart from the rubbing and massaging. William kissed me. I had no will power to stop and kissed him back. He kissed me for a couple of minutes, and my knees started getting weak. My head was swooning as he kissed me and he was still rubbing and massaging. He started walking backward, and I was pulled along without any resistance. He kept kissing me and rubbing me, and I didn't want it to stop. I felt myself falling and was now lying on a bed. His hands were moving from my back to the front, and my shirt was coming off. Next my bra came off, and my breasts were being massaged and kissed. I then felt my pants being unbuttoned, and they came off.

After the seduction was complete, I woke up about an hour later with a sheet on top of me. William wasn't in the bed. A robe was lying on the bed, and I slipped it on. I walked into the kitchen, and he was pouring a glass of wine for me. My eyes were still droopy as I took the wine.

I asked, "What happened? Did I fall asleep?"

"I believe you did. You must have been exhausted from your work today."

"I'm sure it was the work and not the seduction."

"I was just trying to take away some of your stress."

"I'm very relaxed now, and I'm very hungry. What are we eating?"

"I've prepared a nice meal consisting of a nice strawberry feta salad and vegetable lasagna." He said this as he opened to-go boxes from a local Italian restaurant.

"You cheated. You ordered take out."

"I wanted to be sure you came over here for dinner. If I'd met you at a restaurant and seduced you, we may not have been invited back. The restaurant advertises that it's homemade."

"Advertising never lies. The chef probably made it in his home and brought it to the restaurant."

William had a bottle of pinot noir opened, and the wine was breathing. I had trouble telling the difference between a wine that had breathed and one that hadn't.

I took a seat at the counter in the kitchen but was taken by the arm and led to the dining room table. William had a large glass-topped dining room table with light green upholstered chairs with curved wooden legs. The table would seat about ten people, and I was led to one end of the table. William then brought my glass of wine to me that I left on the counter. He brought the plated food to the table with raspberry vinaigrette dressing for the strawberry feta salad. This was two Italian meals in one day if the pizza I ate earlier could be considered Italian. I ate the salad and lasagna together, and it was great. This was my first strawberry feta salad ever, and it was good. I didn't eat salads much.

After several big bites of food, I said to William, "Tell me about your trip to New York."

"There isn't much to tell. It was a business trip. I'd bore you with the details."

"Did you get to play tourist?"

"No, there wasn't time. I was very busy."

"What about food? Did you get to have good food?" Since he hadn't told me yet why he went to New York, maybe the food would give me a clue.

"I dined at a couple of fancy restaurants. The people I met have expensive taste. I'm not sure they'd eat at my restaurants since my restaurants don't have enough stars."

"What hotel were you staying in?" I decided to be more direct.

"I was in the Plaza Hotel."

"Do you need to go back to New York?"

"I'll be in Aiken for a while. I'm hoping you and I will get to spend a lot of time together."

"Is there going to be dessert involved while we spend time together?"

"There is dessert. I believe there is peanut butter pie that's in the freezer." William used his sexy voice again, which gave me a little stir.

"What's peanut butter pie?"

"You'll just have to wait and see. It's for dessert, and it does come after a meal in most cases."

"Don't we need to let the peanut butter pie breathe?"

"The pie was just panned this year, so I don't think it has to breathe."

"Well, I guess I'll wait but not without protest."

"I again want to apologize for having to leave for New York on such a short notice. It was truly unexpected, and I did try to get out of going."

"I'm sure you were needed or you'd have stayed in Aiken." I was thinking that I'd have liked to travel somewhere, especially if I stayed in the Plaza Hotel.

"Was the Lowes' case solved while I was in New York?"

"There was progress. The FBI has identified a prime suspect for the murders, and they're trying to find him. Supposedly there was someone inside the mob that helped them."

It was good to know it wasn't William that murdered the Lowes since they did appear to be such good friends.

He asked about my mother and father and how everything was going with the Aiken County sheriff. I hadn't told him before about my parents' car accident, so I told him the whole story.

He said, "I'm so sorry. I hope they'll make a full recovery."

"So far, they're making good progress."

"Tonight you and I should catch up for the time we missed."

"Does catching up involve peanut butter pie?"

"Yes, it'll involve peanut butter pie."

William watched me eat my last bite and got up. He filled my glass with more wine and cleared the table. He placed all the dishes in the kitchen sink, and I watched him move like a graceful athlete. He seemed so perfect, but there had to be something I wasn't seeing. Maybe he had a wife in New York or a lover. I wondered when he'd go to New York again. I was sure he didn't kill the Lowes, but I still had my doubts about his reasons for getting close to me. I really expected him to kick me to the curb after the FBI took over the case. I was a good investigator, so I'd figure it out.

He came back and took my arm again. This time he led me to the sofa. He placed one of the sofa pillows on one end and gently coerced me to lay my head on the pillow. He moved to the other end of the sofa and placed my feet in his lap. He then turned on the TV to a ball game. I was suspicious that maybe William had disguised the fact that he had a foot fetish. When he started massaging my feet, I didn't care. I had never had a foot massage but sure liked it. I had tingling all over. Just as he had a good start massaging one foot, he got up to leave.

I said, "Wait. Don't go. That feels too good for you to stop now."

William said, "I'll be back in a minute."

In fact, he did take more than a minute, but I didn't quibble over a few seconds. When he came back, he had a case like a makeup case in his hand and a bottle. I now thought he did have a foot fetish and was going to put makeup on my feet and toes. Instead, he opened the case and brought out a foot sander. I knew what it was since I had one. I never took the time to use it though.

"There are calluses on your feet, so I thought I'd give you the full treatment." He sat back down and began using the sander. It felt a hundred times better when he was sanding my feet. He sanded for a while and then massaged for a while. He massaged between the toes, and I lost my breath. Wow, I was becoming so relaxed, and it felt so good. My eyes were getting heavy.

I looked at my watch, and an hour had past. I looked up at William with sleepy eyes and asked, "Was I asleep?"

"You just dozed off for a minute or two."

"I need to go to the bathroom." I got up and started sliding on the floor. I finally got my balance as I looked at the floor and asked, "What's wrong with the floor?"

"There's lotion on your feet. That's why you're sliding."

"I could have hurt myself. That was devious of you."

"I was just trying to help your calluses go away. I'll warn you next time you fall asleep while I massage your feet."

"You did very well with the feet. Your apology is accepted."

He was snickering as I left the room. I didn't see anything funny about me possibly falling and busting my ass. I came back more wide awake and sat on the sofa beside William. As I sat down, he took my right hand and started sanding my index finger. I pulled away and said, "What are you doing with my finger?"

"I'm just sanding down the callus on your trigger finger. You need a sensitive touch for your fast draw."

"Don't be silly. I don't have a callus on my trigger finger." I rubbed my right index finger with my left hand to be sure though. "You're having fun at my expense, aren't you?"

"No, I'm not."

William took my hand again and started massaging it. This could be better than getting my feet massaged. He massaged between the fingers and massaged the palms. For twenty minutes, he was massaging my hands. He then put lotion on my hands and started again. I was getting so relaxed when he stopped.

"Was the hand massage or feet massage better?" William asked as he leaned next to my ear. I could feel his breath, and it tingled.

"I'm not sure. I'll let you do it again tomorrow and then decide."

"I believe it'll be my turn tomorrow."

"I'll watch more closely tomorrow. I don't think I know how it's done yet."

"Are you a slow learner?" William teased.

"In this case, I'm a very slow learner. It may take several times before I learn."

"Would you like your peanut butter pie now?"

"Just give me a small piece."

William got up and went to the freezer. He came back in a couple of minutes with the pie and a fork. The pie was frozen but delicious. It had a smooth texture and a mild peanut butter taste.

I looked at William with a questioning look on my face and said, "You were too good to me tonight."

"I believe the evening will get better." He said this as he massaged my lips with his. This time, the massaging didn't make me sleepy. Instead, I became more alert.

I woke up with no clothes on, with a sheet and blanket on top of me. I put my arm on the other side of the bed, but William wasn't there. I opened one eye and then the other and heard noise in the kitchen. I slithered out of bed and put on my jeans and shirt from the day before. I stumbled into the kitchen and smelled coffee. I was careful this time since I could still have lotion on my feet.

William handed me a cup of coffee and said, "I don't remember you sleeping in your clothes. I distinctly remember you being naked last night. I've been having a lot of dreams about you lately, so it could have been just a dream."

I said, "This is what I'm wearing today if you'll just use your body to press out all the wrinkles."

"Come here, and I'll try. I believe you took all the steam out of me last night, so I hope heat will work."

He pulled me close and pressed me to him. I lost my breath as he pulled me tight. I gasped as he pulled me tighter.

"That's enough. I believe they're pressed." He reduced the pressure, and I could breathe again. He continued to hold me and rubbed my back and shoulders.

"I still feel knots in your muscles. Maybe you should take the day off, and I can massage them out."

I looked at the clock, and it was six thirty.

"I need to go to work. There's a murderer on the loose, and it's my job to hunt him down."

"Breakfast is almost ready, so you can sit down."

"What's for breakfast?"

He went to the oven, opened up the door, and took out a casserole dish. I got a whiff of the food and was hungry. He brought the casserole over to the counter, and it appeared to be an egg casserole. He put a heaping of casserole on my plate. It had eggs, cheese, ham, bacon, peppers, onions, and maybe something else.

I said with a full mouth, "This is good. Is this your concoction?"

"This is a family concoction."

"It's nice. And you can cook too. You're a man of many talents."

"I try hard to overcome my shortcomings."

"You didn't have shortcomings last night."

William laughed.

I ate my breakfast quickly and told William I had to go. I took the rest of my clothes and was walking to the door when he pulled me close and whispered in my ear, "I believe we have more catching up to do. I'll call you later to see what time to prepare the evening activities."

"I don't know what I'll be doing later. I'll know more when you call me. As far as the evening activities, a repeat of last night's activities would be just fine except I'd like to start with the peanut butter pie."

"Even before the seduction?"

"Yes, even before the seduction."

I pulled away and opened the door. After my shower at my parents' house, I went by the hospital for a few minutes to see my parents. My father was feeling good this morning, considering he was still in intensive care. My mother was watching Fox News and having breakfast. My breakfast was much better. Mom tried to interrogate me, but I told her I had to go to work.

Chapter 22

Tuesday Morning—William

Jessie left for work, and I was alone with my thoughts. I hadn't heard that the FBI had a prime suspect until Jessie told me last night. If the information did come from inside the mob, then there could be bigger problems. The person could also identify me as someone linked to the mob, and I could be under surveillance right now. I knew that getting involved with the Lowes could be trouble. I should have stuck to my more remote involvement. It seemed like easy money. All I had to do was find where the Lowes hid the money.

I had $1 million in my safe that I needed to run through my businesses. I was planning to add about $10,000 a week to the income of the businesses. I'd also planned to use cash to buy foreclosures. Some local counties allowed me to use cash. I needed to put these plans on hold for now.

After getting one of the prepaid cell phones from my safe, I called New York, and a secretary answered. The Don also had legit businesses.

"I need to speak to Frank," I said.

"Who may I say is calling?" she politely asked.

"Tell him it's William."

Several minutes passed, and the secretary came back on the line. "He'll call you back," she said, and she repeated the number I was calling from. I was guessing someone would be calling me from a secure or prepaid cell phone.

I answered the phone a minute later, and it was Frank the Don.

"Hello, William, my boy. You're calling to give the million back."

"No, I'll keep the million."

"Then why are you calling?"

"It appears the FBI may have a suspect in the Lowes' case. The problem is the suspect's name may have come from an inside source." I tried to not show my dismay.

"Are you sure someone isn't playing games with you?"

"I don't think so," I said with a little reservation.

"We'll take a look at our organization and let you know. There've been several attempts in the past to slip someone in, and we've been reluctant to allow it."

"Thanks," I said with a little relief.

"I suppose you may want to know if your name was given to the FBI."

"I would indeed."

"Ciao, William." The Don ended the call.

I now had some hope that a subpoena wasn't being generated while I was sitting there.

Chapter 23

Tuesday Morning—Jessie

Bill was in his office when I stuck my head in the door. I was running late but was glad I went to see my parents.

Bill said as he looked up from his computer, "We have a meeting with the captain at nine o'clock in his office. After that, I thought we'd go to the house and do a more thorough look at the office. We should then talk to more neighbors and the two friends we know about. We'll then meet with Jeffery, IT, and Investigator Robinson at four."

We drove to the victim's house. Bill took a different route, going past polo fields and farms. It was a late start, but the captain did have priority. When we arrived at the vic's house, there was a police officer at the entrance. He knew Bill, and we drove up to the house. There was police tape across the door, and we went under it. The house was very quiet, and we went to the office. There were a few documents on the desk, but the office was neat. The floors were hardwood, so we could hear our own footsteps. We turned on the ceiling light and desk light and saw where the computer was located before it was taken by IT. The gun safe was open, so we called to see what was in the safe and were told there had been two rifles and two handguns. We were told that neither of the handguns were the caliber of gun that the vic was shot with, which was a .22.

We spent the next two hours looking through files, and neither of us found anything that seemed to be a lead. The files were for properties, businesses, and personal items. The victim was extremely organized and had individual files for utilities, credit cards, insurance, medical, etc. We looked through the credit card file, and the charges were the expected charges for gas, groceries, etc. There were no travel expenses for the past year. There were no life insurance policies. This didn't mean there wasn't a life insurance policy, but there wasn't one in the files. A life insurance policy was always a good place to start. We didn't find a copy of a will, but that wasn't unusual either since the lawyer would keep the original. We'd ask Jeffery to make calls to the insurance agencies and lawyers to find a life insurance policy and will.

We looked through all the property and business files, and the last information filed for the properties appeared to be deeds or contracts. It looked like all the properties and businesses were sold shortly after his wife died. Jeffery was researching the properties and businesses and could confirm this for us.

We decided to go to lunch and then talk to the friends.

Bill said, "I've got another hankerin' for barbecue. Can you eat barbecue today?"

I thought he was talking about Carolina Barbecue again and remembered how good it was. I also fondly remembered the banana pudding.

I answered, "Barbecue would be good today."

"Then we'll head over to Bobby's Barbecue. I used to eat a lot of barbecue but reckon I'll take it easy today. Bobby's Barbecue has granny-slappin' good barbecue and almost as dang good as Carolina Barbecue."

I was now sure Bill was adding the southern slang just for me. The only thing missing was the chewing tobacco.

Bobby's Barbecue was on Jefferson Davis Highway. I was looking for the confederate flag but didn't see one. Bobby's Barbecue looked like a log house and was next to Langley Pond. The building was bigger than Carolina Barbecue and had regular tables rather than picnic tables. There were two steam tables rather than one and more side choices. My choice was still the pulled pork with a little hash, slaw, potato salad, and vegetables. The sweet tea was not on the table this time. There were choices of barbecue sauce on the table in plastic squeeze bottles, and they weren't labeled.

I asked, "Which is the mild sauce?"

Bill picked a bottle and said, "This one."

Bill then picked up another bottle and said, "This is the hot sauce. It is hotter than a goat's butt in a pepper patch."

"I'll just stick with the mild sauce."

I had my one plate and then had banana pudding and soft-serve ice cream. Bill had two plates and banana pudding.

Bill said, "How was the barbecue?"

"It was dern good. It was almost as dang good as Carolina Barbecue." I added some southern slang.

"You're getting the hang of it. You'll be Kid Rock'd before you know it."

I didn't know what Kid Rock'd meant and didn't want to ask.

Joe lived in a modest-size, ranch-style brick home on a large lot. It was an older home but seemed to be well maintained. We introduced ourselves, and Joe invited us in. The inside of the house looked like it had been refurbished with wood floors and new paint. Joe was bald and had a scraggly, white beard with hair hanging over his mouth and eyebrows that hung down in his eyes. It was distracting. His face was weathered with deep lines around his eyes and on his brow. His eyes were in deep sockets, and were a dark gray. Joe was wearing coveralls and looked like a mountain man. I was waiting for a wolf to show up behind him.

Bill said, "We're here concerning Mr. Burnette. As you probably heard, he died last night. We understand that you and Allen Jones were good friends with Mr. Burnette, and we wanted to ask you a few questions."

Joe said, "I haven't been close to Paul since his wife died. We were very close before then. My wife and I spent a lot of time with Paul and his wife." This was the first person to call Mr. Burnette by his first name.

"Had you visited Mr. Burnette since his wife died or had he visited you?"

Joe hesitated before answering. He appeared to be searching for the right words.

"No, I've only seen him at the gas station or grocery store." He looked away and tensed some as he spoke.

There was something he wasn't telling us.

I asked, "Have you heard anything negative around town about Mr. Burnette?"

"No. Not really."

"Do you know of anyone who may have a grudge or issue with Mr. Burnette?"

Joe hesitated again before answering. He then rubbed his temples.

"No. He has always been liked by everyone."

"What aren't you telling us?" I asked.

"I don't know anything else."

More questions were asked, and I was sure Joe wasn't telling us everything. Bill gave Joe his card and asked him to call if he remembered anything. Joe said he would. I made a note to have Jeffery research Joe.

We went to see Allen Jones. Allen lived on Randolph Street. He answered when we knocked and was the opposite of Joe. Allen had a full head of white hair, was clean shaven, and was wearing khakis and a polo shirt. Allen had lines in his face around his eyes and on his brow, but they weren't as pronounced as Joe's. He had bright blue eyes that were a little cloudy.

Allen said, "Howdy, folks. What brings you to Randolph Street?"

"We're investigating the murder of Paul Burnette. We understand he's a friend of yours," Bill said.

"He was a friend. The bastard stopped being my friend when his wife died. I saw him almost every day before his wife died, and then he turned into a damn hermit."

Allen didn't invite us in, so we stood on the porch while we asked questions.

"Didn't you see him around town?" Bill asked.

"I did, but he wouldn't speak to me. He'd just nod and go on."

"Did you ever confront him and tell him he was a bastard?"

"I called him and left messages, but he never returned my calls. I drove up his driveway about every month and then would change my mind. I remember when Joe's wife died two years ago. Both Joe and I were pissed that Paul didn't come to the funeral. Joe was irate with Paul. We grew up together and were friends all of our lives until Paul's wife died."

We found out what Joe wasn't telling us.

"My wife died six months before Paul's wife died, and Paul was there for me. He helped me get through it. Joe's wife was the sister of Paul's wife, so he should have been there."

"Why do you think Paul changed?" I asked.

"I don't know." Allen shook his head.

"When was the last time you saw Paul?"

"It's been a few weeks. I can't exactly remember."

"When was the last time you drove up his driveway?"

Allen thought for a minute before answering, "It's been about six months."

I thought this was different than the earlier answer.

"How often do you see Joe?" Bill asked.

"I see him every day. He's going through chemo now, and I check on him every day and take him for the treatments. I called Paul and left a message that Joe had cancer but never heard back from him. The bastard."

"Do you own any guns?"

"I sure do. Everybody in town owns guns. I have a couple of rifles and a couple of pistols."

"What kind of handguns do you have?" I asked.

"I have a .38 Smith and Wesson and a .45 Colt."

I didn't ask to see them but thought it may be necessary later.

"Where were you on Sunday night?" I asked.

"These are just routine questions," Bill clarified, sensing Allen was a little irritated.

"I understand. I was over at Joe's. We were watching TV."

"What time did you leave Joe's house?"

"It was about ten thirty. Wait. Maybe it was eleven thirty."

"Was it ten thirty or eleven thirty?" I quizzed, knowing it made a difference.

"It was eleven thirty when I left."

"Did you go home from Joe's house?"

"I did."

"Does anybody live with you?"

"No. It's just me."

I was thinking we now needed to go back and talk to Joe before Allen called him. Allen, Joe, or both could be the killers.

After a few more questions, Bill gave him his card and told him to call if he remembered anything else.

William called while we were leaving Allen's house. I told him I was busy and would call him back.

We decided to go visit Joe and then more neighbors. Joe didn't answer the door when we stopped by. His truck was gone. Bill called the Burnettown police and asked them to drive by occasionally and let us know when Joe was home. We interviewed other neighbors who were mostly elderly people.

Almost all had retired from the mill. There were a couple of houses where no one answered the door, and we planned to try those houses again later. The result of the discussions with the neighbors was the same, with no new information.

We made it back to the office for our four o'clock meeting. The first person I saw was Jeffery the rookie. Oscar from IT was present along with Investigator Robinson.

Bill started the meeting detailing the vic's death and going through a preliminary coroner's report. The vic was shot twice with a .22-caliber gun at close range, which was the cause of death. The vic had guns in a gun safe, but none of them were .22 caliber. He asked Jeffery to check on the guns registered by the vic.

Jeffery said, "I've already checked, and the vic doesn't have any guns registered. I'm guessing he bought them from an individual or he bought them before registration was required."

Bill continued, "The alarm system was on, and there didn't appear to be any forced entry. It's similar to the Lowes' case except the bullets weren't from the same gun. We do have a couple of suspects that we're pursuing. Both were friends of the vic but now aren't. What have you got, Oscar?"

"We've gone through the alarm system, and the alarm was set at ten fifteen Sunday night. The system is just a perimeter system and doesn't have motion activation inside the house. It doesn't look like it was tampered with or anything was out of the ordinary. We've gotten started on the computers and haven't found anything that jumps out. I have printouts of some of the information on the computer." Oscar handed out the copies as he finished.

"What have you got, Jeffery?" Bill said.

"I've made a spreadsheet of all the properties owned by the vic. All of the properties were sold about two and a half to three years ago except for two. One is the house where the vic was killed. The other is the house that burned down. The property has about one hundred acres and was actually deeded to a corporation. The corporate documents didn't show the vic as an officer, and the mailing address was a post office box in Augusta, but the vic paid the taxes on the property so I'm assuming he owned it." Jeffery handed out copies of his spreadsheet with the one hundred acres highlighted.

Michael said, "We'll assume the cases could be linked. I'll let you know what I find."

"So will I."

Jeffery continued, "I asked Wally to help, and he called insurance agencies and lawyers. He didn't find any agency that had a life insurance policy for the vic yet. He found the lawyer that did a will for the vic. He's George Miller. Unfortunately, George and his administrative assistant are on vacation in Europe until a week from tomorrow."

"I thought George was married," Bill said.

"His wife and the assistant's husband are with them," Jeffery clarified.

"Isn't there anybody else that can get in the office?" I asked.

"No, the two of them are the only ones," Jeffery answered.

"We'll wait until he comes back," Bill said.

I didn't like the idea of waiting. Maybe William owned the building and had a key.

"Who're the owners of the corporation that owns the hundred acres?" I asked.

"I don't know yet. I'll check."

"Find out who owned the property before the corporation. The previous owners may be helpful," I said.

"I will."

"Could you research Joe Jackson who lives on First Street and Allen Jones who lives on Randolph Street? Also see what kind of guns they have registered."

"Sure," Jeffery answered as he wrote down the information.

After the meeting, Bill and I discussed the plan for tomorrow. We decided to talk to the neighbors we missed today and do a more thorough look at the house and office.

I called William when I left the office. I didn't have him on speed dial yet, but he could be put on speed dial after one more night like last night.

William answered, "Hello, my favorite investigator."

"Hello, William."

"You could be a little more romantic and call me your sweetie pie."

"I don't do sweetie pie or cutie pie or any other pie except maybe peanut butter. Oh yeah, I also like apple and pecan."

"I'll just have to train you to be more romantic."

"A few more nights like last night and you can sign me up. I hope it's a short course though. I'm very impatient. All my instructors and teachers will attest to it."

"I'll be your teacher, so I'm sure your impatience will not be a problem. When may I have your presence in my house tonight?"

"I want to visit my parents and should be over about eight."

"Will you be expecting dinner?"

"Of course. Good-bye, William." I pushed the end button and headed to the hospital. Mom was having dinner and watching Fox News. She told me she could be coming home in about a week. She said she went to see Dad today and was happy he was making progress. I went to see Dad in intensive care, and he was asleep. The nurse told me he did great today.

I went by my parents' house for clothes just in case I decided to spend the night with William.

I arrived at William's house a few minutes late, and he answered the door. He had a piece of peanut butter pie in his hand with a fork stuck in the top of it. I gently pushed him away and went to the sofa with my pie.

He said, "It's nice to see you too."

"I'll be with you in a minute after the pie."

William watched me as I savored the pie.

"I think you have more feelings for that pie than me."

"It's just fleeting feelings with the pie. It'll be gone soon. For you, my feelings are lasting."

"And what are your feelings?"

"I only have feelings for the pie right now. We'll discuss other feelings later."

William sat on the sofa watching me. I rolled each bite on my tongue before chewing. I could tell this was having an impact on William. He had a look of awe on his face, and I thought I knew what he was imagining. I ate the last bite of pie but didn't lick the plate. I did have a little class.

"Would you care for another piece? The pie could be your dinner."

"What's my other choice?"

"You could have seafood crepes and salad."

"Can I have seafood crepes, salad, and then have more pie?"

"You can indeed have another piece of pie after dinner."

"Good. What's the appetizer?"

"You are, my dear." He said this as he moved next to me on the sofa. This time he started massaging my neck. He then massaged my head, arms, and hands. The hand massages were as good as the pie. Just as I was getting truly relaxed, he started kissing me. I wanted to remind him that he forgot my feet but decided to take what I could get. A few minutes later, we somehow ended up in the bedroom, and I was again naked. I didn't know how this kept happening. I dozed off again afterward, and William was nudging me to wake up. I thought that men were the ones that went to sleep after sex. I was sure it was the pie that made me sleepy and not the sex.

"What time is it?"

"You've been asleep for about thirty minutes. Dinner is ready."

I sleepily got out of bed and put on my jeans and shirt. I remembered doing this same thing yesterday. I wandered into the kitchen and smelled food. The salad and crepes were already on the table. The smell was great, and I felt hungry even after the pie.

"That does smell great. Did you cook it?"

"I did cook the crepes. The salad is from the grocery store. I put ranch dressing on it. I hope that's fine. I remember you ordering ranch dressing in the restaurant."

"You have a good memory. Ranch is fine." This could be a good routine each day. I'd arrive and have pie and sex and then take a nap while my dinner was being prepared. I'd ask later if we could do this every day.

The crepes had shrimp and scallops and something that looked like baby lobster tails. All of it tasted good.

"I recognize the shrimp and scallops, but are these baby lobsters?"

"Those are crawfish."

"I don't think I've had crawfish before, but they're good. Where do they come from?"

"They're usually from Louisiana or Mississippi, but there's also a crawfish farm near here in Edgefield, South Carolina. The ones you're eating are from Edgefield. They're usually in Cajun dishes, but I put them in the crepes."

"I've had Cajun food. It was too spicy for me."

"Is there anything new on the Burnette case?"

"Actually, there isn't much to tell. We don't have any real leads yet except for a couple of ex-friends. It turns out the house where the five guys were killed was the vic's house. I did have a question for you. Do you own the property where George Miller the attorney has an office?"

"I don't. Why?"

"It's not important," I said as I thought about breaking into the Miller offices.

"I made a few calls today but didn't find out anything. I'll make more calls tomorrow," William said.

"We can use all the help we can get."

"It's ten thirty, and it's your bedtime."

I had stretched out on the sofa with my feet in William's lap.

"I'll be fine right here," I said.

I turned over but didn't make any attempt to get up. The next thing I knew I was being carried by William. I was dumped on the bed and reached for a pillow. William rolled me to the other side of the bed, undressed me, pulled down the cover and sheet next to me, and then rolled me back to the other side. He covered me up, got into bed, and spooned me. I went to sleep almost immediately.

William woke me up at six thirty. I was more wide awake this morning and didn't stagger when I got out of bed. My teeth felt furry, and I remembered I didn't brush my teeth last night. I used the toilet, brushed my teeth, and went to the kitchen. William handed me a coffee cup and a plate with the same breakfast as yesterday.

We chatted about the weather and my parents. I wasn't much for chitchat, so I hurried through breakfast and went to the car to get my other clothes. I came back in and showered. I kissed William good-bye and left for the office.

Chapter 24

Wednesday Morning—Jessie

I was at the office about seven forty-five. I was getting to work earlier before I met William. Before him, I'd just pick up breakfast on the way to work or skip breakfast. I checked my messages and e-mails. There were more e-mails from Chicago asking about my parents. The only message was a reminder of the staff meeting today at eight o'clock.

We went to the staff meeting, and the room was full. There were donuts, but I passed. The first item was the safety topic. A fireman discussed fire safety, which was very informative. The captain talked about a bunch of topics with none applicable to me.

I went through the spreadsheet from Jeffery in Bill's office. William was shown on the list as a buyer of three properties. There were thirteen properties on the list. We decided to talk to the people who bought the businesses first. We figured they may not be happy with what they bought.

We were on the road traveling to see more people. The first was Hugh Evans. Hugh had bought the hardware store in Burnettown. The hardware store was still operating, and Hugh was at the store when we arrived. Hugh looked to be about sixty, was about my height, and had white hair and blue eyes. He was in good shape for his age. The hardware store must have kept him active. We introduced ourselves and asked Hugh if we could ask some questions.

Hugh answered, "I assume it's about Mr. Burnette, and I'll be glad to answer any questions."

Bill asked, "Could you tell us about the relationship you had with Mr. Burnette?"

"I didn't really know Mr. Burnette until I bought this business. I retired from the mill the same day that the sign went up for the store. I called the number on the sign, and Mr. Burnette answered. I asked him what he wanted, and he said he just wanted me to pay for the inventory and didn't want any goodwill. He gave me a price, and I told him I'd take it. He wanted to sell the building to me, but I couldn't afford it, so someone else bought the building."

We had the list of people who bought the victim's property, so we didn't have to ask who owned the building.

I asked, "How is your relationship with the owner of the property?"

"The relationship is good. He has stopped by and talked to me several times about the business. He has also given me good advice."

"Did the new owner seem unhappy about the building in any way?"

"No, he seemed quite happy about the property and said I could buy it for a good price when I could afford it."

William was the person who bought the building and certainly had made a good impression on Hugh. I thought William was a tough businessman, but it looked like he also had a nice side.

Bill asked, "Do you know of anyone who had a grudge against Mr. Burnette or could have had a reason to hurt him?"

"No, everybody that I know liked Mr. Brunette."

I asked, "Have you been to Mr. Burnette's house?"

"No. We signed the paperwork for the store in his lawyer's office."

"Who was his lawyer?"

"It was John Thomas, a lawyer in Aiken."

There was silence for a minute. Bill finally told Hugh that we appreciated his time and gave him a business card. We left the hardware store and went to the dress shop.

The dress shop was in a small house on the main street that had been converted to a shop. The house had wood siding and was painted yellow. A sign out front said Carol's Dress Shop and Consignment. We went in the front door, and a woman greeted us. We introduced ourselves, and she introduced herself as Carol. Bill told Carol that we were investigating the death of Mr. Burnette and asked her if she could answer a couple of questions. She said she'd be glad to but didn't usher us to an office or other room.

While we stood in the middle of the store, Bill asked, "Could you tell us about your relationship with Mr. Burnette and your purchase of the business?"

Carol answered, "My only real contact with Mr. Burnette was when I bought the dress shop. I saw a For Sale sign at the shop shortly after Mr. Burnette's wife died. I called the number on the sign, and Mr. Burnette said all he wanted was the cost of the inventory. Someone from Mr. Burnette's lawyer's office let me in the shop and gave me the inventory list and price. I didn't have enough money to pay the price asked and offered to pay less. The lawyer, Mr. Thomas, called me and told me that my offer was accepted. The lawyer also asked me if I wanted to buy the building. I knew I didn't have enough money to buy the building and told him no. I'm sorry about rambling. Is this what you want to know?"

Bill answered, "What you're telling is good. You can keep going."

Carol continued, "Anyway, Mr. Thomas asked me a lot of questions about my name, the name of my business, whether I was going to set up a corporation, and more questions. I didn't know whether I wanted to be a corporation or not and told him I'd let him know. It was only a few hours later that Mr. Bradford called and said he understood I was buying the dress shop. I told him I was, and he said he was buying the building. Mr. Thomas must have called him. We met, and he asked about my plans, and I told him I wanted to run the dress shop. As you can see, I'm pretty talkative, and I asked Mr. Bradford about being a corporation and about setting up the business. Mr. Bradford told me he'd help me set up the business and help me any other way he could."

The front door opened, and a woman came in. Carol excused herself and went over to talk to the woman. A minute or so later, Carol returned.

"Where was I? Oh yeah, Mr. Bradford. Mr. Bradford told me I didn't need to be a corporation and told me to just buy the inventory in my own name. He told me all the other things I needed to do to set up a business. He calls me each month to see if I need anything. He also helped me buy more inventory and suggested that I consider a consignment shop. He's also not real strict about the rent payments, and that has been good. About Mr. Burnette, I've never really met Mr. Burnette. The lawyer took care of all the paperwork, and Mr. Burnette has never been in the dress shop. The only time I talked to Mr. Burnette was when I called the number on the For Sale sign."

Bill asked, "Do you know of anyone who has a grudge against Mr. Burnette or would have wanted to harm him?"

"No." She shook her head.

Bill and I looked at each other and shrugged, indicating that we didn't have any more questions. Bill gave Carol a business card and asked her to call if she remembered anything else or heard anything that could be helpful.

We drove by Joe's house, and he wasn't home again. We wondered if he skipped town. I suggested that we should talk to John Thomas, the victim's lawyer. Bill called the dispatcher and got the address and phone number for Mr. Thomas. We decided to call first, as lawyers could be in court, in a meeting, playing golf, or having hanky-panky with a client. Lawyers have an advantage since their clients come in distraught and need comforting.

Bill called Mr. Thomas's office, and it turned out he was available at one o'clock since he had a cancellation. We had time to get a quick bite and went to Maxine's for lunch. After lunch, we drove to the lawyer's office, and he was available right away with no wait. This was unusual but welcome. We introduced ourselves, and Mr. Thomas invited us to sit down at a table in his office.

Bill said, "We're investigating the death of Mr. Burnette. I believe Mr. Burnette was one of your clients, and we have a few questions if you don't mind."

John answered, "I'll be glad to help any way I can. Although I haven't had any contact with Mr. Burnette since he sold all of his properties and businesses."

"When was the last time you saw him?"

"It was a few months after his wife died when I had the last closing on his properties."

I asked, "Was there anyone that wasn't satisfied with the properties?"

"No, Mr. Burnette was selling everything at a good price, so I'm sure everybody was happy."

"Do you know of anyone or have you heard of anyone who had a grudge against Mr. Burnette or could have wanted to hurt Mr. Burnette?"

"No, Mr. Burnette was a nice gentleman, and everybody liked him."

"Did you do a will for Mr. Burnette?" I asked.

"No."

"Did Mr. Burnette use you to set up corporations?" I asked.

"He did. I set up several for him."

"Did the corporations own property?"

"Sometimes they did."

"What about the properties he sold when his wife died?" I continued to probe.

"We had switched all of them to his name and closed the corporations."

"Did he close all of the corporations?"

"I don't know. He had several."

"Did he ever mention having a life insurance policy?"

"He didn't to me."

After a few more questions, Bill handed John Thomas his business card and asked him to call us if he remembered anything else.

Bill and I left the lawyer's office and got back in the car. We looked at our list of people who bought properties from the victim. The victim had thirteen properties that were sold. Of the thirteen, William Bradford bought three of the properties. Bill called William, and he was available.

We arrived at William's house, and he answered the door. Bill told him we were investigating the murder of Mr. Paul Burnette. William invited us into the living area and asked us to have a seat. Both Bill and I sat in chairs, and William sat on the sofa facing us. William turned his head away from Bill and winked at me. I grinned slightly as I tried to keep my professional face.

Bill looked at me and winked too. I grinned at him too, and he raised his eyebrows several times. I hadn't told Bill about William and assumed he didn't know. I guess he must have figured it out.

Bill said, "Tell us about Mr. Burnette. We understand that you had business dealings with him."

"I bought properties from Paul and ran into him at fundraisers and other events. We weren't close friends. I heard that he was selling his properties, and I bought a few."

"When was the last time you spoke to Mr. Burnette?"

"I went to the funeral for his wife, and that was the last time I spoke to him. He didn't come to the closings for the properties I bought, and I haven't spoken to him since."

"Do you know of anyone who may have had a grudge against Mr. Burnette or would want to harm Mr. Burnette?"

"No, Paul was a gentleman, and I can't think of anyone who would want to hurt him."

I said, "You bought the properties that housed the dress shop and hardware store that Mr. Burnette owned?"

"Yes. I bought both properties."

"In your discussions with the buyers of the business, did either of them say that they were unhappy with Mr. Burnette?"

"No. Both were extremely happy with the deal they got from Mr. Burnette."

"In all your business dealings, have you heard of anyone who wasn't satisfied with Mr. Burnette?"

"No. I haven't heard anything."

There was a short pause, and William asked, "How did you like Maxine's?"

Bill said, "It was nice."

I said, "It was good."

William said, "I was helping in the kitchen today and saw you eating. I'm sorry I didn't have time to visit. I try to talk to as many customers as possible."

I said, "Is Maxine's your restaurant?"

"Yes, I just started it up with a chef who's a friend of mine."

After another short pause, Bill told William we didn't have any more questions for now. William got up and walked us to the door. Bill went out first, and William grabbed my ass as I was walking past. I slapped his hand away and gave him a stern look. William smiled.

"It sounds like he could be a saint except for Allen and Joe. Maybe his demise could be associated with the church," I said.

"We should probably include the pastor in our interviews. Maybe the pastor knows something that'll help," Bill said.

"We'll add him to our list. I'm thinking now it could be Allen, Joe, or one of the people he sold property to or had business dealings with. It could be related to his social life too. That narrows it down. It's either related to his business life or social life. There isn't much left," I said with a hint of sarcasm.

"Yeah. There's not much left after business or social. Speaking of social, do you and William have something going on?" Bill asked as he winked at me.

"I've had dinner with him a couple of times."

"He'd be a nice catch. He's worth a few bucks."

"I wouldn't date him for his money."

"Just saying. I'd be happier if I had his money." Bill lifted his eyebrows a few times and grinned.

After a quiet minute, he said, "Be careful. He's still a suspect in the Lowes' case."

I didn't respond and was now thinking my relationship with William would be all over the station house soon.

Another minute passed, and he said, "Don't worry. I won't spread it around the station."

We didn't say anything the rest of the trip to the vic's house. The same deputy was at the front gate and let us in without showing our badges. The house still had police tape across the front door, and we went under it to enter the house. The house was quiet, and our footsteps were loud as we walked across the wood floors. The sound created an echo in the large foyer. I walked to the office, and it looked the same as yesterday's visit. No one had broken in and left us a message or evidence so we could easily catch the perp. I sat down at the desk and started looking at more documents. I looked through the files for bills and didn't see anything out of the ordinary. Bill was walking through the house, and I heard his footsteps upstairs. I looked through more property files and didn't see anything to follow up on. The names in the property files matched the list the deputy had prepared for us.

We left the vic's house and went back to the office for the four o'clock meeting. Bill started the meeting talking about our interviews that day and the visit to the vic's house. Then he went over preliminary results from the forensics techs. The fingerprints in the house were from the vic, the housekeeper, and one unidentified person. It could be the perp, but the fingerprints weren't in the system. They were checked against Joe and Allen, but they didn't match. Both Joe and Allen were in the military and had prints in the system. The cars had a lot of different hair and fiber samples.

The van had a lot of different fingerprints. So far the only match for the hair and fingerprints in the vehicles was for the vic. The coroner's report showed the vic had a recent meal of chicken and vegetables, and there was alcohol in his blood. The level wasn't even close to be intoxicated. His blood sample also showed his prescription medication for high blood pressure and diabetes and that he probably took sleeping medicine earlier. That probably explained why he was still in his clothes and had his shoes on.

"Could you check the inventory for the vic and confirm it included sleeping medicine?" Bill was looking at Jeffery.

Michael went next. "The five corpses were in pretty bad shape when they were taken to the morgue. The bodies were burned so bad that fingerprints were impossible and facial recognition was impractical. However, we're sure they're the five men who owned the cars left at the house. We'll check dental records tomorrow."

"Have you found out what started the fire?" I asked.

"The forensic fire investigator is still looking. I hope to have an answer soon."

"Oscar," Bill said.

"We printed off everything that was on the computer and phone. It looked like ordinary stuff, but you can check it yourself." Oscar handed out copies of the printouts.

"Jeffery," Bill said as Bill slid the documents to him.

"I checked with the previous owner about the hundred acres, and they said they were contacted by an attorney to buy the property. They couldn't remember the name of the attorney. I checked with the county office, and George Miller was the closing attorney for the hundred acres, so he was probably the attorney who contacted the previous owner. I also checked on the corporate documents filed, and the vic was the sole owner of the corporation."

"What about the construction at the vic's house?" I asked.

"The county doesn't have any record of a permit being pulled. Sometimes work in this county gets done without a permit." Jeffery grimaced as he answered.

"What about Joe Jackson and Allen Jones?"

"I checked Allen, and he didn't have as much as a parking ticket. Joe is a different story. Joe was arrested a month ago for disorderly conduct and possession of a firearm. The gun was a .38 Smith and Wesson Special. He was released without bond since he was undergoing chemo. A month before that, he was involved in a dispute in the Reid's parking lot. There were a few young adults playing loud music, and he confronted them. A Burnettown officer was working near the store at his speed trap and responded quickly and broke it up. I also checked, and neither has guns registered. I'm not surprised since guns are sold at yard sales around here."

"When's Joe's hearing?" Bill asked.

"A date hasn't been set."

"Did you find a life insurance policy?"

"We haven't. Wally has started calling the Augusta agencies."

After the meeting, we undated the murder book and decided to continue the interviews with the buyers of the properties tomorrow.

William called as I was leaving.

I answered, "Hello, William." I used my business voice.

William said, "I want to report a crime. A wonderful lovely woman has stolen my heart."

"I'll need to ask you a few questions, sir, to understand the crime. First, where were you when the crime was committed?"

"I was being interviewed by this stunning investigator in my own home when my heart suddenly disappeared."

"What is the name of this investigator that stole your heart?"

"I believe her name is Jessica Barnes."

"We'll look into it for you, sir. Is it okay if I stop by later and have you fill out a formal complaint?"

"I'm at your disposal. A crime shouldn't go unpunished. What time can I expect you?"

"About seven thirty."

"That would be perfect. We're hosting a dinner for my friends from out of town. The dress is casual."

"Wait a minute. I'm not coming then."

"Just be here at seven thirty. Everything is taken care of. Good-bye, Jessie."

He disconnected before I could argue. I had brought one dress in case I had to attend a funeral. I was certainly glad my parents had improved and a funeral wasn't expected. I left the office, now knowing I had to clean up.

I went by the hospital and saw my parents. There was no change from the last visit. Both parents were awake, and I had a nice chat with each of them.

I went to my parents' house, showered, and shaved my legs and armpits. I found the dress and pressed out the wrinkles. I found my shoes and tried them on and noticed my toenails needed a little work. I clipped and filed my toenails, and they looked better. I also took time to work on my fingernails. I put a couple of curls in my hair and added a little makeup. I usually didn't wear makeup, so my face felt funny with it. I took the makeup off. William did say it was casual. I packed a bag with tomorrow's work clothes just in case I spent the night with William. I thought I had a lot of time to get ready, but it was already seven fifteen.

Chapter 25

Wednesday Night—Jessie

It was seventy thirty when I arrived at William's house. I only had to use my lights and sirens a little. I rang the bell, and William answered the door. He looked at me from head to toe and said, "May I have your name please to see if you're on the guest list?"

"I'm the one who's popping out of the cake."

"Oh yes. Come on in, and you can undress in the hall." He kissed me on the lips and then said, "You look stunning. Wow."

"Don't get used to it. I usually only do this for weddings or funerals."

"Maybe I can arrange one so you can dress up."

I thought he probably arranged funerals. I looked inside, and there were lots of people. I had mistakenly thought that the dinner was for a couple of people. William took me by the arm and led me into the house. I was speechless as he led me into the kitchen. He put a glass of wine in my hand and said, "You look like you may need this."

"I expected only a couple of people, but it looks like there are at least thirty."

"There are thirty-two including you. Dinner will be served in about thirty minutes."

"Who are these people?"

"I'll explain later. You and I have to socialize before dinner."

I took a big gulp of wine, and he took me by the arm and led me into the living area. I was introduced to several people, but their names didn't register. Many looked familiar, but I couldn't put the faces and names together. Of course I didn't know many people in Aiken unless they had been murdered or I interviewed them. William continued through the room, and I kept saying it was nice to meet you. At about eight, William announced it was time to dine. There were tables set up that extended from the dining room into the living area. I was led by William to the head of one of the tables. When we all sat down, William stood back up. He didn't take my arm, so I figured I was supposed to remain sitting.

William said, "Thank you all for coming. This evening is to welcome new residents to our neighborhood. The new residents are friends of mine and will be your friends too as you get to know them. I've known Sandra and Charles Fairfield for many years, and they have visited occasionally. They'll be buying the house next door. It's under unfortunate circumstances that the house is now available, and I know you're just as saddened as I am about the Lowes. But life must go on, and I hope you welcome the Fairfields into the neighborhood. Would you care to say anything, Sandra or Charles?"

Two people stood up that were seated on the other side of William. William had introduced me to them earlier, but I had no clue that they were new neighbors.

Sandra spoke first. "Thank you for your warm welcome. It'll be a few months before we're living here, and I'm now looking forward to it even more. William had spoken of the wonderful people in the neighborhood, and now I know why. Thanks again for your warm welcome."

Charles spoke next. "I also want to thank you for the warm welcome. Thanks also to William for bringing the neighbors together. I also look forward to living here and taking money from William on the golf course and at the poker table."

Both Sandra and Charles sat down, and William shook Charles's hand and kissed Sandra on the cheek. Sandra was a lovely woman with blonde hair and fair skin. She had dimples on her cheeks and looked like she had been pampered and maybe enhanced a little. Both Sandra and Charles had a southern drawl when they spoke. Both appeared to be about sixty-five if I took into account the enhancements for Sandra. Charles was bald except for hair on the sides of his head. I was glad he wasn't wearing a toupee. Charles had darker, weathered skin, so he must have been spending time on the golf course preparing to fleece William.

William touched my arm again, and I turned to him. He kissed me on the cheek as well. I was still in a daze when I noticed the salads arriving for dinner. The salads were a spring mix with nuts, cheese, and strawberries. There were dressings on the table, and I put ranch dressing on the salad. Bread baskets were brought out at about the same time, and I took a roll. William asked me if I needed butter, and I said no. William talked to Sandra and Charles, and I tried to get my bearings. William did pat me on the leg a couple of times, but I was in a trance.

There was fish or steak being served, and I was served fish. The fish was baked and came with a stuffed potato and asparagus. William looked at me and asked if everything was okay. I said, "Everything is fine." I wasn't much for casual conversation. I watched sports, movies, and the news on TV and read the newspaper occasionally but didn't wish to talk about what was going on. The other man next to me wasn't much of a conversationalist either, and we didn't talk except to say hello. I noticed a little later that he appeared to be drunk, so that may have been the reason he wasn't talking. He was not eating much either. I ate my fish and vegetables, and my plate was taken away. I had a few choices for dessert and selected coconut cake. Peanut butter pie wasn't one of the choices. I hoped it wasn't because there was no more peanut butter pie. The wine was flowing freely, but my glass was only refilled once. I noticed that William and the Fairfields didn't drink much wine either. That wasn't true for the rest of our table and the other table.

Coffee was brought out, and most people took coffee. The guy next to me needed it badly since it appeared he was getting pretty sleepy from his drinking. It was now about nine thirty, and everybody was finished eating. William stood up and thanked everyone for coming and told them to have safe trip home. This was the polite way of telling everyone it was time to go. By ten, everyone was gone except Sandra, Charles, and the caterer. The four of us went into the living area and sat on the sofa and chairs. I sat quietly as they talked about the evening and the neighborhood guests. William apologized for the people who became obnoxious after drinking and told Sandra and Charles that these same people were very nice when they were sober. As Charles and William were talking about business, Sandra asked me what I did. I told her I was an investigator and came down from Chicago. She asked me what brought me here, and I told her briefly about my parents and how the Aiken County sheriff had taken me on as a loan. She asked me a lot of questions about Chicago. I felt like I was being interviewed. It was about ten thirty, and I told William that I needed to go since I needed to get up early. That was the best excuse I had. William got up and motioned for me to go into the kitchen, so I followed.

William said as we got into the kitchen, "Aren't you spending the night?"

"You have guests, so I'll go home."

"I really want you to spend the night. It has been a hectic evening, and I'd enjoy a little time with you."

"Don't you want to spend more time with your friends?"

William looked at me with his puppy eyes. "I'd rather spend time with you. We'll say good night to Sandra and Charles and retire for the evening." He took my arm and led me into the living area. He told Sandra and Charles that we were retiring for the evening and they could stay up as long as they desired.

Sandra said, "It's been a long day, and I'm tired. We aren't as young as we used to be." William hugged Charles this time and hugged Sandra and kissed her on the cheek. Charles hugged me and kissed me on the cheek.

Sandra hugged me and whispered in my ear, "William is a great guy."

I whispered back, "I know." I was wondering if Charles and Sandra could have been involved in William's less than legal business. I still believed William was involved in activities that could be skirting the law. I didn't know this for a fact, but my suspicions were high. I'd quiz the Fairfields later about their business ventures and their business dealings with William.

After our bathroom time and change of attire to our sleeping duds, we slid into the king-size bed with the satin sheets. I'd never slept on satin sheets until I met William, and it felt good. I'd expected that everyone in the South slept on flannel sheets. When we snuggled together, his roaming hands were telling me he wanted more. I put my hands on his wrists and said, "Would you explain tonight's reception first?"

"Charles and Sandra are moving next door, so I wanted to introduce them to the neighbors."

"When was this event planned?"

"Two days ago. That's why several neighbors weren't able to attend."

"It looked like all the neighbors that liked to drink free alcohol showed up."

"There are a few neighbors who like to drink, and they drank a gracious amount tonight."

"Why didn't you tell me two days ago?"

"I didn't think you'd come if I told you two days ago."

That was probably true. I'm not much of a socialite and don't like groups that I need to do chitchat. I also might not have come if I had known there were going to be thirty-two people.

"You're right there. I'd have found an excuse not to come."

"Jessie dear, I've gotten to know you a little bit over the past weeks, and I'm learning your quirks."

"Quirks. I don't have quirks. Everybody else has quirks."

"Are you saying I have quirks?"

"Maybe one or two but not many."

"And what are my quirks?"

"Can we get back to the original discussion about the Fairfields? I don't see a For Sale sign next door, so how can the Fairfields buy the house?"

"We'll discuss my quirks later. The probate lawyer who's handling the will and estate is a friend of the Fairfields and also my friend. The Fairfields want to buy the house, and the lawyer has agreed to sell the house to them. He's also the executor of the estate since the neighbors had no known relatives. It'll probably take a few months, but the Fairfields should have the house."

"So the lawyer can just sell the house directly without any other bids?"

"Pretty much. The Fairfields will pay a fair price. Deals are conducted often just like this."

"What about the Atlanta home?"

"I don't know. I'm sure someone will work out a deal for that house."

"What's your relationship with the Fairfields?"

"Charles and I have worked on a couple of business dealings together in the past."

I decided not to ask about the type of business dealings. It was time to move on to the next activity, so I said, "Okay, you're partially forgiven for the dinner party. I'm now willing to have you work toward full forgiveness."

"You looked breathtaking in your one dress. Quite stunning I might add."

"Are we transitioning to the next activity for the evening?"

"I believe we are. I also need to work on full forgiveness. Can I now get back to my foreplay?"

I didn't have a chance to respond as he started kissing me and moving his hands over my back and shoulders. After our lovemaking session, I slept like a baby.

I woke up to find William out of the bed. I slowly made my way to the bathroom and sat for a few minutes extra on the commode, wondering how I ended up with William. We seemed so different but got along so well. I got up from the commode and looked in the mirror. I scrubbed my face, brushed my teeth, and went into the kitchen. William handed me a cup of coffee, kissed me on the cheek, and I sat down on one of the barstools. He told me I should move to the breakfast table for the toast, fruit, and yogurt. There was also a newspaper on the table, and the headlines were about Paul Burnette and the five other murders. The newspaper brought me back to reality.

It was about seven o'clock, so I ate toast and fruit and told William I had to go to work.

Sandra and Charles were coming into the kitchen as I was leaving to take a shower. I showered and put on my jeans and shirt. It felt better than the dress and dress shoes. My feet still hurt a little from last night. I kissed William good-bye, told the Fairfields that it was nice to meet them, and drove to the police station.

Chapter 26

Thursday Morning—Jessie

Bill and I were on our way to interview two of the buyers of Mr. Burnette's properties. We were back on Jefferson Davis Highway heading to North Augusta, South Carolina. We went past Reid's grocery store this time, through the towns of Burnettown and Clearwater. I saw a confederate flag on a flagpole beside the road in Clearwater, so I was reminded I was in the South. We ended up at River Bluff Road on the Savannah River in North Augusta. I could see high-rise buildings in Augusta, Georgia, on the opposite side of the Savannah River. This was a sharp contrast from Aiken.

Bill parked in front of a three-story, brick home located on the river. I saw that it was built off the ground like the vic's home and said, "This looks like a newer home. Why's the home built off the ground?"

Bill answered, "This house is built off the ground for a different reason. Strom Thurmond Lake is about twenty miles up the river, and the house is in the flood zone."

Bill and I climbed one of two curved brick stairways to a brick porch. Bill rang the doorbell, and I knocked on the storm door.

John Wilhelm came to the door and invited us in. We sat on a deck looking at downtown Augusta across the river and looking down at the Savannah River. Augusta was a small replica of Chicago, which made me feel a little homesick. He could have offered us a mint julep. I wanted to ask what time the paddleboat came by but didn't. I did see small boats with four rowers and someone yelling at the rowers with a megaphone.

John saw me looking at the boats and said, "Those are sculls. The person facing backward is the coxswain. The local rowers practice here and on Langley Pond. I've been rowing for a long time. Have you ever rowed?"

"I've rowed in the gym but not on the water."

"It's a lot different on the water. With other rowers, you can catch a crab and get thrown out of the boat."

I thought I knew what catching a crab meant, so I didn't ask. I did ask, "Do you compete?"

"No. It's a good noncontact activity to help me stay in shape."

Bill interrupted our conversation and said, "We need to ask you some questions about Paul Burnette. You bought a property from him a couple of years ago."

"I bought a house in North Augusta from him. It was a Section 8 rental, and I bought it to have another rental property. I read about Mr. Burnette in the newspaper. I hope you catch the killer."

I knew what Section 8 rentals were since some of my relatives were in them in Chicago but asked, "Were you happy with the property and the price?"

"I was extremely happy. I bought the property at a great price."

"When was the last time you saw Mr. Burnette?"

"I never met Mr. Burnette. He wasn't at the closing, but I did talk to him on the phone when the property was put up for sale."

Bill asked, "Do you know of anyone who would want to harm Mr. Burnette?"

"No. I don't."

I didn't want to leave the deck, but I ran out of questions. I thought Bill would be annoyed if I asked John about his coxswain.

Bill thanked him for answering our questions and gave him a card. I reluctantly left.

We left John Wilhelm's house and drove north on Martintown Road. Bill turned on Hammond Drive and pulled in the driveway of a ranch house similar to my parents' rental house in Aiken. The exception was there were flowers, and the yard and bushes were neat.

Bill rang the doorbell, but there wasn't a storm or screen door for me to knock on. Mike Carlisle answered the door and ushered us inside. The living area was in the rear of the house, and I looked out the window. The view was the rear of the neighbor's house.

Bill said, "We're investigating the murder of Paul Burnette and would like to ask you some questions."

Mike said, "I read about Mr. Burnette in the newspaper. What happened?"

"That's what we're trying to find out. When was the last time you met Mr. Burnette?"

"I've never met him. I called about this house when I saw the sign and talked to Mr. Burnette. He didn't come to the closing, so I never met him."

"Were you happy with the property?"

"Yes, I got it for a great price. Mr. Burnette had it as a rental property, but I bought it to live in. The property was in good shape even though it was a rental."

I asked, "Do you know of anyone who would harm Mr. Burnette?"

"No, I don't even know anybody that knew Mr. Burnette."

Bill thanked him and left Mike a card. Jeffery had also included the sales price and value of the properties in the list prepared for us. Mike had bought the property about 20 percent under market value, so he should have been happy.

We decided to take a lunch break. Since we were in North Augusta, Bill decided on the Sno Cap drive-in restaurant in. Bill told me the Sno Cap had been around for over fifty years. We decided to go inside rather than have drive-in service. The restaurant looked like it was from the 1960s. I ordered a club sandwich with fries, and Bill ordered a burger and fries. The restaurant was busy, with the car hops taking food to all the drive-in customers.

We talked about our morning interviews and decided they weren't very informative. The afternoon would be more interviews.

Lunch was great, and I cleaned my plate. I thought about a hot fudge sundae or a chocolate-dipped cone but didn't order one.

After lunch, Bill showed me around North Augusta and then took the back roads to Aiken since we had time before our next interview. I was sure I wouldn't be in Aiken long enough to learn all the back roads.

The interview was with Tammy Allgood and had the same results as the two previous interviews that day. We didn't learn anything that could help. It certainly appeared that the victim sold the properties at good prices. Everybody was happy with their deals.

We left Tammy Allgood and went to see Jeff Thomason next. Unfortunately for us and fortunately for Jeff, he was also happy with the transaction with the victim. He had never met the victim and only saw a lawyer at closing.

The list of persons who had brought properties who hadn't been interviewed was now down to four, with another interview scheduled for three o'clock. The three o'clock interview was with Jim Snyder. We arrived at Jim's house and were invited into the living room. Jim did know the victim and had been to the victim's house before the victim's wife died. He stated that the last time he saw the victim was at the funeral for the victim's wife. Jim didn't know of anyone who would harm the victim and said everybody thought highly of the victim.

We left Jim's house and went back to the office for the four o'clock meeting.

Bill started the meeting with a review of our interviews.

Oscar was next and said there wasn't any more they planned to do for now.

Jeffery spoke next. "I checked the county records, and the vic paid cash for the property about two and a half years ago. The tax records show the building was constructed about ten years ago as a hunting lodge. I couldn't find any building permits after the vic bought the property, so there were no official changes made to the building after it was bought."

Jeffery continued, "We went through the printouts from the computer. Nothing seems unusual so far. The vic hardly e-mailed anybody. The e-mails were usually related to online orders, which were typically books or CD books. There were older e-mails about the property sales over two years ago. There weren't any personal e-mails in the past three years."

"I'm assuming there weren't any threatening e-mails that could help us solve this case," Bill said.

"No. We didn't find any."

Michael interrupted, saying, "Jeffery can talk about the cell phone in a minute. The five vics that were in the burned house have been identified. The dental records for each were matched today. The three from Columbia were Ralph Scott, Charles Collier, and Andrew Bynum. Ralph was a professor at the university, Charles was a lawyer, and Andrew owned a construction company. The two from Augusta were Nathan Reynolds and Melvin

Compton. Nathan owned a medical practice, and Melvin was a chef and owned a couple of restaurants."

I said, "What were they doing at the house?"

"I interviewed the relatives in Augusta today, and Nathan and Melvin were supposed to be at a golf outing at Hilton Head. Both were supposed to be home Sunday night. According to the family, neither was answering their cell phone when they tried to call Monday morning."

"Did they have any clue why they were in Aiken County?" I asked.

"The relatives said that both were members of a hunt club in Aiken County, but they weren't supposed to be there this past weekend."

"What were the causes of death?" I asked.

"All five were shot with a .22-caliber handgun. The bullets match the ones that killed your vic."

"Does anybody have a guess why all six were killed and at two different locations?" I asked.

Jeffery answered, "Maybe they were making meth at the house and a buy went wrong."

Oscar said, "Maybe they were in a cult and someone went crazy."

"Joe and Allen could have decided to kill our vic and his friends. Especially since the vic abandoned them," Bill suggested.

"Joe and Allen are our most likely perps for now," I said.

"I don't think we can get search warrants or tap their phone lines just because they didn't like your vic," Michael said.

Jeffery said, "We also checked the cell phone records of Mr. Burnette, and all five names were in his cell phone. Both Ralph and Nathan had calls to Mr. Burnette last week and typically every week. Each call was less than a minute. Otherwise, Mr. Burnette didn't use his cell phone. We checked his home phone records, and he used the phone to make medical and dental appointments but nothing else."

"Did you look at the inventory to see about sleeping medicine?" Bill asked.

Jeffery answered, "I did. The vic had prescription sleeping pills listed. It was recently filled, but there were only a couple of pills left in the bottle."

"That sounds a little strange," I said.

"He could have taken some to the lodge," Jeffery suggested.

"Maybe so," I said.

After the meeting, Bill made calls and lined up interviews with the three remaining persons on the list who had bought properties. Tomorrow was Friday, and all were available.

I went to the hospital to see my parents. My mother said she could be released next week although she'd still need a lot of physical therapy. It turned out that my parents' house was pretty close to a rehabilitation center. Dad would also need a lot of physical therapy when he was released.

I hadn't heard from William that afternoon, so I decided to call him. I didn't remember if he had made plans for me. He didn't answer, so I left a message. I said, "I'm calling about a police matter. Please let me know when you're available for interrogation."

I decided to go to the gym rather than home. I knew that I wouldn't want to come back to the gym if I went home. An hour of working out and sweating made me feel much better. Back at home, I heated a frozen dinner in the microwave while I sat and watched the news.

William called about eight thirty and apologized for not calling. He said he was working on a project all day. He was taking the group he was working with to dinner and asked if I'd like to join them. I declined and said I'd probably see him tomorrow. He said he'd be busy tomorrow, but we'd have dinner tomorrow night.

I watched the news and then turned on ESPN. I must have dozed off and woke up about an hour later and went to bed.

Chapter 27

Friday Morning—William

I was meeting some associates last night, so I didn't see Jessie. My meeting was to discuss plans to open a brewpub in Augusta. I had a Georgia general contractor, a commercial real estate agent, and an interior designer. I had worked with all three before. We decided on a general location and square footage needed. The real estate agent would research properties, and we'd meet again in a few days.

I missed Jessie last night. I admit I'm getting accustomed to having her spend the night. I expect the sleepovers will be reduced when Jessie's mother gets to come home from the hospital. I hope I can convince her to let me pay for home care since I have some extra cash.

I'm almost thinking the pretend marriage shouldn't be pretend. A lot of women in my adult life have wanted me to propose, but I always convinced myself that I shouldn't. Maybe it was fate that I didn't, and now I can have a pretend marriage to Jessie.

I was eating breakfast alone with my coffee and newspaper when my prepaid cell phone rang. I'd been carrying it with me waiting for the call.

"Ciao," the Don said.

"Ciao."

"I need your help."

"How can I help?"

"We found the guy who had a conversation with the cops."

I knew he meant the FBI, so I didn't ask for clarification.

He continued, "We convinced him to provide the details without much effort. No torture involved, which disappointed me. He was a new guy in our accounting department and was a plant. He was supposedly only working on our legit businesses, but one of our more experienced idiot accountants had this new guy wire money for the Lowes' hit. We had the funds wired back and the other account closed, but there's a trail."

"What do you need from me?"

"We fired the new guy, and I need you to let him have an accident."

I've caused accidents before for the Don, so he knew I could.

"Are you sure I wasn't mentioned by the new hire?"

"I was in the room and was convinced he told us everything."

"I'd have guessed he'd wait until he was more entrenched before feeding information," I said.

"He was trying to impress. A young know-it-all."

"What activities does this young fellow have?" I was asking since an accident is more believable if the person is doing his normal activities when the accident occurs.

"Don't know. One of my guys can find out for you. I'll have him call you."

"What's your timetable?" I was hoping it wasn't soon.

"No schedule. A month or six months."

"Okay."

"Ciao." The Don ended the call, and I agreed to another job. We didn't discuss payment since we had a regular fee. I'd try to put it off as long as I could. Maybe the new guy would have a real accident.

Chapter 28

Friday Morning—Jessie

The first interview on Friday was in North Augusta with Jim Bowers. Jim had bought a tract of land in North Augusta from Mr. Burnette. Jim hadn't met him and didn't know of anyone who had a grudge against Mr. Burnette.

The next interview was at noon back in Aiken with Linda Stevens. Linda bought land from Mr. Burnette located north of Aiken. We stopped for an early lunch at a Subway on the way back to Aiken. Bill and I split a twelve-inch meatball sub. Another Italian meal.

Linda lived north of Aiken next to the land bought from Mr. Burnette. Her house was a double-wide trailer with brick underpinning and a large porch. We arrived at noon, and Linda invited us in. She offered coffee, tea, or soft drinks, but we declined. We sat down in the living area. The trailer was actually very nice inside, and Linda had nice furniture. We asked about Mr. Burnette and got the same answers. Linda had never met Mr. Burnette, and he didn't show up at the closing. She said she called about the land the same day a sign was put on the property. She was very happy with the price and the land. We asked her if she knew of anyone who had a grudge against Mr. Burnette, and she said she didn't.

We thanked her, and Bill gave her a business card as we left the house. The next interview was at two o'clock in New Ellenton with Randy Smith. New Ellenton was south of Aiken. While we were driving to New Ellenton, Bill told me that New Ellenton was established around 1950 after the town of Ellenton was taken over by the federal government to build the Savannah River Site nuclear facility. He drove me through downtown and showed me houses that had been moved from Ellenton around 1950. It had to be tough on the families to have their houses moved. New Ellenton had one traffic light and several businesses. Bill pointed out the Carolina Barbeque restaurant where we ate a couple of weeks ago. He drove all the way through town and went into a driveway off the main highway south of town. The name on the mailbox was Smith. Along the driveway were many large trees. Bill said the trees were pecan trees.

Bill parked in front of a house similar to Mr. Burnette's, except the area under the house was open. An older gentleman I assumed to be Randy Smith sauntered out to the car. We introduced ourselves, and Bill explained that we were investigating the death of Paul Burnette.

We asked him about the property he purchased from Mr. Burnette. He responded that the property was next to his property and pointed north to show us where it was located. He said he had never met Mr. Burnette. We asked him if he knew of anyone who didn't like Mr. Burnette, and he said he knew of no one. Bill gave him a business card, and we started driving back to Aiken.

It was now about two thirty, and Bill asked, "What do we do next? Our interviews are done, and we don't really have any leads."

"We haven't interviewed the pastor at his church. Maybe there's a church connection. Mrs. Fields mentioned that she did see him at church a couple of times."

"It sounds like a good idea."

Instead of going back toward Aiken, Bill turned off on a Chime Bell Road and drove on country roads past farms. I asked him where we were going, and he said it was a shortcut to Burnettown. I knew right away that I was lost. The roads only had numbers and no road signs.

After a lot of back roads, Bill ended up at the Burnettown Baptist Church. The church was a large brick building with a steeple on the top. There were also a few other buildings around the church. One of the other buildings had a sign that said Church Office. We went to the church office, and the church secretary introduced herself as Connie Franklin. Bill asked Connie if the pastor was around, and she said he was in his office. She pushed a button on her phone and said that two sheriff's investigators were here to see him.

Within a few seconds, the office door opened, and an elderly, white-haired man came over and introduced himself as Thomas Wright, the pastor of the Burnettown Baptist Church. He invited us into his office, and we sat down. The pastor went behind his desk and sat down.

Bill explained that we were investigating the death of Paul Burnette and asked the pastor to tell us about him.

The pastor answered, "I've known Paul for many years. He was a member of this church when I became the pastor twenty years ago. Paul and his wife, Evelyn, were very active in the church before Evelyn died. Paul was a deacon, taught Sunday school, and helped the church with projects. Evelyn was also very active with the church and volunteered a lot of her time. I considered Paul and Evelyn good friends. After Evelyn died, Paul stopped being active in the church. He came to church occasionally but kept to himself. I talked to him several times, and he said he was just going through a phase and he would be fine. In the past two years, he stopped coming to church altogether. I called him, and he said he was very busy. I went to his house a couple of times, and he seemed fine. He said both times that he would be coming back to church soon."

I asked, "Did he seem different to you the last time you talked to him?"

"After Evelyn died, he was different. Paul and Evelyn had a great relationship and marriage. He did seem much more at ease the last time I talked to him. He seemed much more like his old self."

"Did he seem stressed?"

"No. He was quite calm and relaxed. He actually seemed content. I asked him whether he wanted to talk about any problems or concerns, but he said he didn't have any."

"Did you know of anyone who had a grudge against Mr. Burnette or disliked him enough to harm him?"

"No, he was well liked, and I don't know anyone who would want to harm him or who had a grudge."

We talked to the pastor for a while longer and asked him to tell us about Mr. Burnette's friends. The pastor told us the names of the friends we already knew. After our discussion, Bill gave the pastor his business card, and we left the church.

After leaving the church, we went to see Joe. He was home and invited us in. He still had on his coveralls, but some of his scraggly eyebrows and beard were gone. He had probably let the hair grow until the chemo made it fall out.

Bill got right to the point. "We talked to Allen, and he mentioned he was at your house on the night Paul was killed. Is that right?"

"Yes."

"What time did he leave your house?"

"It was eleven thirty. It was right after the eleven o'clock news," Joe said confidently.

"Are you sure it wasn't after the ten o'clock news?" Bill asked.

"No, I watch the Channel 6 news, and it's on at eleven. I don't watch the Channel 54 news."

I assumed the Channel 54 news came on at ten.

"Allen stated that he was upset with Paul about your wife's funeral and Paul's isolation. Were you upset with Paul too?" I asked.

"I was. He acted like we didn't exist after his wife died. Allen and I were the ones he needed to help him through it. Then he wouldn't come to my wife's funeral. He pissed us both off."

"Did you ever try to contact him or go see him?"

"I called him many times and left messages. He didn't call back. He's a dirtbag."

"Can we see your guns?"

"Sure. I guess. Let me get them."

Joe brought out a 30-30 Winchester rifle, a Beretta M9 and a Glock 42.

"Have you ever owned a .22?" I asked.

"I had a .22 rifle when I was young. About fifty years ago."

"What gun did you have with you downtown when you were taken to jail?" Bill asked.

He seemed surprised that we knew.

"I had a .38 Smith and Wesson Special, but the police took it. I had just come from the range. The police checked."

"Do you always carry a gun?"

"No."

"Did you have a gun when you were quarreling in Reid's parking lot?"

"No."

"Are you sure you and Allen didn't go over to Paul's and shoot him for being such an asshole?" I asked.

"No, I'm trying to stay alive myself. I wouldn't kill anybody." He looked me in the eyes and was believable.

"Paul had you pissed at him for years. Are you sure the anger didn't build up?"

"No, I was pissed at the bastard, but none of us deserve to be killed." I believed him again.

We made it back for the four o'clock meeting. Bill started the meeting by telling the group that we didn't learn anything new today and didn't get Joe to confess. Bill said Joe or Allen could still be the perps though.

Michael said, "I interviewed the relatives of the three vics from Columbia. All three were supposed to be at a golf outing at Hilton Head and were supposed to be back Sunday night. All three were also part of a hunt club in Aiken County. Jeffery and Wally will be looking at their cell phone, home, and office phone records. We've also got their computers for Oscar to go through. It's strange that none of the relatives knew Paul Burnette. The relatives in Columbia knew the other two from Columbia, and the relatives in Augusta knew the other vic from Augusta. The only link is the hunting lodge."

Michael paused and then continued, "The forensic fire investigator reported that the fire was set using gasoline that was poured throughout the house and on the mattresses where the vics were found. Whoever set the fire wanted it to burn everything, and it did."

"Were containers found?" I asked.

"There were three five-gallon gas cans in the house that were probably used. We're checking to see if the gas and cans were bought recently."

Jeffery said, "There's a lot of calls made from the five vic's cell phones. It'll take a while to go through all of them."

After the meeting, Bill said, "I have a date tonight and need to leave. Let's plan to meet tomorrow."

I said, "That's fine with me. What time do you want to meet?"

"Let's make it 11:00 a.m. If everything goes as planned, I hope to be busy in the morning too."

"I don't need to know any more details."

I told Bill good night and left for home. I called William on the way but had to leave a message.

About ten minutes later, William called back.

I answered, "Hi, William."

William said, "I thought you were going to use sweetie pie or cutie pie."

"I'm working up to it."

"It looks like it'll be a real late dinner. I still have the final details to work out on another project and don't know how late it'll be. The group will be leaving early tomorrow, so we need to finish tonight."

"Call me when you're done. I'm going to visit my parents."

"Tell my future mother-in-law and father-in-law hello."

"I'll do just that," I said sarcastically.

I pressed end on the phone and drove to the hospital. My father was asleep, but William's future mother-in-law was awake and watching TV. She had a new vase of flowers in the room.

I asked, "Who are the flowers from?"

She answered as she smiled, "The card says they're from William. You should read the card."

The card was addressed to my future mother-in-law with a note that said to get well soon for the wedding.

"It's a nice card and nice flowers."

"Is this the fellow you mentioned?"

"Yes, Mother. It's the guy I've been dating."

"It sounds like more than just dating if I'm to be a mother-in-law. Are you in a family way?"

"First of all, I'm not in a family way. And second, William is just instigating trouble."

"When will I get to meet this instigator?"

"I'll bring him to see you soon." I knew this was the wrong thing to say immediately after I said it. Mother was now going to remind me every day until she met William.

"That would be dandy. You can bring him tomorrow. I'm getting my hair done in the morning."

"He stays very busy, so I'll check to see if he's available." I knew I messed up again. Now Mom would want to know what William did and why he was so busy.

"What does he do that keeps him so busy?"

"He has restaurants and flips foreclosures."

"Oh, he's one of those."

"He doesn't do foreclosures on properties. He's someone who buys foreclosed properties as investments." I knew Mom was thinking he was someone who took people's properties.

"That's better. I was thinking for a minute that I didn't want William as my son-in-law."

"I'm sure you'll like William."

"We'll see. All of the guys you dated so far haven't met my standards. I want someone for you as great as your dad."

Tears came to my eyes, and I bent down and hugged her.

"Me too, Mom."

We finally left the subject of my dates and William and talked about her and the news from back in Chicago. She said that a couple of her friends from Chicago had called and caught her up on the local news.

"Did you know your first cousin Tamara is getting married?" Mom always reminded me of all my cousins that were getting married. This was just another way of reminding me that my biological clock was ticking.

"No, I didn't." I didn't keep up with my cousins in Chicago.

Mom went on telling me about all the other local and family news in Chicago. I hoped the caller had unlimited long distance since there was a lot of news.

Mom asked, "What are you doing this weekend?"

"I'll be working."

"Are you working on the Burnettown murder case?"

"Yes."

I was saved from more interrogation when my phone rang. It was William.

I answered, and William said, "How is the love of my life?"

"I'm fine. I'm with my mother."

At about the same time that William said that he wanted to speak to my mother, my mom said she wanted to talk to him. I put the phone on speaker.

William said, "Hello, Mrs. Barnes. It's nice to meet you. Your daughter has spoken highly of you." I hadn't told William much about my mom, but William was allowed to exaggerate.

"Jessie has told me only a little about you." Mom gave me a look.

"Did you get the flowers?"

"Yes, they were beautiful and such a nice card. Thank you so much."

"I need to get back to a meeting. I just wanted to let your lovely daughter know that her future husband would be working later than planned. Did Jessie tell you where we're having our wedding and where we're going on the honeymoon?"

"No, she didn't."

"You should ask her. Good-bye, Mrs. Barnes and my sweetie pie."

The phone went dead, and I was now faced with my mother.

"I need to go. I'll see you tomorrow."

Mom used her motherly voice. "Not so fast, young lady. Tell me about the wedding and honeymoon."

"William was just instigating trouble again."

"Are you sure? William sounded serious."

"Believe me. There is no wedding or honeymoon planned."

"You know all of your other cousins are getting married. This could be the right one, and your biological clock is getting louder every day."

"I need to go see Dad. I'll see you tomorrow." I kissed her good-bye and went to see Dad. He was asleep, so I went home.

Chapter 29

Saturday Morning—Jessie

I got up early. Since Bill and I were going to have a late start, I decided to go to the gym and then go see my parents. I hoped Mom had forgotten about William, but I was sure she didn't. It was too early to drink or I would have had a couple before going to the hospital.

Dad was awake, so I spent time with him. He was still a little groggy. I thought maybe I needed his pills before going to see Mom. William didn't send him flowers, and Dad didn't interrogate me. Dad was doing a little better. He was scheduled to have another surgery after he recovered more.

I reluctantly went to see Mom next. I knew the interrogation was coming, and Mom didn't disappoint me. I didn't have time to tell her that her hair looked nice before the questions started.

Mom said as I came in the door, "Tell me more about William. You left before I got more details."

I said, "I'm breaking up with William."

"Are you crazy? He's perfect for you."

"You don't know him yet, Mom. How do you know he's perfect?"

"I need grandchildren, and he would be perfect for that."

"I should have some say about who I have children with."

"So tell me what's wrong with William."

I thought for a few seconds. "I don't know yet, but I'm sure there's something wrong with him."

"So there's nothing wrong with him. That makes him perfect for you."

"I know he's purposely hiding his faults from me. Under that great physique is a fat and bald guy." Dad was still fairly trim and had all of his hair, so I could talk about fat and bald guys with Mom.

"So William has a great physique."

"His physique is good."

"Is he smart?"

"He's smart."

"Does he manage his money?"

"It looks like he does. He lives in a nice home and owns properties. But he could be bankrupt for all I know."

"Can you check out his finances?"

"I'm not going to check out his finances."

"Why not?"

"Because it's sneaky. It's not the right way to build a relationship."

"So you admit you're building a relationship."

"I admit nothing."

"When can I meet him?"

The door to the room was propped open, and I heard a familiar voice at the door. William said, "Is this the maternity ward?"

I said to William in a mean tone, "What are you doing here?"

"I came to see my future mother-in-law."

Mom said, "Is this William?"

"I'm William and you must be the lovely Wanda. Your hair looks lovely." Mom put out her hand for William, but William reached over and hugged her. I thought Mom was going to pull on his hair to see if was real.

Mom spoke to William and ignored me. "I just had my hair done this morning. Jessie didn't even notice."

William looked at me and said, "You're a bad daughter. You should be punished." I thought he was going to say I needed to be spanked.

Mom then took the opportunity to start asking questions. "Tell me about you. I need to know more about my future son-in-law." Mom looked at me as she said this.

William said, "Can we talk downstairs?"

Mom answered with a quizzical look, "I guess so."

"I've arranged for a mani-pedi for you. They're waiting downstairs for you now. You need lovely nails to match your lovely hair."

Mom said, "Are you serious?"

"I'm very serious. Jessie will help you get in the wheelchair, and I'll push you downstairs."

Mom said when William stepped out of the room, "I told you he was perfect."

William must have overheard because he said from the hall, "That's what I've been telling Jessie."

I didn't respond to either of them and got Mom in the wheelchair. I now had both of them to deal with. I was going to see if there was a bar in the hospital while Mom had the mani-pedi.

When we went into the room where mani-pedis were done, William went over to one of the ladies and told them my mom was here. Mom was able to get in the pedicure chair with help from Jessie and the pedicurist. After she was put in a chair, the pedicurist told me to get in the next chair. I thought they wanted me next to Mom, but the pedicurist told me to take my shoes off and to place my feet in the water. I protested a little, but both Mom and William gave me the look. I now knew Mom and William would team up on me. I didn't feel so bad when I saw William get in the other chair next to my mother and take his shoes off. The pedicurist showed both my mother and me the controls for the massaging chair. William had his controller out and had already turned on his chair. The pedicurist asked me what nail polish I wanted on my toes, and I said none. William then told the pedicurist to do French nails. I wasn't asked by the pedicurist if that was fine with me.

William then looked at Mom and said, "What did you want to ask me?"

Mom said, "Just start at the beginning and tell me your life story."

"My life didn't begin until I met Jessie."

Mom's eyes became wet while I gagged.

"That's so sweet. Does Jessie know how you feel?"

It was obvious I was going to be ignored by Mom now. They were probably going to talk about me just like I wasn't there.

"I've told her, but she's resistant. You know how she is."

"Yes, I know. She can be difficult at times."

I said, "I'm sitting right here." Neither of them paid any attention to me.

William said, "Maybe you can talk sense into her."

"I'll try."

I put my fingers in my ears and hummed.

"This is a condensed life story. I was born in West Virginia, raised in southwest Virginia on a farm, worked my way through college by working in the coal mines, came to Aiken to work at the Savannah River Site, started restaurants and other businesses, invested in real estate, and then met your wonderful daughter and future mother of my children."

"I told Jessie her biological clock was getting loud."

"Between us, I think we can convince her it's time to make you grandchildren."

I put my fingers back in my ears and hummed more. The pedicurists that were working on Mom, William, and me were smiling as they overheard the conversation.

William asked, "How many grandchildren do you want?"

"I'd like three."

"Three would be great with me."

I was ignored again while they decided how many children I'd have.

Mom got personal and asked, "When can I expect my first grandchild?"

"Nine months from tonight if Jessie will cooperate. Can you go ahead and have the mother-daughter talk so that Jessie can start having children?"

"I had the talk with her years ago, but she wasn't very attentive. I'll talk to her again today."

"That would be great. We may end up having to adopt if we don't get started soon. Tick-tock, tick-tock."

"I agree. It's time to start. Almost all of her cousins in Chicago are already married and have children. I was just told that one of her younger first cousins is getting married. Jessie will be an old maid soon."

"What would you like to name your grandchildren?"

"I'd like one to be named Richard and one to be named Mary after my mother."

My pedicurist said, "I like the names Richard and Mary." I gave my pedicurist a look, and he did the sign where he was zipping his lips.

I hummed again. It was getting worse. My pedicurist was now getting involved. William was such a troublemaker.

William had ordered the full pedicure treatment, so we were getting a lava scrub and a calf massage, which helped ease the discomfort.

William said, "You and I should go ahead and set the date for the wedding. When do you think it should be?"

Mom said as she continued to ignore me, "We need to wait until her dad is out of the hospital so he can give her away. Let's plan on three months from now. It should be on a Saturday."

"Should the wedding be here or in Chicago?"

Mom thought for a moment. "It'd be best if was in Chicago, but it depends on Jessie's father. If he's able, the wedding will be in Chicago."

I was humming again with my fingers in my ears. All three pedicurists were grinning.

"I'll make reservations in Aiken and Chicago. We can cancel one later."

"If it's Chicago, there'll be a lot of people who'll come."

"I'll book a place that'll handle a lot of people."

"Jessie's father and I aren't very wealthy, so we do need to limit the cost of the wedding."

"I'll take care of all the costs. Jessie is worth it."

"That's so sweet. Her father will be pleased."

William's pedicurist was finished since William didn't get French nails.

William said, looking at Mom, "I need to go. Can I stop by tomorrow and we can discuss more details for the wedding?"

"Please do. Thanks so much for the pedicure."

William put his shoes on and got out of the chair. He came over to my chair and leaned down to kiss me. I turned my head and let him kiss me on the cheek. He said, "Will you be available for dinner tonight?"

Mom and the pedicurists looked at me as I said, "I'll call you later."

William leaned down and kissed my mother on the cheek and left the room.

Mom now noticed I was in the room and said to me, "William is such a wonderful fellow."

"He's a troublemaker."

"You two will make a great couple."

I didn't say anything and sat quietly for a couple of minutes.

Mom finally said, "What are you thinking, sweetheart?"

"I was just enjoying my pedicure." I was actually thinking of how to get even with William. I wondered if anyone would miss him if he was tied up for a few days.

"It was nice for William to do this for us, and he's going to pay for the wedding."

The pedicurists finished and gave us plastic flip-flops to put on while our nails dried. We helped Mom out of the chair and back into the wheelchair. A pedicurist pushed Mom over to a manicure table. Our pedicurists now became our manicurists. Thank goodness my manicurist's table was across the room from Mom's manicurist's table.

I took Mom back to her room after the mani-pedi and helped her into bed. It was time for me to leave for work, so I told her I'd see her later.

Mom said as I was leaving, "Bring William back with you."

I didn't respond and left for work. I drove through Burger King and got a whopper and fries. I deserved it after this morning's ordeal.

It was almost eleven when I arrived at the station. I went straight to Bill's office, but he wasn't there. I left him a note on his chair and went to my office. I was responding to e-mails when Bill walked into the office at eleven thirty.

Bill said, "I'm sorry I'm late. It was a wild night."

"Too much alcohol?" I just blurted it out without thinking.

"No, too much sex. The woman I dated last night just got her legal separation yesterday. She wanted to catch up, and I was there to help her. Now I have trouble walking. I couldn't ride my motorcycle today."

"Are you able to work?"

"As long as I don't move suddenly."

We went back to Bill's office slowly and started looking at all the e-mails and documents from the vic's computer. Jeffery had already gone through them, but we wanted to look too. After a couple of hours of looking, we both decided that there weren't any other leads worth pursuing.

It was almost two when we were through with the e-mails and documents. I asked Bill if he wanted to go back to the house today, and he said he needed to go home and sleep. He said he had to help the legally separated lady catch up more tonight and needed to be well rested.

I asked, "When do you want to get together again?"

"Let's meet Monday morning at eight."

"I'll see you Monday."

I sat and thought a few minutes and decided to go to the dojo to work out. I called, and there was an advanced class starting at six, which Choi asked me to join.

Since I had time, I went to see Mom and Dad at the hospital. Dad was awake, so I spent time with him and saw that he was making progress. I then went to see Mom.

Mom asked as soon as I came in, "Where's William?"

"I don't know. I haven't heard from him since this morning."

"I was looking forward to seeing him this afternoon."

"What about me?"

"I always like to see you." William was now at the top of the list for my mother, and I was second. I was assuming I was second.

I told her I was going to a martial arts class and kissed her good-bye.

William called me on the way to the dojo, and I answered, "Hello, William."

"You can call me honey or baby if you want."

"I don't want."

"You just need a little more time. I'll discuss it with your mother."

"I'm not sure I want you to see my mother again. The two of you cause trouble."

"Your mother and I just want the best for you."

"And you're the best."

"Yes."

"If you say so."

"Dinner tonight?"

"I'm going to a martial arts class at six. How about seven thirty or eight?"

"I'll keep your dinner warm. See you at seven thirty or eight. Good-bye, my cutie pie."

I was at the dojo just before six. The class had all guys, and I paired up with each of them before moving to the next. When the class was over, Choi and I did *kumite* as a demonstration to the class. Choi stopped our sparring frequently to explain to the class what he or I was doing. This was good since I was tired from the evening. After the demonstration, I bowed to Choi and thanked him for the workout and allowing me to join the class.

After class, Choi again offered me a part-time job teaching classes. I refused again. Choi reminded me again that instructors get together on Sunday afternoon, and I should join in. I told him I'd try to come, and he told me the location for the next one.

Chapter 30

Saturday Night—Jessie

I decided to shower at William's house. I rang the bell, and he came to the door. He looked at my *karategi* and said, "Did you come to fight?"

"I just came from martial arts class."

"That's a relief. I wasn't prepared for a fight."

"I'd like to beat you up for getting my mother wound up."

"I do like your mother. She's great."

"She does get on my nerves sometimes."

"She's your mother. She's allowed to get on your nerves."

"I need to take a shower, and I need food and wine to talk more about my mother." I went to the master bath and took a shower. William didn't join me.

After the shower, I came into the kitchen, and William handed me a glass of wine as he said, "Dinner is on the table. We'll talk about your mother and pick out a wedding dress after we eat."

I gave William the look just like my mother gives my father the look. Then I realized I acted just like my mother, so I gulped the rest of my wine.

"I need dinner. I've worked up a hunger."

"Then let's begin the feast." William took my arm and led me to the dining room table. Dinner was a garden salad and spaghetti with meatballs. There needed to be peanut butter pie or I'd sleep in a guest room.

William watched me devour my food and didn't speak. Sometimes he knew when to be quiet.

After I had my fill of spaghetti, William got up and went to the refrigerator and brought back a piece of peanut butter pie.

I ate again with earnest. The pie was just as tasty as I remembered.

After cleaning my pie plate, I said, "That was a great dinner. What's the plan now?"

William handed me a book. "It's time to pick out a wedding dress."

"No."

"Your mother is expecting you to start planning your wedding."

"What wedding?"

"You saw how the thought of your wedding cheered her up. Do you want to cause a relapse?"

"I want her to be happy, so I'll play along." What was I thinking? I didn't want to plan a wedding, especially mine. I added, "Since it's just a pretend wedding, I'll pretend I picked out a wedding dress."

"Have it your way, sweetie pie. We'll pretend we picked a dress."

"While I pretend I'm looking for a dress, could I have my feet massaged?"

"Lay down on the couch, and I'll get my accessories. I want to see how your French toenails turned out."

I put my feet on William's lap, and he started doing the magic on my feet. I felt myself getting drowsy. I woke up about thirty minutes later when I heard noise from the kitchen. William was cleaning up. I got up from the sofa, aware that I had slippery feet. I slid into the kitchen and asked if I could help. William told me he was almost done.

I said, "I'm sleepy."

"Are you ready for bed?"

I nodded as I yawned. After I did my face and teeth, I climbed into my side of the bed. William was already in bed and rolled over and kissed me. I told him that I was tired and just needed to sleep. This was the first night we didn't make love when I stayed over. William might have needed sleeping pills to go to sleep.

It was Sunday morning, and I smelled coffee and breakfast. William was at the breakfast table reading the Sunday paper when I got up. A carafe of coffee was on the table and an empty cup. I kissed William and poured coffee.

I said, "Anything on the six murders in the paper today?"

"There's a short article on page three that says the murder investigations are progressing."

"I haven't seen a lot of progress."

"What do you know so far?"

I went through all the details we knew so far. I also told him about Bill's services for the legally separated lady, and William smiled. He said he thought it was an important community service.

I talked more about the Burnette case. It was better than talking about my mother. William asked a few questions but didn't have any suggestions. He said he would ask around more.

William had fixed another casserole for breakfast, and I ate it heartily. After breakfast, William took my arm and led me back to bed. The after-breakfast morning sex was great. It was just as good as the before-breakfast morning sex.

I didn't fall asleep after the sex and was actually more energized. It was now about eight thirty, and I told William I was going to visit my parents. William got up with me, and we took a shower together.

When I was dressed, William was waiting for me in the kitchen.

He said, "I'll drive."

I said, "I don't think so. You're not going."

"I need to meet my future father-in-law."

"If you go, you have to promise to behave."

"I promise."

William led me to the garage, and we got into his BMW. I hadn't been in the garage before. He also had a pickup truck in the garage. It was a three-car garage, and one spot was empty. I guessed that was my spot. What was I thinking?

He turned on my heated seat and put jazz on the radio. I hadn't thought of the music that William liked before. I was more of a soft rock fan. I decided to just listen to the music and relax as we went to the hospital. William didn't speak as he drove. He looked like he was thinking, so I didn't disturb him.

At the hospital, we went to see Dad first. He was awake but still groggy. I kissed him on the cheek and introduced William.

Dad asked, "Is this my future son-in-law?"

I said, "Have you been talking to Mom?"

"She told me everything. That makes me want to get better faster. Tell me more about your plans."

William looked at me and smiled. I sneered.

"William and Mom are making the plans. You'll have to get more details from Mom."

William said, "Jessie was looking at wedding dresses this morning."

I reached over to pinch William, but he moved.

"Your mother said William was a great guy and would be perfect for you."

"Mom is still on drugs." I gave William another look.

Dad asked, "So how's everything else?"

I told him about the murder cases. Dad liked to hear about my cases while Mom didn't. Dad asked William what business he was in, and William told him about the businesses and houses. Dad seemed to be impressed. After a while, I told Dad we were going to see Mom and kissed him on the cheek. Dad told William he was glad to meet him and looked forward to having him as a son-in-law.

Mom was in a great mood when we arrived. I wasn't. As we went in, Mom spoke to William first and then to me. She kissed William first and then me. She told William to sit in the cushioned chair so I had to sit in the folding chair.

William said, "Jessie was looking at wedding dresses this morning."

"What kind of dress did she pick out?"

Mom was almost glowing, so I wasn't going to burst her bubble. Maybe I needed to find a pretend minister for the pretend wedding. Then I could find a find a pretend lawyer for a pretend divorce. I'd then need someone to catch me up on sex after the pretend legal separation.

William answered, "The dresses she's leaning toward have a lot of sequences and lace. They have a high collar and a long train. We should have brought the bridal books with us so she could show you."

Mom didn't even look at me.

"If Jessie comes back later today, have her bring the books. I'd like to see the dresses she's considering."

"I'll make sure she brings the books." William went on, "I also started narrowing down choices for the wedding. It'll be a spring wedding, so some places are already booked."

Mom was only looking at William. "I'm sure you'll pick a nice place. Have you thought about a caterer, flowers, bridesmaid dresses, and invitations? There's so much to do for a wedding. I'll be home next week, so I can help."

"I'll be working on those items this week. Maybe you and I can work out the details together."

"I'd like that very much. I can't wait to get out of here. The first thing I need to do is get a new cell phone. Our cell phones were busted in the wreck."

William said, "We can get you a replacement cell phone today. What kind of phone would you like?"

Mom said, "I just had a plain LG phone that was destroyed in the wreck. One like it would be great."

"We'll get you one today." William looked at me and smiled.

William said he had to go to the restroom, so I moved to the cushioned chair. Mom would probably make me move after William came back.

Mom said, "Tell me about the wedding dress."

"They're just like William said."

"I know you're excited. I remember when your father and I were married. I gave my wedding dress to one of your poorer cousins since I wasn't sure you'd need it."

Ouch. Mom was being a little nasty.

"I'm excited, but my work is coming first right now."

"William and I will handle everything when I get out of the hospital."

I gritted my teeth. "That would be grand." Changing the subject, I said, "I went to see Dad this morning, and he seemed to be doing better."

"I told him about the wedding, and that seemed to perk him up." My pretend wedding was now bringing happiness to everyone but me.

"Yes, he did appear to be happier."

"The wedding gave him more motivation to get better. I think all of his injuries made him depressed. This is the happiest I've seen him since the wreck."

Maybe I was getting mad at William when I should have been glad he created this fake wedding. Mom and Dad were the happiest I'd seen them since the wreck, and I should probably go along with the sham. I decided to keep up the pretending at least until both of my parents were out of the hospital. I'd then be a runaway bride.

William came back in and sat in the folding chair. I waited, but Mom didn't tell me to get up, so I kept the good chair.

I said to William as I took his hand, "You and I should spend time discussing the wedding details this afternoon. It's best to have everything planned as early as possible."

William looked at me like I was off my rocker and said, "You're right, sweetheart. We need to get the planning done."

Mom said, "Remember I'll be available next week to help."

I said, "It's going to be a beautiful wedding."

Mom had moisture in her eyes as she said, "I've been looking forward to Jessie's wedding for a long time."

Mom told us she thought she would be released on Tuesday or Wednesday and that the doctor had arranged for therapy to start the day after she was released. Mom thanked William for the mani-pedi and said she had starting telling relatives in Chicago about the wedding. We said our good-byes and left the hospital.

William said after we were out of range of Mom, "What happened in there? Were you taken over by a spirit? You sounded like you were going to help plan the wedding. What's your motive?"

"I just realized when I was talking to Mom that the wedding had made both Mom and Dad very happy. I figured I'd play along."

"You know it isn't going to be as much fun for me now."

"I'm sorry it'll ruin your fun. Mom and Dad are more important than your fun." I then asked, "When do I get to tell your mom?"

"Let's wait a while to tell my mom."

"So it's different with your mom."

"Your mom is in the hospital, so she needed the wedding. My mom doesn't need to be cheered up."

"When can we go to see your mom?"

"Soon."

"How soon?"

"Soon."

At the Verizon store, I explained to the guy waiting on us about Mom's phone. I didn't ask about Dad's phone since I didn't think he needed it yet. The guy was hesitant at first but became more helpful when he saw I was with William. We picked out a replacement phone exactly like she had before. We left the Verizon store and were driving back toward the hospital.

I asked, "Where are we going?"

William said, "I'm going back to the hospital to give the phone to your mother."

"If we go back to the hospital, I'm giving the phone to my mother."

"I told her I'd get her a phone, so I should give it to her."

"I need points with my mother. You don't. Let me out at the entrance, and I'll take her the phone."

"You can take the phone to your mother, but tell her I let you."

William dropped me off at the entrance to the hospital, and I took the phone to my mother.

Mom said as I gave her the phone, "That William is so nice. William just called to tell me you were bringing the phone up."

I should have known William would call but didn't think about it. I left Mom's room and went back to the entrance. William was waiting with a smile on his face.

William said, "Was she happy you got a phone for her?"

I said, "You rat. You called her before I went to her room."

"I could have taken the phone to her and could have given you full credit."

"I'm sure you would have."

As we left the hospital, William was headed in the opposite way from his home.

I asked, "Where are we going now?"

"I just want to look at a house that's being auctioned. It's near the hospital."

William stopped at a two-story, brick house that looked abandoned and in need of repair. The front door was ajar, so we toured the inside, which was almost destroyed.

"Don't buy this one. It's in awful condition," I said.

"It's perfect for me. The price should be cheap, and the repairs are cosmetic."

"It looks like a disaster to me," I said.

We stopped for lunch at Cracker Barrel. I had meatloaf, French fries, and macaroni and cheese. William had a vegetable plate. We didn't have dessert.

At William's house, I told him I wanted to go play with the martial arts instructors. He suggested that I should work out with him. I thought he was talking about more bedroom time and said, "I'll romp with you in the bed when I come back."

"I thought you could teach me martial arts."

"I could. Do you want to go with me today?"

"We can do it here."

"Where?" I asked.

William took me by the hand and led me out through the garage. Attached to the back of the garage was a large room with exercise equipment, free weights, and mats.

"Will this do?"

"It'll do nicely. Let me go put on my *karategi*."

"I washed it for you. It's in the laundry room."

"Where's the laundry room?"

"I'll show you."

I found the laundry room with William's help and got my *karategi*. I put it on, and William put on workout pants and a T-shirt. I showed William how to warm up and stretch. I was still a little stiff from yesterday but would work it out. I showed William how to stand and how to punch and kick. I had him do shadow punching and shadow kicking. After a while, I decided to show him some throws. I showed him how to use the other person's movement to make the throw. I had William grab the sleeves of my *karategi*, and I proceeded to throw him on the mat. I then had him throw a punch at me, and I grabbed his arm and threw him on the mat. I then had him try to kick me and put him on the mat again. William asked to take a break and limped over to a refrigerator for a bottle of water. He tossed me a bottle too.

I asked, "Have you had enough?"

"If you promise not to hurt me, can we do sparring?"

"I think you need to practice a lot more."

"I'll learn faster if I spar."

We started sparring, and I blocked all of William's punches and kicks. At first, I didn't throw any punches or kicks. When I threw the first punch, William took my arm and threw me on the mat.

He said, "Is that how it's done?"

I said, "You're a fast learner."

I got up and took my stance again. This time I'd be prepared. We started sparring again, and I threw a punch. William dropped down and swept my legs, putting me on the mat again. I got up and decided it was time to stop playing. I took my stance again and waited for him to start. William feigned a kick, feigned a punch, feigned another kick, feigned another punch, and then kicked me in the chest, knocking me backward. I came at him with several kicks and punches, and he blocked them all. He was a fast learner. I tried more kicks and punches, and he blocked them too. The third time I came at him with kicks and punches, I was flipped to the mat after my last punch.

I said, "I think you know more than you told me."

"I didn't tell you how much I knew. I just asked you to teach me. You assumed I didn't know much."

"I did but won't anymore. Let's do real sparring."

"That's fine with me."

We faced off on the mat and went at each other. I didn't take him for granted now and was prepared for anything he threw at me. Unfortunately, he was just as fast as me and stronger. I did put him on the mat one time, but he put me on the mat several times. We were both sweating after a while.

I said, "You're as good as Choi."

"Choi was one of my instructors."

"Are you a black belt?"

"Yes."

"Why didn't you wear your *karategi?*"

"It's best to not let your opponent know your strengths."

"Would you like to spar more?" I asked.

"I'm ready. You should be since you've spent a lot of time on the mat." He grinned.

"Get prepared for your time on the mat."

Unfortunately, I ended up more on the mat than William. It was a good workout, and I was tired. There were showers in the exercise room, but we elected to use the master bathroom where we could shower together.

After, I decided to go back and see Mom and Dad. William said he needed to work, so I went by myself. I took the bridal gown books.

When I got to the hospital, I showed Mom the books, and she was beaming. We had a great time picking out wedding dresses, shoes, and bridesmaid dresses.

I called William, and he suggested that I stop and get a pizza on the way. He said he wanted to relax and watch a movie, eat pizza, and drink a beer or two. I agreed with the plan.

Chapter 31

Monday Morning—Jessie

On Monday morning, I arrived at work about seven thirty. There were a few e-mails and a couple of messages. One was from the captain asking Bill and me to come to his office at nine.

Bill looked better than he had on Saturday. I sat down in his office and asked, "Did you see that we had a meeting at nine with the captain?"

"I did, and I invited the whole team to meet with the captain," Bill answered.

After the meeting with the captain, I suggested going to the vic's house. I still had the feeling we missed something. There was police tape still up, but there wasn't a deputy at the entrance. We parked and went under the tape. The house was locked, so we used a set of keys. It was quiet and warm inside. The power was still on for now.

Bill went to the garage and outbuildings. I went into the office and started going through the desk and files. As I was going through files, I thought I heard a noise underneath me and behind me. It was faint, and I was sure I heard it. I put my head to the floor and could hear a thumping noise. It could be the heating unit, but I wasn't sure. I got up and looked behind me, and there were the bookcases. I put my ear to a bookcase and could hear the noise more. I walked out of the office, around the steps to the upstairs, and into the kitchen. The steps going upstairs and walls on each side of the steps separated the office from the kitchen. I walked back into the office and looked at the other wall for the steps going upstairs. Most houses used the space under stairs for a coat closet, storage, or pantry, but the area under these stairs wasn't used. This was where I heard the noise.

I went back into the office and checked the bookcases. I could still hear the thudding noise like someone was hitting a wall. I got on my hands and knees and looked closely at the floor. There was a faint scratch on the floor that made an arc away from the bookcase. I ran my finger along the arc, and it ended at the end of the bookcase at the wall. The shelves were full of books, and I started removing them and stacking them on the desk.

Bill came in while I was stacking books and asked, "What are you doing?"

"Just help me. I'll explain in a minute."

Bill helped, and we removed all the books from the end section of shelves.

I took out a pen light and starting searching the shelves. Underneath a shelf about three feet up was a lever just under a shelf. It would be impossible to find with the books in place. I pulled the lever and pulled on the shelves. The shelves swung open.

Behind the shelves was a door with both a regular doorknob and two deadbolts.

"Look in the desk for keys," I told Bill.

Bill found a ring of keys, and I started trying them. One of the keys fit the locks. I opened the door and saw a stairway going down. There was a light switch just inside the door, and I switched it on. The walls were painted a light brown, and the steps were wooden.

We went to the bottom of the stairway and opened the door. The lights were already on when we opened the door. The room was a large living area with sofas, chairs, end tables, a coffee table, a TV, and a stereo. I listened but didn't hear anything. There was a light on to the left. A broom was lying on the floor, and I almost tripped on it. There were six Latina teenage girls at a table eating. They were dressed in pants and shirts just like typical girls. They looked up when we came in, and then all six left the table quickly and ran through a door off the kitchen.

I turned to Bill and said, "You need to wait outside the house. Call for help. We'll need counselors and medical. Make sure they're all women. I'll be bringing the girls upstairs soon."

Bill understood and went back outside.

I walked through the door the girls had gone through, and there were four doors off the hall. The first door was closed, and I knocked on the door. "I'm Jessie. It's just me, and I'm with the Aiken County sheriff."

The door was cracked open, and I showed them my badge. The door opened further, and all six of the girls started crying, holding themselves and rocking.

"All of you are safe now." The crying continued. Some started holding each other, but none of them spoke.

One finally got up and came over and hugged me. Eventually, all came over and huddled around me.

"You're safe now. I'm taking you out of here. Follow me upstairs." I took the hand of one girl and started leading her toward the stairs. The other girls followed.

The girls were still crying as I led them into the living area of the house. They stayed together in a group, and none sat down. I could hear sirens in the distance.

"Is anybody hurt? Medical is on the way. Is everybody okay?" I asked.

None answered.

"You're safe now. We're here for you now."

They were still crying.

I kept reassuring them that they were going to be okay now.

A female officer from Burnettown arrived first and repeated my assurances to the girls that they'd be okay. The female officer asked whether they were hurt, but none responded.

Several minutes later, two female EMTs came and started checking the girls to see if they were hurt. The girls had to sit down for the EMTs and remained sitting after being checked. The crying was lessening.

About thirty minutes later, a female psychologist arrived from Aiken. The psychologist was trying to talk to the girls, but the girls weren't talking.

I looked out the window, and there were Aiken County sheriff's cars, Burnettown Police cars, ambulances, and a news van.

I opened the door to go outside, and one of the older girls spoke with a Latino accent, "Don't go."

"I'll be right back. I need to make sure arrangements are made to get you away from this place."

I walked up to the captain and Bill. I was shaky.

The captain said, "I have a van coming to take the girls to the Aiken County Hospital. It's a twelve-passenger van, so you, the EMTs, and the psychologist can ride with them. We'll leave the keys in the van for you."

The Burnettown captain said, "Our female deputy will follow them."

Our captain said, "I can't believe this is happening in Aiken County."

Our captain's cell phone rang, and the captain answered it and talked for a few seconds.

"The van will be here in a couple minutes, and the hospital is waiting for the girls. I'll have everybody moved away from the house so you can bring the girls out."

I said, "I'll go back inside and tell them we'll be leaving soon."

I went back inside and only heard sobbing. The girls not with an EMT were back in a group and were holding hands and swaying.

I said to the group, "We're taking you to the hospital. You won't be coming back here ever. Does anybody have any questions?"

The same girl said, "Can we go now? We don't like this place."

"It'll be just a few minutes. You don't need to bring any clothes or anything else. Everything will be provided for you."

The girls, the EMT, and the psychologist followed me out and loaded in the van. Everybody else was away from the house and out of sight. I could see several cameramen in the woods, but they weren't close. I'd been to the hospital many times since I'd been in Aiken, so I knew the way.

On the way to the hospital, the girls told us their names. They were Victoria Alvarez, Alejandra Ramirez, Maria Sanchez, Gabriela Delgado, Sofia Ramos, and Daniela Castillo. That was all the information we got out of them.

The hospital had us take the girls through a side entrance and up a freight elevator. The hospital had rooms for all the girls on the same floor. An Aiken County sheriff's female deputy was already on the floor restricting admittance. Nurses arrived right away.

One of the nurses was telling two of the girls that a doctor would be coming soon. I went down to the lobby, and it was swarming with reporters, cameras, and police officers. I had microphones and cameras stuffed in my face as I made my way outside. The microphones and cameras didn't follow me. I saw the captain and Bill standing outside and walked over.

We moved further away from the hospital, and the captain asked, "Did the girls talk to you?"

"No. They only told us their names. Maybe they'll talk later today."

"I want you to lead the interviews. They'll probably talk to you since you were there first."

"I'll check with them in an hour or two. I'd like the psychologist with me."

"We'll move them to a house in Aiken for abused women when they're released from the hospital. The staff is only females. We'll be calling the FBI too, so expect them to be involved."

Bill and I went to the hospital cafeteria, and Michael joined us.

"Do you think there are more men involved?" I asked.

Both said, "We can't be sure until we talk to the girls."

"I'm still bewildered from seeing the girls in the basement. That was a shock."

"There're some strange people in all parts of the world, including our part." Bill was attempting to be profound and did okay at it.

I knew I should eat, but my appetite had disappeared. I thought about the young women upstairs. Their stories would depress me even more. I went back upstairs, and the medical staff was with all the girls but two. The hospital had two to a room, and I knocked on the door.

"This is Jessie with the Aiken County Sheriff. Can I come in?"

"*Si*," one of the girls said.

I opened the door, went inside, and shut the door.

"I need to ask a few questions."

"Can it wait? We'd like to be together when we talk to you," one of the girls responded.

"I can wait. When do you want to talk?"

"Tomorrow."

"Fine. We'll talk tomorrow." I didn't want to create more stress for them.

I went back downstairs and told Michael, Bill, and the captain that the girls wanted to wait until tomorrow to talk, and they wanted to be together when they talked to me. The psychologist was still upstairs with the girls, and the captain said he'd make sure she was available tomorrow. I told them

I'd be here early tomorrow to interview them and see when they could be released.

"An FBI Child Abduction Rapid Deployment team will be here this afternoon. I'm sure they'll want to be involved with the interviews. They'll also bring a forensic team and cadaver dogs," the captain said.

I wanted to go back in the basement, but it didn't look like it'd be today since multiple forensic teams would now be there.

I decided to spend a little time with both of my parents while I was at the hospital. Mom and I talked about the pretend wedding and all the people in Chicago she had been talking to on her cell phone. She informed me about all the news and gossip, but it didn't take my mind off of the girls. My dad and I talked about the wedding, the house, and the yard. I fibbed a little when I said I had been keeping the yard in good shape.

William answered when I called, "Hi there, my little dandelion."

I said, "I don't feel like a flower. I found six girls in Mr. Burnette's hidden basement, and I'm pretty depressed."

"What can I do?"

"Nothing for now. You can cheer me up later."

"I can do that. Call me later?"

I was the last to arrive at the four o'clock meeting. I drove the van and had trouble parking it. It didn't fit in a regular space, so I had a long walk to the station.

Two FBI agents were in the meeting when I arrived. Agent Lorena Valdez and Agent Bob Brown introduced themselves to me. Agent Valdez was Latino, so that would help with the interviews. She was about five foot four with dark hair and dark eyes. She was petite but in shape. Agent Brown was about Bill's height with blond hair and green eyes. He had short hair the same length all over. He was big boned and also in shape. Both were wearing the FBI uniforms.

Bill started the meeting with a discussion about the six girls. I tried to recall the names of the girls but didn't try to say them. Agent Brown asked for the history, and Bill and Michael summarized their cases.

Oscar went next and said they were continuing to go through the computers and cell phones. He handed out printouts of information. There were ten stacks of paper placed on the table.

Jeffery took the stacks and said, "It'll take a while to go through them."

Agent Brown said, "We may be able to provide resources. We'll be concentrating on the abductions."

I was expecting the FBI to take over the murder cases, but they didn't.

"I'll be going back to the hospital tomorrow morning at eight to talk to the girls," I said, expecting the FBI agents to tell me I wasn't.

"I'll meet you at the hospital," Agent Valdez said.

"A local child psychologist was with us yesterday and will be there tomorrow."

"We checked her out, and she's fine. A couple of our psychologists should be here tonight. We'll be going back to the house after this meeting. Our forensic team is already there," Agent Brown said.

"We'll meet you at the house," Bill said.

I didn't know who was going but I assumed it included me.

After the meeting, we met at the Burnette house. An FBI agent and a sheriff's deputy were at the street and waved us through past the news vans and reporters trying to stop us. There were several FBI vans parked outside the house. A couple of vans had satellite dishes. A tent was set up with tables and chairs, and Buck's pizza boxes were on one of the tables. An FBI agent at the house came over to Agent Brown and Agent Valdez when we arrived. Introductions were made. The agent was Agent Tim Marlow, and he was in charge of the forensic team.

"We're taking samples from the entire house. We've matched fingerprints to Paul Burnette, but none of the other fingerprints match. We found lots of fingerprints in the van, with the only match being Burnette."

"What's in the basement?" Bill asked.

Agent Marlow answered, "The basement was constructed like a single-story house with three bedrooms, a kitchen, dining area, and living area. Each bedroom had a separate bathroom. There was also an exercise room."

Bill and I stayed for another hour answering questions but not being allowed in the house. I repeated how I heard the noise and found the mark on the floor and the latch. Agent Marlow went inside and checked. He said it was a nail that was working out of the bottom of the shelves that was causing the mark.

"When can I go in the basement?" Bill asked.

"Meet me here tomorrow morning at nine. I'll probably have more questions I'll think of tonight," Agent Brown said.

William had pizza, wine, and a foot massage ready for me when I arrived. I didn't eat the FBI pizza, so I gobbled three slices, drank two glasses of wine, and headed for the couch. I told him about the girls as he massaged and rubbed. He convinced me to go to the bedroom before I dozed off. I paid him for the pizza, wine, and foot massage. I was restless all night thinking of the young women locked in a basement.

In the morning, William had breakfast and the *Aiken Standard* newspaper on the table. The headlines were about the young women being held at Paul Burnette's house. CNN was on the TV, and the Aiken abductions were headline news. Agent Brown and Agent Valdez held a press conference where they stated that all resources of the FBI were being used for the abductions. Pictures of the girls and me were shown coming out of the house. I hadn't been invited to the press conference and was glad.

Chapter 32

Tuesday Morning—Jessie

On Tuesday morning, I went to the hospital. A sheriff's deputy was sitting in a chair in the hall. He knew me, so he didn't get up. Agent Valdez and Tammy were waiting in the hall. Two FBI psychologists with Agent Valdez introduced themselves as Sally Straight and Kimberly Charles. I went in the first room, and there weren't any girls. I checked the second room and the same. I knocked on the door of the third room, and one of the girls opened the door.

"Hi, Jessie," Victoria said in her Latino accent as she swung the door open.

All six girls were either on the bed or in chairs. They seemed happy. I walked in, and all got up to hug me. Three said gracias, and three said thank you.

"I'm so glad we found you," I said.

"We are too," Victoria said.

"I need to ask you some questions."

"We'd prefer to be out of the hospital first."

"I understand. I'll check with the nurses to see when you can be released."

I went to the nurses' station and asked about their release. The nurse said they could be released this morning, but there was paperwork to fill out. She directed me to the admittance office. I waited in line and finally was called. The admittance lady gave me several pages of documents for each girl. I asked for six clipboards and pens. The girls and I would figure it out.

I took the stairs up to the rooms and told Agent Valdez and the others about the required paperwork. I knocked on the girls' door again. Victoria opened the door.

"The hospital needs paperwork for each of you." I handed out the clipboards with the documents, and I kept one set.

I read down the document and gave them the sheriff's address to use as their address. I told them it was okay to leave blanks if they didn't know the answers to the questions. Many of the questions were about medical conditions or family history. The forms were completed in a few minutes, and I took them back downstairs. The handwriting was better than mine on the forms, and most of the questions were answered except for the family history. I asked for copies but was told I couldn't have them. The admittance lady asked about payment, and I didn't know the answer.

"Check back with me in about thirty minutes."

After updating Agent Valdez and the others, I went to visit Mom and Dad for thirty minutes. Both asked questions about the young women. After, I went back to admittance. I stood by the same window waiting for the lady to finish with a customer. I ignored the stares from many of the people waiting. The admittance lady told me she had all she needed and the girls could be released.

When we got to the home for abused women in Aiken, there were two ladies waiting on us outside the house. The seven of us got out of the van and went inside with the two ladies. Agent Valdez, Tammy, and the two FBI psychologists followed us inside. There was a large area in the house with tables and chairs. One of the two ladies told us that it was a common area. She continued throughout the house, showing us the other rooms and where the bedrooms were located. The house was old and large. I only saw women and girls as we toured the house.

We went back to the common area, and everybody sat down.

One of the ladies said, "My name is Charlotte, and this is April. We're here to help you. You'll have to share bedrooms since we have many women and girls already here. There's a big closet full of clothes down the hall that you can pick from. There're also toothbrushes, toothpaste, hairbrushes, soap, and whatever else you need in the same closet. There're more clothes in the attic. We do have rules. One, you need to tell us if you're going to leave the premises for any reason. You're allowed to leave, but we would like to know where you're going. Two, you need to let us know if you have any problems. We'll talk to you or get more help."

I got up and said, "I do need to talk to you to understand everything. When do you think we can sit down and talk?"

"I can after I eat," Daniella said.

"What about the rest of you?"

All the girls said they could talk after they ate.

"Can we have a McDonald's meal?" Sofia said.

"I'll get us all a McDonald's meal. I'll be back shortly."

Charlotte said, "We'll save the living room for you so that you can have privacy."

"Thanks." I looked at the girls and said, "I'll see you soon."

There were no hugs this time.

William called while Agent Valdez and I went to McDonald's. Tammy and two FBI psychologists stayed.

"How are you doing today? Yesterday was hard on you," William said.

"I need to interview the girls in little while. We moved them to Aiken into a home for women and girls."

"I know Charlotte and April. Tell them to call me if they need anything for the girls."

"I'll call you later." I wondered how William knew Charlotte and April.

I didn't know what to buy at McDonald's, so I bought a lot of everything. I figured the staff and others could eat the remainder. April met us outside, and the three of us carried the food to the room saved for us.

The girls appeared to be in a good mood. We made a second trip to get the drinks. The girls saw the McDonald's bags of food and dug in.

Maria said as she put her hand on my shoulder, "Let me get you something. What do you want?"

"I want a Big Mac, fries, and a Coke."

Maria found me a Big Mac, fries, and a Coke while the rest of the girls were getting their food.

Agent Valdez was hanging back, and Maria asked her what she wanted.

"I'd like a grilled chicken sandwich and a diet coke."

Maria got the sandwich, fries, and a Diet Coke for Agent Valdez. Maria was a trim girl just like all of them except Daniella. Daniella was a shorter and a little heavier than the others. Maria appeared to be the attentive one.

She had dark hair and eyes, a round face with a wide mouth, and a pudgy nose.

Maria finely got her food, and we ate together. Tammy arrived and found herself some food. Nobody said anything while we ate. I took my time eating so that the girls weren't rushed. I was normally a fast eater. I noticed Tammy and Agent Valdez were taking their time also. The two FBI psychologists had finished their meal. They probably wanted to get started while I wanted the girls to enjoy themselves.

I had bought McDonald's apple pies and was thinking of them. I started to get up for an apple pie when I was pulled back down by Maria.

"I was getting an apple pie," I said.

After I ate the apple pie that Maria got for me, all of the girls seemed to have finished eating.

I said, "You've met Tammy Street and FBI Agent Lorena Valdez. This is Agent Straight and Agent Charles. All of us will be talking to you."

Victoria said, "We've talked, and we're ready to talk about everything."

"The first priority is to get you back home, so let's talk about that first. Agent Valdez and I will be recording our conversation. Victoria, will you start and let me know where you're from?" I figured I would start with the easy questions first.

Victoria said, "I'm from Phoenix, Arizona. I'm eighteen years old, and my parents are Rosa and Carlos Alvarez."

Alejandra said, "I'm from Scottsdale, Arizona. I'm seventeen years old, and my parents are Sara and Hector Ramirez."

Maria said, "I'm from Glendale, Arizona. I'm seventeen years old, and my parents are Clarisa and Ricardo Sanchez."

Gabriela said, "I'm from Tempe, Arizona. I'm seventeen years old, and my parents are Claudia and Eduardo Delgado."

Sofia said, "I'm from Peoria, Arizona. I'm sixteen years old, and my parents are Natalia and Luis Ramos."

Daniela said, "I'm from Phoenix, Arizona. I'm fifteen years old, and my parents are Diana and Javier Castillo."

"What are the addresses of your homes?"

Each of the six girls gave an address.

"What are the telephone numbers?"

Each of the six girls told us telephone numbers.

The pattern became apparent. The girls were all teenagers from Arizona. I remembered that Phoenix was close to the top of the list for kidnapping, and now I was seeing it. I knew there were over eight hundred thousand missing persons reported last year, and Arizona was a big contributor.

Victoria asked, "Can we call and talk to our parents?"

Agent Valdez answered, "The FBI will try to contact your parents first. Let's take a couple-minute break while I pass along the information."

After Agent Valdez returned, I asked, "Would anybody like to talk about how they were brought here from Arizona?" I knew this could be a touchy subject, so I asked for volunteers.

Victoria said, "I can tell you my story. My parents were planning to leave Arizona because of the new immigration law. They said they had a guy who was going to give them work in California. I told them I didn't want to go since all my friends were in Phoenix. I was sixteen years old and thought my parents were old-fashioned. On the night before my parents were leaving, I told my parents I was going to see one of my girlfriends, but I spent the night with my boyfriend. During the night, I decided to go with my parents and told my boyfriend I was leaving. The next morning, I went back home, and my parents were gone. There was an older guy on the porch when I arrived. He told me his name was Pablo and said he would take me to my parents. I told him I needed to go in the house to get my clothes I had packed. As I went to unlock the door, I felt a sharp sting in my back and went numb. When I woke up, I was in a big sack in the back of a van or enclosed truck. I could tell the van or truck was moving. My hands and feet were tied, and I had tape over my mouth. In four or five hours, the van or truck stopped, and the doors were opened. I was taken into a room with bars on the door and a window. I was untied, and the tape was taken from my mouth. There was a commode and sink in the corner, so I used the commode and washed in the sink. There were cameras in each corner of the room. I was given clean clothes and food. I was left in the room for about a week. After the week, four guys came in and tied me up and taped my mouth again. I was put into a sack and put back into a van. The door opened two more times, and I found out later that Alejandra and Maria were being put in the van. We were in the van until we were taken into the place that you found us."

"Would anybody else like to tell us how they got here from Arizona?"

Alejandra said, "I'll go next. My parents had also decided to leave

Arizona due to the immigration law. I was planning to go with my parents. My parents had told me and my two younger brothers that arrangements had been made for work in California. On the night before we were to leave, two guys with guns came to our house and took me. I was tied up with tape on my mouth. I was put in a van or truck and taken to the place where Victoria was also kept. I stayed in the cell for about two weeks and then ended up in the van with Victoria."

"Does anybody else want to tell us how they got here?"

We heard similar stories from the other four girls. All the stories seemed almost like they were rehearsed. I expected more emotion when they explained how they got here.

"Whose parents were illegal aliens?"

All of the girls raised their hands.

"How long ago did you leave Arizona?"

Victoria said, "Alejandra, Maria, and I've been here about a two years."

Sofia said, "Daniela, Gabriela, and I got here about two months after the others."

"Let's take a break before we talk more."

I stood up, and all six girls came over and hugged me as each left the room.

I asked Tammy, Agent Valdez, Agent Straight, and Agent Charles, "Is everything okay so far?"

Tammy said, "You're doing fine. Keep getting them to volunteer information without forcing them."

Agent Valdez said, "You're doing okay."

Agent Straight and Agent Charles also said I was doing fine.

"Ask questions too if you want."

"The girls respect you. I suspect it may be just the girls and the psychologists later," Tammy said.

"You're certainly welcome to join in. We may get to some difficult discussions, and I may need help."

I actually expected Agent Valdez to ask questions. She probably would soon.

"I need to go to the ladies' room. I'll be back in a minute." I left, and then when I came back to our assigned room, I didn't see any of the girls.

I saw movement out the window, and all six girls were standing outside.

I pointed it out to Tammy and Agent Valdez. The girls were looking up at the sky and trees as they walked around. Daniella and Sofia were holding hands and moving in circles. Maria was picking blooms from an azalea bush and showing them to the others. Gabriela was picking a rose and letting everyone smell it. I walked and watched. All of them smiled at me with their bright white smiles.

I said, "Let's go back inside."

When we were inside, I said, "Does anyone want to talk about what happened in the basement?"

Victoria said, "It was where we lived. We ate and slept there. We had TVs, stereos, and played games."

I was confused since I thought the vic and others came down to the basement and took advantage of the girls. I looked at Tammy and Agent Valdez, and they were confused too.

"Did you have anybody that visited you in the basement?"

Victoria said, "No, we just lived in the basement like I said."

I was more confused.

"Were you ever taken out of the basement?"

Victoria said, "Yes. Can we talk about that later?"

I now understood better and wasn't as confused. I now suspected they were taken to the hunting lodge.

"I don't need any details. I would like to know where you were taken when you left the basement."

Victoria thought a minute, sighed, and then said, "We were taken to a house out in the woods."

I didn't know how much to ask, and Tammy wasn't jumping in. "How far did you travel to get to the house in the woods?"

"It was about twenty minutes."

"Could you take me to the house?"

"No. We were always in an enclosed van without any windows."

I was sure what happened in the lodge and knew it was the house that burned down. I had to assume the girls didn't know the house burned down. I was now thinking there must have been a seventh person involved.

"How often did you go to the house?"

"Almost every weekend. We would go on Friday or Saturday and come back on Saturday or Sunday."

"So you spent the night at this house in the woods?"

"Yes." Victoria hissed the end of yes and pursed her face. Some of the other girls shuttered.

"On the last trip a week ago, did you come back on Saturday or Sunday?"

Victoria hesitated a few seconds. "We came back on Saturday."

Tammy gave me a look, but I asked anyway. Agent Valdez had a poker face.

"Can you describe the people you met at the house in the woods?"

Victoria said, "We can, but we'd like to do that later." The other five girls nodded in agreement.

"Did you see the van driver?"

"Yes. We did. Can we talk about him later too?" I assumed the driver was also a participant at the house in the woods.

"We'll need to get descriptions of the driver and others, but that can wait."

Victoria said, "Tomorrow would be better."

"Let's end for today and pick back up tomorrow. What can I do for you today?"

Daniela said, "I'd like to go to a movie."

I looked at Tammy and Agent Valdez for help. "Are you sure you want to go out in public?" I knew this probably didn't come out right.

Gabriela said, "We have to sometime."

I was waiting for Tammy or Agent Valdez to help, but they didn't. "Don't you think it's too early?"

Alejandra spoke this time. "If Jessie is with us, it'll be okay."

I asked Maria and Sofia, "What about you?"

Both said we should go.

I looked at Tammy, Agent Valdez, Agent Straight, and Agent Charles, but they were quiet.

"We'll get today's newspaper and pick a movie."

Tammy brought back a newspaper, and we decided on a movie. The movie started in two hours.

I said, "I'll come back and pick you up in about an hour, and we'll go to the movie."

Victoria spoke for the group again. "We'll be ready. You *will* be staying with us." This sounded more like an order rather than a question.

"I'll be with you the whole time."

I rose to leave, and they all hugged me again. Maria squeezed the tightest.

I called Bill and told him I was headed back to the office. Bill said he would be waiting. Agent Valdez went to meet Agent Brown. The three psychologists stayed to consult with one another.

I went to Bill's office, and he said we were meeting in the captain's office. We went to the captain's office and sat in our usual chairs at the table. I told them what I had heard so far.

"What about the parents? Have the parents been located?" the captain asked.

"The FBI is making calls, but I don't know what they've found out. Maybe they weren't reported missing."

"That's probably the case since the parents were illegal aliens."

"I'm sure there could be more details than the girls knew. There could have been some kind of deal."

I then said, "The girls were probably taken and then sold. It sounds like the girls were bought when they were taken to the house with cells and cameras. There're probably a lot of these girls other places too."

The captain said, "Keep me posted. I'll be questioned on why we didn't find them earlier."

This was my second murder case in Aiken County and the second one that the FBI became involved in. Aiken County was strange so far.

We were leaving for the movie in fifteen minutes, so I called William. I went over the latest details with him. He said he left his credit card at the movie theater for us to buy tickets, food, and drinks. He said we could also go by Marble Slab Creamery ice-cream shop afterward if we wanted. I told him it was too cold for ice cream. He said it was never too cold for ice cream. I told him thanks and I'd see him later.

Tammy, Agent Valdez, and I went to pick up the girls, and all the girls had changed clothes. The two FBI psychologists didn't want to come along. They were standing outside when we arrived. Maria came over and hugged me when I got out of the van.

Victoria asked, "Were any of our parents located?"

Agent Valdez answered, "We haven't located any of the parents. The phone numbers must have been changed. Hopefully we'll know more after the movie."

"That's great," Victoria said.

I said, "It's time to leave. We'll take the van." I hoped they wouldn't object since it was a van. This van did have windows.

The girls didn't object, so we took the van to the movies.

We got to the movie theater about ten minutes before the previews started. William had left his credit card as promised, and I used it to pay for the tickets and food.

I was surrounded by the girls as we watched the movie. Agent Valdez and Tammy were now becoming part of the group. After the movie, I asked if anyone wanted ice cream, and the group said yes, including Agent Valdez and Tammy. We went to Marble Slab Creamery and ate ice cream. The girls were doing wonderful out in public. After ice cream, I took the girls back to the house. The girls hugged me and told me thanks.

There were men at the movie and at Marble Slab Creamery, but the girls didn't getting upset. I expected them to cringe when they were close to other men and shy away. This didn't happen, and they were acting like normal girls out for a movie and ice cream.

Chapter 33

Tuesday Night—Jessie

I went to William's house although it was late. I needed someone to fuss over me, and I wasn't disappointed. William already had his feet scrubbers out and the lotion. I kissed him quickly and took my position on the couch. William sat down and placed my feet on his lap. I told him about the movie and ice cream and told him I would pay him back in trade. I was asleep in about ten minutes. I woke up, and the lights were out, and the TV was on a ball game. I spoke to William, but he didn't hear me. I looked at him, and he had earphones on. There was no sound from the TV, so I guessed he had wireless headphones. I nudged him with my foot, and he took the headphones off.

I said, "Did I go to sleep?"

"You were asleep for about an hour."

"It was a nice sleep. Thanks for doing my feet."

"Would you like more?"

"I would. I was cheated since I fell asleep."

"I'm here to please you, fair lady. You deserve much more for saving the girls."

"I was just glad they weren't hurt. They seemed like they were in good health."

William rubbed and sanded my feet more, and I was asleep again in about fifteen minutes. I woke up later as William was carrying me to bed. The bed covers were folded over, and William put me down. He undressed me and helped me into bed. I curled up and went back to sleep.

The morning came with the smell of coffee and breakfast. I slid into the kitchen, and William handed me coffee and the *Aiken Standard* newspaper. CNN was on, and Agent Brown and Agent Valdez were talking about the young women, the abductions, and the link to the five deaths at the hunting lodge.

Breakfast was fruit this morning, so I asked, "Where's my hardy breakfast?"

"The fruit will counteract the food you had yesterday."

"It tasted great though."

"Great tasting doesn't mean healthy."

"I'm not sure that's true."

"It was true for your meals yesterday."

"Maybe so, but it did taste great. The girls enjoyed it too." I looked at the clock, and it was seven. I didn't have time to go to the hospital to see my parents.

William must have known what I was thinking. "I'll go see your parents this morning. Maybe you can see them at lunchtime."

"I'm not sure how long we'll be with the girls. I hope to get away for a while at lunch."

"I'm sure the girls will have you eating another healthy lunch." William grinned.

I took a shower but didn't have a change of clothes. I'd go by my parents' house on the way to the office. When I was out of the shower, there were my pants, shirt, socks, and underwear laying out for me in the bathroom. I dressed and went back into the kitchen. William was at the breakfast table reading the newspaper.

"Where'd my clothes come from?"

"I went by your house and picked them up."

"Where'd you get the key?"

"I have a key to the house."

"Why do you have a key?"

"I own the house."

"My parents rent from you?"

"They do. Are you supposed to be taking care of the yard?" He sounded a bit like my father.

"Yes."

"I'll have someone go today and work on the yard. Your mother will be coming home soon."

"That's right. Can you find out this morning when she's coming home?"

"I'll let you know."

"You're wonderful. Some woman will be lucky to get you."

"You're the lucky woman."

"Oh yeah. We have a wedding coming up." I grinned and rolled my eyes.

"Your mother and I'll be doing more planning today."

"That's great, but my schedule doesn't have an opening for a wedding this year."

"Your mother and father need this wedding to keep them happy."

"Have fun planning the wedding."

"Thanks, your mother and I will."

I gave William a wet kiss and left for the office. He wanted more, but I pushed him away.

I went to Bill's office at eight, and he was at his desk. Since Bill was the lead investigator, he had been in contact with Agent Brown, who was the FBI lead. According to Bill, the FBI had made progress on locating some of the parents. Two of the sets of parents had been found. The FBI was planning to meet with the parents today to get more details.

"The FBI forensic team went through Mr. Burnette's basement yesterday and collected a lot of trace evidence. The cadaver dogs were used at both the Burnette house and the burned house but didn't find anything. There was another exit from the basement through the garage. A door was behind a large tool chest that could swing out from the wall."

"Do you think that was how the girls were taken from the basement each week?" I knew the answer but wanted Bill to agree.

"The girls could be loaded into the van in the garage without anyone noticing. It makes sense."

"Into the van and drive out. When they brought the girls back, they would be unloaded in the garage," I said.

"Do we know who was driving the van?"

"I have my suspicions, but I'll wait until the girls tell me."

"How was the movie?" Bill asked.

"The girls had a good time and seemed to do fine. We also had ice cream afterward."

"I was surprised the girls wanted to go to a movie so soon. What's the entertainment plan for tonight?" Bill asked.

"I don't know. I'm sure the girls will have suggestions."

"So who murdered Mr. Burnette?"

"I'm glad you aren't calling him the vic. The girls are the victims and not Mr. Burnette. I was thinking it was a business deal gone wrong or Joe before finding the girls. I'm now sure it has something to do with the girls. I'm now thinking it was a seventh guy that either came to his senses or was kicked out of the private sardonic club. The girls should help us find out."

"I'll be with Agent Brown again today," Bill said.

"Hopefully Agent Valdez will keep me involved. So far she's let me ask the questions."

I'd told Agent Valdez and Tammy Street we'd start interviewing again at nine. Agent Valdez had arranged for a woman sketch artist to come over at noon.

When I arrived at the house, the girls came outside to meet me. Maria hugged me and took my hand to lead me into the house. April met us and told me we would be in the same room as yesterday.

We sat down, and I had Victoria and Maria on each side of me. The three agents waited for everyone to take a seat, and then they took the empty seats. I had a feeling the psychologists were going to be needed more today since we'd be talking about more sensitive information.

I said, "There has been progress finding some of your parents."

Agent Valdez said, "We've found Maria's and Daniella's parents, and they were told you'd call them this morning. Both of you can come with me, and we'll make the calls."

I was sure the calls were being recorded by the FBI.

Maria and Daniella followed Agent Valdez into another room. Both looked at Victoria as they were leaving the room.

"We'll wait for them to come back. What did you think of the movie?" I asked.

The four were very vocal about how they enjoyed the movie and the ice cream. I asked them what they wanted to do tonight, but they said they hadn't decided. I asked about the house we were in, and they said it was fine.

"When can we go home?" Sofia asked.

"I'm guessing in a day or two. It'll be up to the FBI," I answered. The two FBI psychologists didn't elaborate on my answer.

Maria, Daniella, and Agent Valdez returned.

Maria said, "I talked to *mi* mama and papa. I can't wait to see them."

Daniella said, "I talked to *mi* mama and papa too. I told them I'd see them soon."

The other four girls hugged Maria and Daniella.

After everybody was seated again, Victoria said, "We talked this morning, and we're ready to tell you anything you need to know."

It was now obvious that Victoria was the spokesperson for the girls.

I said, "I know this may be difficult, but we need details on what happened at the house you were taken to in the woods."

Victoria said, "We talked about it, and I'll be talking for all of us."

"Could you just give a quick overview of what happened during a weekend?"

"I'll start from the basement. We were told a time we would leave for the house so we would be ready to go. We left the basement and went up the stairs out of a door and into the van that was in the garage. Mr. Woodward, Paul, or Mr. Jameson, Nathan, drove the van. When we were at the house in the woods, the van was backed up to the entrance. If we arrived on Friday night, the guys would play poker. There was food for all of us to eat. We would get drinks for the guys and watch them play. There was also a couple of TVs, so we watched TV sometimes."

I interrupted. "How many guys were there?"

"There were a total of six. A lot of times there was less but never more."

"Were two of them Mr. Woodward and Mr. Jameson?" I knew that the guys weren't using their real names, so I figured Mr. Woodward could be Mr. Burnette since his was using Paul.

"Sometimes Mr. Woodward or Mr. Jameson wasn't there, but there was always one of them there."

"What were the names of the other guys?"

"Their names were Mr. Smith, Ralph, Mr. Jones, Andrew, Mr. Thomas, Charles, and Mr. Johnson, Melvin."

It sounded like all six were using their real first names. I didn't understand why.

"Were there always six?"

"No, there were three until Daniela, Sofia, and Gabriela came."

"Who were the first three?"

"Mr. Woodward, Mr. Jameson, and Mr. Smith."

I said, "Go on with the rest."

"After the guys played poker, we would go to bed with them. There were six bedrooms with their own bathrooms. Sometimes we would just sleep with them and sometimes we would have sex." Victoria was telling it casually without getting emotional. I was getting more emotional than she was.

After a short pause, Victoria added, "On Saturday morning, we got up and exercised. The guys exercised with us. We then had breakfast together. Mr. Johnson would usually cooked breakfast with us helping. After breakfast, we usually had tests on what we studied for the week. Mr. Smith would give us the tests."

I interrupted again, "You had tests on what?"

"Mr. Smith said they were home schooling classes. He said we could get our GED someday and go to college. I was doing advanced studies."

I was getting more confused. How could they go to college?

"How long have you been studying and taking tests?"

"Since we came here."

"I know we'll have more questions later, but continue on."

Victoria continued, "While we were taking tests, some of the other guys would leave. Mr. Smith would then go over the tests and then teach us on the subject he picked. We usually took a break for lunch while Mr. Smith was teaching. Mr. Smith would then have us paint or write. We painted with different mediums and wrote short stories and poems. About half the time, we would go back to our basement on Saturday, and about half the time we would stay Saturday night. If we stayed on Saturday night, we would get dressed nice and have dinner. Mr. Johnson would cook and teach us as we were helping. We would have appetizers, salads, dinner, and dessert. We would sometimes watch a movie or we would play games like Monopoly or Rummy. We would then go to bed. On Sunday morning, we would exercise again and have breakfast. If we came on Friday, we would go home Saturday night or sometimes Sunday. If we came on Saturday, Mr. Smith would give us tests and teach us on Sunday. We'd then go home later Sunday."

"Were you ever beaten?"

Victoria seemed surprised at the question. "We weren't beaten."

"I do know the sex was physical abuse," I suggested.

"The guys didn't hurt us while having sex. They were always gentle with us."

I had lots of questions, and I knew Agent Valdez and the psychologists did too. I decided to stay away from sex questions although I wanted to know more.

"Tell us more about the basement. Yesterday you said you didn't have visitors in the basement. How did you know the time you were going to the house in the woods?"

"There was a plastic pipe that came down from above, and a piece of paper would come down with dates and times. That was how we were told."

"How did you get food?"

"When we went to the house in the woods, the guys would have groceries for us. We would bring the groceries back with us."

Agent Valdez asked, "What about clothes and toiletries?"

"The guys would have those for us too. We'd give them a list each week."

I asked, "What if something broke in the basement. Let's say a sink or commode started leaking."

"Mr. Woodward taught us how to fix a lot of things. We were taught how stuff works and how to fix it. We had tools and could fix the basic things. We would let Mr. Woodward know the parts we needed, and he would leave them at our door or send them down the pipe if they were small. If it was something that we couldn't fix, someone would come into the basement while we were at the house in the woods and fix it."

Agent Valdez asked, "Why didn't you try to escape?"

"We thought about it a lot, but there were usually two guys around. We only saw the basement and stairway in the house, so we didn't know if there were guards or dogs. At the house in the woods, we saw the big fence around the house, and the house was always locked. The windows and doors had bars. After a while, we resolved that we weren't going to escape."

I asked, "What happened when you were sick?"

"We didn't usually get sick. If we did get sick, Mr. Jameson would examine us and give us shots or pills. Mr. Jameson also checked our eyes and hearing. He also gave us birth control pills. He even checked our teeth and made sure we were taking care of ourselves."

This almost sounded like an experiment with society. A doctor, a teacher, a cook, and a builder created a place where girls could be educated and shielded from the world. I wondered whether the girls were forced to have sex when they first came. I asked, "When you first came here, were you required to have sex?"

"No. We started having sex after a couple of months." We all noticed that she said she wasn't forced to have sex after a couple of months. This sounded like an area for the psychologists.

Agent Valdez's cell phone vibrated, and she indicated she wanted to take the call.

"Let's take a ten-minute break."

Tammy and I got a drink from the kitchen. The girls went outside, so I asked Tammy whether a bond had developed.

Tammy said, "This is a textbook example of the Stockholm Syndrome. In this case, the girls have emotionally bonded with the guys. I'd be surprised if they said anything negative about the men."

The girls started coming back in, so Tammy stopped talking. Based on the short conversation with Tammy, I would stay away from saying nasty things about the six guys although I was thinking them.

I asked on a hunch, "Were any of you promised that you would be released?"

Victoria said, "Mr. Woodward said that I would be released soon." I looked at the other girls, and they were all staring at Victoria.

"Did the other girls know you were going to be released?"

"No. Mr. Woodward told me not to tell anyone."

"Where was Mr. Woodward going to take you?"

"Mr. Woodward said he would be finding my family and taking me back to them."

I looked at the others. "Were any of you told that you would be released?"

All the other girls said they were promised that they'd eventually be released.

I figured Victoria was Mr. Woodward's girl. I wasn't sure anybody could have found these guys if the girls were released. The girls would probably not help since they were emotionally bonded.

Agent Valdez asked, "When were you going to go back to your family?"

"Mr. Woodward said it would be within a few months. I gave him the phone numbers for my parents. He said he called but didn't get any answers."

Agent Valdez asked, "Did Mr. Woodward tell you he was making progress on finding your parents?"

"He said he hired someone to help."

I decided to confirm my hunch about Victoria and Mr. Woodward and asked, "Who was Mr. Woodward's girl?"

Victoria said, "I was."

"Did you share guys?"

"No. We only had one."

I then decided to play another hunch and asked, "Did you tell Mr. Woodward you would prefer to stay with him rather than being released?"

I got looks from Agent Valdez and the psychologists.

"Yes. I told him I'd stay. He told me I should go back to my parents and that he would send me money to go to college. He said I was too smart to stay here."

This was weird. This was certainly in the psychologists' area and not mine. It was going to be hard on Victoria if Mr. Burnette was actually Mr. Woodward. Since Mr. Burnette was involved with construction and a hardware store, it certainly sounded like Mr. Burnette was Mr. Woodward. I was thinking back to yesterday, and the girls could have been crying and upset because they didn't want to be found. I wouldn't ask that question.

I again assumed Mr. Burnette was Mr. Woodward and asked, "Did Mr. Woodward ever take you in the house above the basement?"

Victoria hesitated before answering. She probably didn't think she'd be asked this question.

"Yes, a couple of times."

Agent Valdez seemed surprised at the question and the answer.

"How long would you stay upstairs?"

Victoria looked at Alejandro before answering, "Only an hour or two."

Tammy said to the girls, "It would be a normal tendency to like these guys. We can discuss why that happens later."

I was confused enough, so I said to the girls, "Let's take another break. Who would like to go out for lunch?"

All the girls said yes. I told the girls we'd leave at eleven. It was ten forty now. The girls left the room, and Agent Valdez, the psychologists, and I remained. I closed the door.

I said, "An FBI sketch artist is coming around noon. I hope the girls will help with the sketches. I was totally mistaken thinking the girls would now hate guys."

Tammy said, "They seem pretty attached to the guys. This is a normal reaction."

"I should have listened more in the psychology classes."

Agent Valdez said, "You can read about it, but it's different when you see it in person."

"No wonder they didn't have any problem going out in public last night."

Agent Straight said, "Agent Charles and I have been involved in cases just like this. The girls are attached to the men and are dependent on them. In this case, it seems to be even stronger since the men are educating them and teaching them skills. They probably think they're better off there than with their parents."

I said I needed to make a couple of calls and left the room. I called William first.

William answered, "Hello, gorgeous."

I said, "Hello, handsome."

"That's more like it. Pretty soon, you'll be calling me pet names."

"I'll start thinking of some. How were my parents?"

"Your parents are doing fine. Your mother and I found someone to make your dress, decided on the flowers, and talked to a caterer to do the wedding in Aiken."

"Did you decide on the invitations too?"

"We're down to two choices. You can help decide."

"You and Mom can decide. I hate to change the subject, but we're breaking for lunch. The girls want to go to Chick-fil-A today, so we'll be there in about fifteen minutes."

"May I join you?"

"I think you can. The girls appear to not be guy haters. I'll tell you about it later."

"See you at lunch. I'll buy again."

"Thanks, my little scorpion."

"That's not a pet name I was thinking of. Work on it more."

I then called Bill and caught him up on the discussions with the girls. I told him that we were going to Chick-fil-A and that I would call him after lunch. He said that Agent Brown and he were coming back to Aiken so we should meet.

The two FBI psychologists, Tammy and Agent Valdez, didn't go with us to lunch. The rest of us loaded into the van and went to Chick-fil-A. I told the cashier that it was on one ticket and hoped William would arrive in time to pay. He did. I ordered a grilled chicken sandwich combo. I wanted the fried spicy chicken sandwich combo but compromised. Since William was watching, I almost ordered a salad, but my sanity prevailed. William ordered a grilled chicken garden salad. I wouldn't let him have any of my waffle fries. The girls got their orders first and sat together. We sat away from the girls.

They didn't notice William since we sat across the room. I didn't talk to him about the case, but we did talk about Mom and the pretend wedding.

William said, "Your mom will be released from the hospital tomorrow morning."

"I should be able to pick her up. Did she say what time?"

"It'll be after the doctor does rounds, so there isn't a definite time. I'll go with you in the morning."

"I can manage, but it would be nice."

We talked more about Mom and Dad and the pretend wedding. I kissed him good-bye, and we went back to the house.

The sketch artist had set up his equipment in the same room we were in, and the girls took seats. Agent Valdez stayed with the sketch artist and the girls while I went outside and called Bill. I asked him if George Miller had returned, and he said it'd be later today. I gave him more details about the conversations this morning but didn't tell him how naïve I was. Agent Valdez walked outside shortly after me and made a phone call.

I asked Agent Valdez, "Have you been involved in a case like this before?"

Agent Valdez said, "I've been involved in hostage cases, but the cases were resolved quickly enough that I didn't see this type of emotional attachment."

"Me too. I haven't seen anything like this. It's difficult to understand."

"The guys treated the girls well, educated them, and were teaching them a lot."

"It's still very confusing to me."

I went into the house with the girls. The sketch artist was still busy working with the girls on a rendering. One was finished, and it was for Mr. Woodward. The sketch looked like Mr. Burnette. I had thought the girls wouldn't cooperate with the sketch artist, but they were. I motioned for Tammy to come out of the room. Agent Valdez followed us out too. When we were outside, I asked her how it was going.

Tammy said, "The girls are helping so far. For Mr. Woodward, Victoria wasn't very involved, but the other girls were. I suspect this scenario will be true for all the sketches. I need to leave and go back to my office. What are the plans?" I looked at Agent Valdez since I didn't want to speak for her.

Agent Valdez said, "I thought we would start again at nine tomorrow. Can you be here?"

Tammy answered, "Yes. I'll be here."

Agent Valdez then asked, "What do you think about Agent Brown being here tomorrow?"

Tammy answered, "Before today, I would have thought it would be a bad idea. After the interviews today, I don't think the girls would care whether a man or woman is interviewing them."

"Agent Brown will most likely dominate the questioning tomorrow, so I wanted to let you know."

Tammy responded, "I'll watch and see how the girls react. If the girls don't respond well to Agent Brown, I'll jump in."

I said, "I'll tell them we're meeting in the morning. It looks like the sketch artist will be with them for the rest of the afternoon."

We went back into the room, but the girls weren't there. We saw a second sketch that was in progress. In a few minutes, the sketch artist came back and said they had taken a break. I asked the sketch artist how it was progressing.

The sketch artist responded, "The girls have a very good memory and a good attention to detail. This is going faster than I thought it would."

"Can you finish all the sketches today?"

"At the pace we're going, we'll be done."

All the girls came back and took seats. I stood up and told them that we would meet with them again tomorrow morning at nine. I asked them if they wanted to do anything tonight.

Victoria answered, "We'd like to go to a movie again, and we'd like to have pizza."

I asked, "What movie would you like to see?"

Victoria told me, and we decided to meet them at five. I called William to tell him about the pizza and movie.

William answered, "Hello, my cutie pie."

"Hello, my slithering snake."

"I don't think you have quite got it yet. I'll give you a list to practice with."

"I have my own list."

"I'm not fond of your list so far."

"I'm saving the good ones."

"Could you please get to the good ones soon?"

"I'm taking the girls out again tonight. We're having pizza and then going to a movie."

"No ice cream?"

"Maybe."

"Who's going with you?"

"No one yet."

"I'll go."

"Are you sure?"

"It appears it's the best way for me to be with you."

"We're picking up the girls at five. I'm going to see my parents now."

"Your mom has the wedding details we worked out today. Be sure to ask her about them."

"I'm sure the subject will come up without asking. See you later, my little apricot."

"A little better."

Chapter 34

Wednesday Afternoon—Jessie

I went to visit my parents in the hospital. My dad was awake and was doing a little better. He said the doctor thought he had improved enough to schedule the next surgery. He said it would be later in the week or early next week. Mom was wound up due to William when I came in her room. She had lots of wedding magazines and other magazines. William must have brought her the two wedding planning books that were on top of the stack of magazines. One wedding planning book had Aiken on the cover in black letters, and the second one had Chicago in black letters on the cover.

As I sat down, Mom said, "William called and said you were coming. He now has me on speed dial."

"William is so thoughtful." I was being sarcastic, but Mom took it the other way.

"I agree. He's so wonderful. Let me show you the plans we've made so far. We have to plan for a possible Aiken wedding or a possible Chicago wedding, so it's twice the work."

Mom showed me all the stuff they had been working on. She went through each wedding planning book with me. I didn't know there was so much to do for a wedding. This pretend wedding was certainly making my mom feel much better. Mom then caught me up on all the happenings in Chicago. I now knew more about what my cousins were doing than I did when I was in Chicago. Mom reminded that she was being released in the morning after the doctor did rounds. I told her I would be there early and would take her home.

I stopped by my parents' house to check on the house and do a little cleaning before Mom came home. I thought I was at the wrong house when I pulled in the driveway. The yard had been cut, the bushes were trimmed, and there were flowers in the yard. The outside of the house also looked cleaner. I went into the house, and the inside had been cleaned too. Everything was orderly. There were fresh flowers on the tables. My stack of dirty clothes had been washed and put in my room. The bathrooms were clean, and the tops of the vanities were organized. I blinked my eyes a few times to make sure I wasn't dreaming. This was spectacular. I was wondering whether Mom had someone do the house, but it was probably William.

Bill called and said we could go through the basement, so I drove down Jefferson Davis Highway to the Burnette house. The FBI still had vans parked in front, and I found Bill under the tent. There were Subway bags on the table this time.

Bill said, "I'll show you the basement."

We went into the office and down the stairs. This time there weren't any girls to find. There was a large living area as we exited the stairs. The furniture was modern with two leather couches and two upholstered chairs. There was a TV in the living area with surround sound and a stereo system with a rack of CDs. There were six desks at one end of the room with shelves full of books. The room where I found the girls was a kitchen with a wooden table and six wood chairs. The kitchen had modern appliances that were stainless steel. There was a hallway off the kitchen with three bedrooms. Each room had two twin beds and two dressers. A wall-mounted TV was in each bedroom along with a stereo system. A walk-in closet had lots of clothes in each bedroom. The rooms had wood floors with the same light brown paint. The bedspreads were bright with flowers. Each bedroom had a minimal bathroom consisting of a small vanity, a commode, and a standard tub-shower combination. The tile floor in the bathrooms matched the tile floor in the kitchen. The fourth room off the hall was an exercise room with two universal machines, mats, and weights. A door in the exercise room opened to a stair that went up to the garage. I walked up the stairs, and the tool chest had been moved out of the way. The door at the top of this stairway had similar locks as the other door. I walked through the garage to the tent. I could now picture the young women coming up the stairs, getting in the van, and driving to the hunting lodge. The neighbors had watched the girls drive past their houses for the past two years.

Bill got a call from Jeffery while we were standing at the tent.

"I see. Tell him we'll be there in about twenty minutes," Bill said.

"Where are we going?" I asked.

"George Miller is back and waiting for us at his office. He's made a copy of the will for us."

I followed Bill since I didn't know where George Miller's office was located.

George met us at the front door and ushered us into a conference room. He handed each of us a copy of the will.

"First of all, I'm shocked at finding out Paul had abducted girls. My wife and I were appalled. Paul had me change the will about a month ago. I didn't know any of the people he included, but I changed the will as he instructed. He didn't tell me anything about the women he was leaving the estate to."

"Give us a couple of minutes to read it."

As I read it, I saw that the will left the house and lots of money to Victoria Alvarez. I wondered if Victoria knew that Mr. Burnette had included her in the will. There were a few others that were included. Mrs. Rodriquez was to be provided $50,000. The SPCA was to be provided $50,000. Alejandra Ramirez was to be provided $100,000. Maria Sanchez was to be provided $100,000. Sofia, Daniela, and Gabriela were to receive $50,000 each. I now had six suspects. Seven if you included Mrs. Rodriquez. They were Victoria, Alejandra, Maria, Sofia, Daniela, and Gabriela.

George saw that we were finished reading and said, "I didn't place the names in the will until we got back to the States today. It's hard for me to understand why Paul and the other guys did it."

"It's hard for us to believe it too. Thanks for coming to the office," Bill said.

After seeing the will, I was now thinking the girls had something to do with it. Unfortunately, the house in the woods burning down had to involve someone else. There must be a link between the girls and someone else.

Agent Brown and Agent Valdez were at our four o'clock meeting. Bill handed out copies of the will to everybody and gave them a few minutes to read it. Bill said he went back to see Joe Jackson today, and Joe was in the hospital. The chemo had made him sick.

Michael said, "We've interviewed lots of friends and family and don't have any solid leads. We checked on several of their golf trips, and there wasn't a record of them golfing. Andrew Bynum and Nathan Reynolds had condos at Hilton Head, so they could have stayed at the condos. I suspect they spent more time at the hunting lodge than Hilton Head."

Jeffery spoke next. "We've gone through lots of records on their computers and cell phones and provided some possible leads to Michael. All of the information seems to be routine. Ralph Scott did have charges for home schooling, so he was probably buying the education materials for the girls."

"Were there any child pornography sites or other sex sites on the computers?"

Oscar answered, "We didn't find any. The FBI has the computers and cell phones now."

"Did you see any links where they may have bought the girls?" I asked.

"No, I figured they didn't use their personal or business computers, but I don't know what they used," Oscar responded.

Agent Brown was next. "We'll go through the computers too. We've found two more parents for the girls. The two girls, Maria and Gabriela, called their parents this afternoon. We'll be flying them home as soon as we finish questioning them. We moved the forensic team over to the hunting lodge, but the lodge was destroyed. We hope to find some trace evidence. We're processing some evidence at the scenes, and we've sent some to Atlanta. I expect to get results quickly."

Agent Valdez said, "The six sketches were completed and were a close match to the six guys. The girls described them very well. What's the plan tomorrow?"

Bill said, "The captain wants to see us at eight."

"I'm seeing the girls at nine," I said.

"We'll see you in the captain's office at eight," Agent Brown said.

It was now time to take the girls to the movies. I called William and told him that I'd meet him at the house with the girls. He said he knew where the house was located. I was at the house at about ten minutes until five, and the girls were outside. The girls came over and hugged me, and I hugged them back. I asked about the time with the sketch artist, and Victoria said it went fine. I asked if they were finished knowing the answer. About this time,

William drove up in his 700 series BMW. The girls stopped hugging me and looked at the car and the guy.

Victoria asked, "Who's that?"

"That would be William. He was with us at lunch today."

"Who's William?" Alejandra asked.

I thought about saying fiancé but couldn't get it out. I wanted to say boyfriend but didn't want to have that be public yet. I finally said, "A friend who's going with us for pizza and the movie."

"I'll ride with him."

The rest of the girls said they would ride with him also.

I was shocked that the girls wanted to ride with a man they didn't know.

"Someone has to ride with me," I said.

Victoria settled it by saying, "The four oldest will ride with William, and the two youngest will ride with Jessie."

Daniela and Sofia both said, "Darn."

Sofia then said, "The two youngest should get to ride back with William."

William was on his cell phone when he got out of the car, so I didn't go over and kiss him. He held up his finger, and I told Victoria to tell him we were going to Pizza Hut. I told Victoria that I was going ahead to get a table. Daniela and Sofia reluctantly rode with me.

I saw William hang up his phone as I was driving out of the driveway. When I parked at Pizza Hut, William was already there. He must have known a shortcut. William came over, smiled, and said, "Where have you been?" The girls were laughing at me.

I said, "I came the only way I knew."

We went into Pizza Hut, and the server said a table was ready for us. William must have called ahead to have a table ready. One of these days, I would be organized too.

William and I waited for the girls to find seats. They didn't leave two seats together, so I made a couple of girls move. William sat down beside me and said, "Hello, honey."

The girls stared at us, and Victoria said, "Friend?"

William said, "Friend?"

I said, "Very close friend." I shrugged.

A server came over, and we ordered drinks. William told the server that he should bring pitchers. The girls discussed the choices on the menu and decided on pizzas. Three large pizzas were ordered with different toppings.

William said, "Remember to leave room for popcorn."

I said, "I will."

"I meant the girls."

Victoria said, "Some of us are women."

"My apologies. You are women."

"I would certainly not call you a boy."

"I'm still a boy at heart."

"There's a little boy in every man," she said as she made a trilling noise with her tongue. She raised her eyebrows and pushed out her breasts. She was wearing a low-cut blouse.

I was glad Victoria wasn't sitting beside William. If William looked at her breasts, I'd pinch his leg until it bled.

William saw where this was headed and finally said, "Jessie is actually my fiancée. We'll be married in a few months."

Victoria said, "That's great. Do you have a brother?"

Maria said, "Maybe two brothers."

Alejandra said, "Maybe three brothers." Alejandra used a sultry voice and trilled the R in *three* longer than needed.

When I rescued the girls from the basement, I thought I needed to protect them from men. Now I was thinking I needed to protect men from the girls.

Drinks came, which broke the estrogen cloud that had settled over the table. The girls didn't look at the male server. He must have been too young for them.

Everybody had their drink, and I changed the subject by asking about the movie last night. Each of the girls gave their opinion on the movie. All six of them spoke well and thoughtfully. This made me wonder whether Victoria was there as the spokesperson or as the one selected to talk to make sure the story was consistent.

Victoria tried to work on William again by asking in a sexy voice, "What do you do?"

Victoria probably wanted him to say that he would do her, but he said, "I flip houses and have rentals."

"Is that like the *Flip This House* show on TV?"

"It's similar."

Alejandra said in a sultry voice, "You can teach us."

Maybe the sultry voice was her natural voice, but I doubted it.

I was waiting for one of them to say that they'll have a lot of money to invest soon, but none of them blurted it out.

William didn't know what to say and looked at me. I finally said, "William has to teach me first after we're married."

William smiled at me.

The server brought the pizza to the table and saved us. The rest of the meal was fine with everyone devouring pizza. The girls ate heartily while I tried to eat lightly. William paid for the pizza, and we left the restaurant. The same girls rode with William. I noticed Victoria was in the front seat with him. I was glad there was a wide center console in the car to keep Victoria away from William.

William paid for the movie tickets and our snacks. Victoria would be able to buy her own tickets soon. William made sure he sat on the end of the row, and I sat beside him. If they had the chance, the girls would probably devour him like they devoured the pizza.

After the movie, we stopped for ice cream at the same place. I had a small scoop of chocolate. We dropped the girls off at the house, and I went to William's house.

William poured each of us a glass of wine, and we sat on the sofa.

William said, "Put your feet up. You've had a long day."

"You need to let me do your feet after your ordeal with the girls."

"They're women."

"They're certainly mature girls."

"They've been trained."

"I want to run a scenario by you, but I want to thank you for doing the yard and having the house cleaned."

"I may be too sleepy after you properly thank me, but let's go." William was pulling me up.

"I'm not thanking you that way right now."

"When will I get thanked that way?"

"After the scenario, if you pay attention." I glared at him a little.

"Proceed quickly."

I said, "Here's what I think happened. Tell me where there are flaws. It's my theory that Victoria or Victoria along with the other girls killed Mr. Burnette. I believe Victoria and Mr. Burnette became very close over the past two years, and Victoria was allowed to come upstairs. She admitted today that she was brought upstairs. I believe Victoria was told about the will or Victoria found a copy of the will in the office."

William raised his hand, and I acknowledged him. He asked, "What will?"

"We obtained a copy of Mr. Burnette's will this afternoon. Victoria will get most of the assets, with the other five girls getting money."

"How much money?"

"Fifty thousand to one hundred thousand each."

"Go ahead with the scenario."

I went on, "I believe Victoria probably took a set of keys. We found one set of keys in the desk. Locks come with extra keys, so there was probably another set. I believe Victoria used one of Mr. Burnette's guns she got out of the safe. I believe she got the combination to the gun safe from Mr. Burnette or watched him open it. I'd bet she had the extra keys on her when we brought her out of the basement. The keys were probably discarded at the hospital. I believe the girls also burned the hunting lodge."

"Have you thought about Paul having a gun in his truck? Lots of country folks carry a rat and snake gun in their truck."

"What's a rat and snake gun?" I asked.

"It's usually a small-caliber gun kept in a glove box. Victoria could have found it in Mr. Burnette's truck."

"I'll adjust my scenario to have the gun in the truck. That's more logical."

"Tell me how you think they burned the lodge."

"The lodge was burned on a Sunday night. Victoria said they came back on Saturday before the lodge was burned on Sunday. I think she was lying. I think the girls and probably Victoria shot all five guys at the lodge and then burned it." I was thinking out loud.

"How could they control six guys?" William asked.

"I think they used sleeping pills. We found almost an empty bottle in Mr. Burnette's medicine cabinet, and I'll bet the girls had asked for sleeping pills. The girls said they usually fixed a nice dinner on Sundays, so I'm thinking they laced the wine or water with sleeping pills."

"That could work, but how would they get Mr. Burnette back to his house?"

"They drove the van and carried him to his bedroom or woke him up when they were back to the house." I was sorting through the scenario as I spoke.

"If it was me, I'd tie him up and promise to do special things to him. I'm speaking for Victoria of course."

"So she shoots him when he gets in bed?" I asked.

"Was he clothed when he was shot?"

"Yes."

"Did he have alcohol and sleeping medicine in his system when he was autopsied?" William asked.

"Yes, and he had chicken and vegetables from dinner on Sunday in his stomach. She probably untied him after she shot him."

"When did they burn the lodge?" William asked.

"I think they killed Mr. Burnette and then went back and burned the lodge. Mr. Burnette probably had gasoline there, which they used. They could have bought gas too, but we didn't find anyone that saw them buy gas that night."

"I'm guessing Paul had lots of gas at his house and maybe some at the lodge," William said.

"Why wouldn't they set fire to the lodge before they left with Mr. Burnette?" I asked.

"They needed the gasoline, which was probably at Paul's house."

"So they brought Mr. Burnette back and shot him. Then they went back and burned the house. They'd already shot the other five, so there wasn't a hurry. It also gave them an opportunity to throw the snake gun and extra ammo away. The gun and ammo were probably hauled to the county dump days ago and are now impossible for us to find," I said.

"Fingerprints and other traces of her will be found upstairs, but she won't care. She'll have told you already that Paul brought her upstairs with him," William said.

"She did tell me she was allowed to come upstairs."

William said, "So Victoria killed Mr. Burnette and then drove down to the house in the woods and burned it down. I would guess that last Sunday wasn't the first time she drove to the house in the woods."

"Mine too. After burning down the house, Victoria came back to the basement, and the girls waited for someone to rescue them. They didn't want it to happen right away but wondered if it would happen. When I heard the thudding, it was probably planned by the girls; enough time had passed for the gun and ammo to disappear."

"They certainly couldn't come out by themselves. All of the girls had to know the plan and probably knew about the will. I would have thought Mr. Burnette would have kept a copy of the will in his safe or files. Did you find one?"

"No, but that gives me an idea. Mr. Burnette's files were organized alphabetically with each file having the tab spaced from the next file. He was very anal about his files."

"Doesn't everybody organize their files that way?"

I gave him a look. "Are your files like that?"

"It saves time when you're looking for a file."

"I should go back and look at Mr. Burnette's files. My other question about the will is whether Victoria and the girls are allowed to receive Mr. Burnette's assets if they killed him. That could be why the girls thought the murder needed to look like someone else did it."

"The girls must have researched it since South Carolina has a slayer statute, as do all states. The slayer statute prevents a murderer from profiting from the crime. The question is whether you'll charge them with a crime. I suspect you won't, and the girls will get the property and money from the will. You should call George Miller to get his opinion since I'm only a shade-tree lawyer."

"You're a wealth of knowledge. I suspect we won't charge them. What else am I missing?"

"It was actually a pretty good plan. Will you get them to confess?"

"It was a good plan except that the girls were the logical choices based on the will. I can see the headlines when we put all six girls in jail. It wouldn't be well received."

"You know they'll never admit that they saw the will."

"I know it."

"One more detail."

"What?"

"Your mother tomorrow."

"I forgot about her. I have a meeting with the captain at eight, and I'm seeing the young women at nine. I'd like to go check Mr. Burnette's files before eight."

"You check the files, have your meetings, call the probate lawyer, and meet the girls. I'll take your mother to her house. There's more planning to be done for the wedding."

"Now I'm ready to give you a proper thank you."

"And don't forget to thank me for helping with your scenario."

"You will get additional attention."

William was already on his feet and pulling me up. We went directly to the bedroom. William left the wine glasses on the coffee table, which he wouldn't usually do. I washed my face and brushed my teeth quickly and jumped into bed. Both of us had our birthday suits on. I gave William special treatment for all the help lately. He fell asleep right afterward, which was positive feedback.

Chapter 35

Thursday Morning—Jessie

The next morning, I went to the kitchen, and William handed me coffee and the newspaper. He kissed me on the mouth. The newspaper headlines were about the girls, Mr. Burnette, and the lodge. The FBI must have had another press conference so that the newspaper had the latest information. It was six thirty, and William was already dressed.

I asked, "Why are you dressed?"

"Your mother."

"Oh yeah. Thanks. I'll reward you later."

"I'm planning on it. I was thinking I would spend the night with you at your mother's house."

"My mother will be there."

"I'll sneak in after she goes to sleep."

"You're sick."

He came over and kissed me on the lips again. William then said, "Since Victoria and the girls will be coming into a substantial amount of money, have them call me, and I'll advise them." William handed me a business card as he was talking.

I took the card and tore it up. I said, "More than the business card will be torn up if you help these girls. Before you know it, they'll be in your will."

"My will now has your mother getting everything."

William left the room as I thought about the girls. I did feel sorry for the girls and wouldn't wish their nightmare on anyone. I showered and dressed. I went to Mr. Burnette's house and checked his files. Sure enough,

Mr. Burnette's files were tabbed as left, middle and right and then repeated. There was a file missing between the 212 Wardlaw Drive property and the 433 Woodfield Road property. It was probably the will. It was just before eight when I got to the captain's office. I called George Miller, and he answered the phone.

I said, "I need to ask a hypothetical question."

George Miller said, "I'll try to answer it."

"Let's suppose there was this man who was holding girls captive in his basement. One or more of the girls killed the man. The man had a will that left money and property to all of the girls. The question is whether the girls would get the money and property if they killed the man."

George Miller said, "This is hypothetical, of course."

"It is."

"If the girls were convicted of the crime, they wouldn't receive the assets from the will even if the will was executed before the crime was committed. I'd certainly advise the recipients to sell off the property quickly before they were charged. This is only hypothetical, of course."

"Thank you."

"My pleasure to help."

It was eight o'clock, and I went to the captain's office. Bill, Agent Brown, and Agent Valdez were already there.

Agent Brown started off by telling us that he appreciated our help so far. The captain told Agent Brown and Agent Valdez that their help had been outstanding.

I said, "I would like to discuss a scenario."

Agent Brown said, "Go ahead." He rolled his eyes like I was wasting his time.

I went through the scenario I honed with William's help. I thought it sounded very plausible, and I had convinced myself that it was likely true. I told them about the missing will and my discussion with George Miller.

There was quiet in the room for a minute as the captain, Bill, Agent Brown, and Agent Valdez came up with questions.

Bill spoke first. "It does sound logical, but there are a lot of things we can't prove."

"I believe that's what the girls hoped for, so that they wouldn't be charged," I answered.

Agent Brown said, "What about the emotional attachment from the interviews yesterday?"

"There was emotional attachment, but I believe the property and money became more important than the attachment."

Agent Valdez said, "Victoria told us yesterday that Mr. Burnette was going to release her, but I'm not sure it was true. The other girls seemed surprised when she said it."

"I think that was part of the ruse. Even if it were true, I think the will changed Victoria's thinking. She probably didn't want to wait for him to die even though he was sixty-five. The will was changed just a month ago."

Agent Brown said, "Let's say that this scenario is true. There's no way that Victoria or any of the girls will be charged with murder."

"I agree. Victoria could have been found standing over Mr. Burnette with the gun in her hand and would still not be charged. I believe in their minds they thought they could be charged."

Agent Brown said, "Why don't you start out the conversation by explaining what we know and that they won't be charged with killing Mr. Burnette. Let them know about the will and say the will wouldn't change if they did kill Mr. Burnette. Then we can ask them questions."

I said, "I can do that."

Agent Brown asked Agent Valdez, "What are your thoughts?"

"I also believe Victoria or one of the girls killed Mr. Burnette. It was probably Victoria. Based on the girls' reactions yesterday, I don't think Mr. Burnette was planning to release her. I don't expect the girls to admit it, but I do believe they killed Mr. Burnette and the others and burned down the lodge."

Agents Brown and Valdez and Bill had a few more questions until it was time to leave for the house with the girls.

Chapter 36

Wednesday Morning—Jessie

It was time to see the girls' reaction to the scenario. The girls were already in the room and seemed happy. I introduced Agent Brown and Bill. The girls didn't look at Agent Brown and Bill the way they looked at William.

After we sat down, I said, "Thank you for your help so far. I think it's time we gave you information. First, the reason I became involved was due to Mr. Burnette being murdered. Mr. Burnette is Mr. Woodward." I looked for a reaction, but there was none.

"Mr. Burnette or Mr. Woodward was killed in his sleep on Sunday night ten days ago. He was shot with a .22-caliber handgun." There was still no reaction.

"The house in the woods was burned down the same night as Mr. Burnette or Mr. Woodard was killed. This happened after Mr. Burnette or Mr. Woodward was killed." I didn't know this for a fact, but it matched my scenario. There was still no reaction.

"Mr. Burnette had a will that'll provide each of you money and Victoria property. A copy of the will was removed from the files in Mr. Burnette's office. I believe Victoria removed the will." This did get a small reaction, and the girls looked at Victoria.

"I believe that the thudding on the stairs on the day I found you was intentional. You needed someone to find you so that you weren't accused of killing Mr. Burnette. I almost tripped on a broom in the living area that was probably used." All of the girls looked at Victoria but said nothing.

"I've talked to a probate lawyer, and you'd still receive the money and property even if you killed Mr. Burnette as long as you weren't convicted of the crime." This resulted in a couple of small grins, and the girls looked at Victoria again.

"The FBI and the police wouldn't charge you with killing Mr. Burnette if you did kill him. Under the circumstances, it would be considered justified." Victoria was looked at again. Victoria was obviously the mastermind.

"I believe the sketch artist drawings were accurate since you knew all six men were dead. To sum it up, Victoria or one of you killed Mr. Burnette. Whoever did it was justified in doing it. Victoria or one of you drove to the house in the woods ten days ago and burned it down. I suspect that all of you went. Victoria or one of you threw the gun away while you were driving to the house in the woods. When you came back to Mr. Burnette's house to go back in the basement, you locked yourselves in the basement, waiting for someone to find you. When nobody came, you started making noise to get my attention. After you left the basement, you pretended to not know what was happening when you actually did. Victoria, was this what happened?"

Victoria paused for several seconds and then said, "We were locked in our basement when Mr. Burnette and the others were killed and the house was burned."

"Did you know Mr. Burnette or Mr. Woodward had a will?"

"Mr. Woodward said he would help me with college, but I didn't know about a will." Victoria was looking away when she answered.

"Did you burn down the house in the woods?"

"We were locked in the basement and couldn't burn the house."

"If you tell the truth, the results will still be the same. You won't be charged with a crime, and you'll still get the property and money from the will."

"We're telling the truth."

Agent Brown said, "As Jessica said, the results will be the same if you're truthful."

"We're telling the truth. Why don't you believe me?" Victoria acted emotional.

Agent Brown said, "Let's take a ten-minute break." The girls left the room, leaving Agent Brown, Agent Valdez, Bill, the three psychologists, and me.

Tammy spoke first. "Based on what I heard, the girls probably did what you said. From a psychological perspective, they probably got as much reward from covering it up as doing it. I don't think you'll get them to admit doing it."

I thought to myself again that I should have listened more in the psychology classes.

Agent Brown said, "I'm not sure it's worth the effort to grill them anymore. They've been through a lot of trauma already. Our psychologists will keep talking to them, along with Tammy."

I said, "I'd suggest turning the girls over to them now."

Agent Brown said, "I agree. When the girls come back, all of us should leave but the psychologists."

Bill said, "Will the FBI still be looking for the other parents?"

Agent Brown said, "Yes. We'll let you and the girls know if we find the other parents. They can decide whether they want to stay with their parents. The FBI will fly them home as soon as the psychologists say they can go."

I suspected the girls would be home soon.

Everybody left the room except for the psychologists. I stayed outside the door, waiting on the girls. I wanted to say good-bye. The girls came back, and I told them I was leaving. The girls hugged me and thanked me. I held Victoria's arm and held her back from going in the room. I pulled her outside so that no one could hear us.

I said, "The FBI and the police have decided not to ask you any more questions. First of all, all of you are brave women, and I respect you. Second, did you and the girls do more than you're telling us?"

Victoria answered, "I did what I had to do. The girls depended on me."

"It'll be our secret, Victoria."

Victoria smiled. "Thanks for finding us."

"You're welcome. The probate lawyer now knows who you are, so he should be contacting you soon. He'll advise you to sell the properties and to not waste the money. All of you will need a good advisor right away."

"I know. We've decided to divide the assets equally between all of us."

"That's nice of you. I've got to go now. I'll see you later."

We hugged for a minute.

I left and called William. He said he was taking my mother home now. I told him I would meet him at my parents' house. I arrived as William was pulling in the driveway. I went over to the passenger side of the car to help my mother out. William was getting a wheelchair out of the trunk.

Mom said, "Let William do it. He knows where I'm hurting."

I said, "I know where you're hurting, Mom."

"Let William do it, Jessica."

I knew when I was called Jessica it was time to let mom have her way.

I moved out of the way, and William moved into my spot. He stuck his tongue out at me. I pinched him on the butt.

As we rolled Mom into the house, Mom said, "The yard looks good, Jessie." I was back to being Jessie. I was in front of Mom, turned around, and stuck my tongue out at William.

Mom saw it and said, "Behave, Jessica." I switched back to being Jessica that fast. William smiled and stuck his tongue out at me. Mom couldn't see William.

We rolled Mom into the house and helped her into a lounge chair in the family room. She noticed the clean house and fresh flowers and thanked me. William helped her put the feet support up on the chair, put the back down on the chair, and put the remote for the TV beside her. I looked on the wall, and there was a new, large, flat-screen TV. I was hoping to get credit for the TV too, so I didn't say anything.

Mom said, "That's a nice TV, William. Thank you very much." I pursed my lips, narrowed my eyes, and gave William a dirty look. William smiled.

William and I sat on the sofa. We talked to Mom about finalizing the wedding plans, visiting Dad, and the physical therapy that would start tomorrow. Mom was asleep in a few minutes. She probably didn't sleep much last night, knowing she'd be leaving this morning.

After she was asleep, William asked, "Did you get the girls to tell you what happened?"

I said, "They didn't when we were interviewing them, but I talked to Victoria outside afterward, and she all but admitted it. I think she wanted to talk about it but was still worried about being accused of murder."

"I need to leave now. I'll be back later to spend the night."

"I don't think so."

William said, "That's what I expected. I've got a date tonight anyway."

"Are you trying to sow your wild oats before the wedding?"

"I hope not. The date is with your mother. I'm taking her out for dinner. Maybe I'll ask her about spending the night with her daughter tonight. This could be the night a grandchild is conceived. Do you want to join us?"

"Let me think about it."

I left Mom a note that I would see her a little later. William and I left together. I went back to the station, and William went off to buy or sell something.